Summer at the Lakeside Resort

The Lakeside Resort Series (Book 2)

SUSAN SCHILD

Summer at the Lakeside Resort
The Lakeside Resort Series (Book 2)
Copyright © 2019 by Susan Schild, Longleaf Pine Press

For more about this author please visit https://www.susanschild.com/

For permission requests, write to the author on Facebook at: https://www.facebook.com/authorsusanschild/

Editing by The Pro Book Editor
Interior Design by IAPS.rocks
Cover Design by Cover Affairs

ISBN: 978-1-7328249-3-5
    1. Main category—Fiction>General
    2. Other category—Fiction>Women's

First Edition

CHAPTER 1 — BUCKLING DOWN TO BUSINESS

WEARING A FLANNEL NIGHTGOWN, HER longest down jacket, and the old red cowboy boots she'd found at the annual Heron Lake Fire Department rummage sale, Jenny Beckett held a cup of coffee and stepped outside into the frosty March morning. Clutching the doorframe with one hand, she braced herself, trying to avoid being swept along in a running-of-the-bulls type stampede that happened first thing every morning as her two dogs and tiny horse barged out the door for their morning constitutional. Pulling her coat tighter, she broke into a smile as she watched them race around.

Buddy and Bear, her two eighty-plus-pound shelter dogs, trotted and zigzagged around the lakefront clearing, noses to the ground, sniffing for traces of raccoon, possum, fox, or deer that might have visited last night. Both looked puppy-like even though they were gray-muzzled and would, in human years, be middle-aged men who'd recently begun wearing khakis with the secret stretch waists and started dreaming of trading their SUVs for vintage 'Vettes.

Levi, her miniature horse, lifted his nose and sniffed the air coming off the water, then dropped to a spot of frosty grass and did a lazy, exultant, back-scratching roll.

Glancing at the old red Texaco pump thermometer she'd hung on the cabin, another exceptional rummage sale find, Jenny saw that it was 33 degrees. Cold for this time of year in the Carolinas. Blowing out a puff of breath to watch it freeze, she took a sip of coffee and sighed contentedly as she looked out at the expansive view from this high bluff. The morning mist hung like a soft cloud of white cotton over the deep blue water of Heron Lake. The only sounds she could hear were the rustling of squirrels in the woods behind her, the lapping of waves, and the soft rush of wind through the treetops. The muted colors and quiet soft edges of morning soothed her.

Jenny sent a prayer of thanks up to Jax, who was probably talking persuasively with new buddies about an otherworldly business venture or organizing a big craps game in the sky. She shook her head, remembering her larger-than-life daddy, and thought about how her life had changed in just six months. After her then-fiancé dumped her before their Christmas wedding, she had been evicted from her chicken coop cottage. She'd hit rock bottom, or so she'd thought. She shuddered inwardly, recalling that low point. But the tide had turned when Jenny learned that Jax, her rolling stone of a daddy, had died and left her the Lakeside Resort—eight partially finished cabins meant to be weekend rentals on scenic Heron Lake. Jenny had closed her tutoring business, packed her bags, hooked up her old Airstream trailer, loaded the animals, and moved to the lake to start a new life. Best move she'd ever made. She'd left the town of Shady Grove and all her unhappy memories in the rearview mirror. Along with a brother and sister team of contractors, she'd helped finish the cabins and was now the proud but very inexperienced proprietress of the Lakeside Resort.

Glancing over at the four cabins she had rented this weekend, Jenny saw no lights and no wood smoke coming from the chimneys. Good. Folks were sleeping in. That's just what she wanted for them on their lakeside getaway.

Softly, she called up the animals, and they headed back inside. Time to get this day going.

Jenny had a pep in her step as she went about her chores. Having four of the seven cabins rented in late March seemed promising, and all of her guests this weekend seemed like nice people. Temperatures had dipped into the high twenties both nights, and she guessed folks slept cozily under the fluffy down comforters she'd put in the cabins. Though the days had only gotten a few degrees warmer, no one seemed bothered by the cold. She smiled as she dipped kibble for the boys and fed Levi. People liked making crackling fires in those robin's-egg blue cast-iron Nilsson wood stoves Jax had installed in each cabin. So comforting.

After a quick shower, Jenny tidied up. Guest checkout was at eleven and for now, the office for the Lakeside Resort was the kitchen in her cabin, the Dogwood. She liked it to look as neat and professional as a kitchen office could look. Snatching up the underwire bras she'd hand-washed and hung near the wood stove to dry, she put them away and scooped up the dogs' Nylabones, tripping hazards for sure. She cracked a window, hoping to air out the smell of the pound of bacon she'd fried earlier. Though she'd eaten some of the bacon on top of a warm English muffin topped with egg and cheese, Jenny promised herself she'd ditch the carbs and start a Keto-ish diet the next day. After vacuuming, a quick job in a three-hundred-square-foot cabin, she was done. Hands on hips, she looked around. Tidy and shipshape.

The Strattons, the outdoorsy family staying in the Redbud, were checking out early so they could stop at the National Whitewater Center in Charlotte on their way home to Greenville, South Carolina. Megan, their precocious ten-year-old daughter, had chattered about it to Jenny when she'd taken them clean towels yesterday. "It's got the most challenging man-made whitewater river in the world and a kajillion rock-climbing walls."

When the family arrived to check out, Kip Stratton greeted her with a smile and a vigorous, pumping handshake that left Jenny feeling oddly invigorated. "Top of the morning to you. Hate to go, but we're off to our next adventure."

"I enjoyed having you all visit and hope you come visit again. I'd be real grateful if you'd review your stay here," Jenny said, her voice cracking a little. It still made her nervous to ask for reviews, but she absolutely needed to, according to what she'd read.

"Be glad to tell anybody. This place is top-notch for the outdoor types." After paying their bill, Kip gave her one more bone-crushing, cardio-pumping handshake and strode off.

Jenny followed him out and waved at the Strattons as they tooled away. Back inside, Jenny fixed herself a cup of Earl Gray and thought a little enviously about the Strattons. Saturday morning, they'd roared off in their truck to go geocaching, a scavenger hunt kind of activity, they'd explained, in which they used clues and latitude and longitude coordinates to find a hidden object. The parents and their eight- and ten-year-old girls also had taken long walks and used the binoculars they'd given each other for Christmas to watch ducks and geese and see if they could spy eagles. The tight-knit family enjoyed each other's company and seemed so all-American. Jenny added a teaspoon of honey to her tea and stirred it. So different from what it was like growing up in her family. The business deals and sure-fire new ventures Daddy'd chased had meant the only thing she and Mama could count on was his unreliability. But in the here and now, Jenny reached out and touched the solid log wall of her cabin, reminding herself that Daddy had done the best he could and had sure come through for her when she needed him the most.

"Yoo-hoo! Helloooo, Jenny!" a woman called out as she rapped on Jenny's door.

"Good morning." Jenny smiled as she swung open the door.

Lola Russell, a blonde woman in a faux-fur vest, bounced inside, followed by her husband and the Steins. The two couples looked to be in their mid- to late sixties and had been friends since the men had met while stationed at Seymour Johnson Air Force Base. Jenny had put them side by side in the Mimosa and the Hydrangea.

"I heard a lot of chatting and laughing going on. I'll bet y'all stayed up late," Jenny said in a mock reproving voice, then broke into a smile.

The four chuckled as the men handed Jenny their credit cards.

Lola beamed as she caught her girlfriend's arm and squeezed it. "Oh, we had a wonderful time. We reminisced and caught up and had to talk double time because we hadn't seen each other in years."

"Every meal we cooked was a feast," said the pretty brunette in the Fair Isle sweater. "We got the woodstove going so hot that we had to open all the windows. Such fun!"

"Had a Texas Hold'em tournament and a few games of Monopoly that got cutthroat," Mr. Stein said as he ran a forefinger across his neck, hiding a smile.

"Please come again, and if y'all would please review us on the travel sites, I'd be so grateful," Jenny said as she handed them their receipts. These were just the kind of guests she hoped would become regulars at the Lakeside Resort.

"Oh, we plan on it. I'll email you as soon as we get home and look at dates for next time." Lola had a determined look in her eye. "Life is too short not to spend time with your closest friends."

Jenny's neighbor down the street, award-winning mystery writer Ella Parr, had sent her the last guest to check out. Corinne Stewart was a cozy mystery writer finishing the last book in her series set in a bed-and-breakfast on North Carolina's Outer Banks. Jenny had put her in the Camellia, the cabin as far away from other guests as she could. Corinne had been there for the whole week, staying holed up in her cabin most of the time except for mornings when she'd sat in her porch rocker and watched the sun rise as she'd swilled down coffee from her extra-large thermos cup.

Corinne arrived at Jenny's door just before eleven, looking wan and thinner than she had when she arrived. Sporting a messy, wind-tunnel-inspired hairdo, she beamed as she held up her thumb drive. "Done. I'm done!" Raising her arms, she did an awkward little victory dance that Jenny decided was River Dance meets polka, complete with hops and heels kicked together. "I'll be back for my next book," Corinne promised as she settled up. "Something about the serenity here made me write like someone turned the faucet on."

Jenny waved as she watched Corinne tootle away in her little car. Writers seemed to be good guests: quiet, undemanding, and appreciative. She'd talk to Alice, her close friend and web designer, to see if she could figure out a way to draw more writers to the resort. A writers' retreat? A writers' workshop? She'd let it percolate.

Back inside, Jenny felt elated, buoyed about the money flying though the ether to her business account. Throwing a log in the woodstove, she took a moment to pat Buddy and Bear and used her fingernails to scratch Levi's wiry winter coat. After she handed them each a few carrots, the three of them clambered onto the couch and began crunching their treats.

In the bleak, cold month of January, Jenny had made a few concessions to country living. She'd installed a signal booster for cell service in all the cabins that had improved reception some, but it was still spotty. Knowing she needed to be able to call 911 if necessary and handle business over a phone without calls dropping mid-sentence, she'd shelled out the money for a landline for herself. She'd also bought a nineteen-inch wall-mounted television that she'd put in her loft and discretely hidden behind a tapestry because she'd decided not to put TVs in the cabins and didn't want guests to spot it. While she was determined that the resort be a place where guests could disconnect, she'd also experienced how lonely the winter months could be and, sometimes, she was just too tired to read. If there were no storms and it was a relatively cloudless night, she could watch shows on PBS or catch *Maine Cabin Masters* and *American Pickers*. That was a comfort.

With the delicious shiver of anticipation she got whenever she connected with her beau, Jenny sank into the couch to call Luke. Toeing off her shoes, she snuggled under a warm throw and smiled when Luke answered. "Morning, you. How are you? How's business at the store?"

"Good morning, Jen." Luke's voice was warm as a caress. "We're busier than you'd think for a hardware store in late March. The do-it-yourselfers are taking advantage of the cold weekends to get inside projects done."

"Good." Jenny reached over to pat Bear. "How did your dad's doctor's appointment go this morning?" Over the last few months, Luke's father, Frank, had had several scary incidents related to an undiagnosed health problem. Right after the New Year, Frank had blacked out while behind the wheel coming home from the Tractor Supply store. Luckily, he'd been driving slowly when he lost consciousness, and his truck drifted into a fallow field and a few round bales of hay. He'd come out of it with a gash on his forehead and a mild concussion, but subsequent medical tests had revealed he'd had a stroke and also had several other problems, including scary high blood pressure. All were being addressed medically, but this seemingly hale and hearty man had to make lifestyle changes.

"He's improving, but the doctor told him that unless he started taking better care of his health, the next stroke could kill him. That got his attention."

Holy smokes. That would sure get her attention. Jenny heard voices in the background and guessed Luke was getting a rush of customers. "I'll let you go. Supper tonight's at six. I'm trying out a recipe for stuffed green peppers."

"Does it have quinoa in it?" There was a smile in his voice.

"Yes, as a matter of fact." She was trying to cook healthier this year and though Luke groused about it, he cleaned his plate every meal.

"See you soon, darlin' girl," he said, and ended the call.

Darlin' girl. Jenny gave a swooning sigh and sent up a quick prayer of thanks that she'd walked into Frank's Friendly Hardware that October day last year and met Luke working behind the counter.

Shrugging on a coat, Jenny gathered her bucket of cleaning supplies and rubber gloves and headed to the now-vacant cabins to clean them. As she gathered used linens and towels, she saw that all her guests, bless them, had left their cabins fairly clean.

After putting fresh sheets on the beds, Jenny vacuumed. She sprayed nontoxic grapefruit-scented cleaner on the counters and looked around, admiring the mismatched, reclaimed barn board they'd put on one wall as an accent. With Luke and his sister Alice as her contractors, they'd completed the partially finished cabins and added interesting touches like the accent walls. They'd put in stairs to the lofts instead of ladders, added handsome rough-hewn log posts to the living rooms, and kept the furnishings simple so as not to detract from the rustic aesthetic of the cabins. Then, in an embarrassment of riches, Jenny and Luke had slowly fallen in love, and Alice had become one of her closest friends.

Moving to the next cabin, Jenny wiped out the immaculate refrigerator and cleaned the stove, marveling at how life could turn on a dime. One thing she'd learned over the last year was that no matter what your plans were for your life, God or the universe or maybe even your guardian angels might present a much better plan for you if you stayed open to the possibilities.

Stepping outside, Jenny shivered in the bitingly cold air and hurried back to her toasty cabin. Stowing the basket of laundry as best she could under the stairs, she paused to admire the yet-to-be-hooked-up gleaming stainless-steel commercial washer and dryer that were conveniently located in the middle of her already compact living quarters. Luke and Alice had promised to come out on Saturday morning and finish up the new spacious laundry shed they'd roughed in directly behind Jenny's cabin. Finally, the appliances could go to their new home.

Later, when she had enough money to hire a housekeeper, she or he could handle the laundry without coming through her personal space. Jenny ran her hand along the cool, smooth steel, and tried again to decipher the high-tech-looking dials and the choices for settings.

After the Christmas and Valentine's Day rush of guests, Jenny'd realized she had to break down and buy a commercial washer and dryer to handle all the sheets and towels generated by eight cabins. These beauties had cost a pretty penny even at the President's Day sale, but she and Luke had talked and decided it had to be done because doing laundry now took her the better part of a day. Trying to wash all those sheets and towels in her stackable washer-dryer just didn't work, and schlepping a carload of laundry to the next town over to Wanda's Washeteria meant spending the better part of a day in the dingy laundromat with religious music playing, fluorescent lights flickering, and grown-up people walking around in pajama pants.

Jenny put both hands on the small of her back and tried to stretch, but her back still hurt just from a little vacuuming. Good grief. Though being forty-three didn't seem old most days, some days it did. Last month, she'd ended up in bed with an ice pack after leaning down to pick up the dogs' Kong toys from the floor. Sliding onto the rug, Jenny tried to get rid of the kinks in her back with a few of the stretches she vaguely remembered from a yoga class she'd dropped out of years ago. Child's Pose and Cat Cow did help. Levi watched with interest, Bear did some stretching of his own, and Buddy tried to kiss her. Feeling slightly less stiff, she made herself a cup of coffee and slid into the chair at her computer. The boys curled up on the rug to snooze.

Jenny blew out a sigh. She'd rather weed poison ivy with her bare hands than do bookkeeping, but it had to be done. In her previous career as a middle school and high school tutor, once the teachers, guidance counselors, and principals got to know her as a resource and started referring students, her work was fairly steady. She could count on a certain income every month and knew to set aside money for summers when school was out. But now, she needed to plan for the slower months and scratch around to find ways to bring in more business.

After distracting herself with checking email and comforting herself with viewing a montage of sleeping bunnies on Facebook, Jenny reluctantly clicked back to her books. Nibbling a nail, Jenny thought about her old job again. Maybe she was forgetting money challenges she'd had in her past. Now she remembered lean months punctuated by stomach-churning unexpected expenses, like needing four new tires on her SUV or having to get a crown put on with no dental insurance. Finally, Jenny had started making extra money running study groups for the SATs and offering one-on-one sessions for students getting ready to write the essays and present their best selves for admission to college. She sat up straighter, feeling a spark of hopefulness.

But back then, her only expense was the rent on her small

office in a not fancy part of town. Jenny rested her chin in her hand. Running the Lakeside Resort was a much bigger deal expense-wise than her old job. She had eight buildings and the grounds to keep up. The beds, bedding, and furnishings all sat on her Visa bill. She was nibbling away at that balance, but still, she dreaded even looking at her monthly statements. Property taxes were breathtaking. Good insurance was an expensive must. She wrote a sizeable check online every month to Goodlife Bank for the construction loan she was still paying off, and she had quarterly taxes to pay to the State of North Carolina and to Uncle Sam. To top it off, she'd had to buy the washer and dryer.

Since she didn't know what she was doing as a hotelier, the hardest task of all was figuring out ways to generate business. Closing her eyes, Jenny inhaled and exhaled a long, slow breath and tried giving herself an internal pep talk. *You can do this. You've figured out other hard things. You can read books and articles and get marketing ideas.* Jenny's eyes fluttered open. It wasn't working. She didn't believe what she was telling herself. What she needed to do was to take a hard look at exactly what income she saw coming to offset all those expenses.

Squaring her shoulders, Jenny mentally braced herself as she pulled up her *Welcome Inn* reservation system. The good news was that she already had some bookings for the heart of summer, Memorial Day through Labor Day. But she had a lot of empty cabins to fill on either side of the high season and wide open spaces between now and then. Just because she had lucked out with full houses at Christmas and Valentine's Day didn't mean she was in high cotton. Numbers swirled around in Jenny's head. She was a rookie with few ideas for growing her business. Jenny raked her fingers through her hair. What had she gotten herself into?

CHAPTER 2 — EAU DE SKUNK

FTER FRETTING, IMAGINING THE WORST, and eating half of a family-sized bag of M & M's she kept on hand for emergencies, Jenny gave herself a good talking to and decided she'd make the forty-five minute drive into town for groceries. Getting moving would be good for her.

Pulling on her jacket, she grabbed her purse and headed out. Chicken breasts were on sale and so were small turkeys, both of which Jenny would have liked to stock up on, but the freezer in her cabin was small and always packed to bursting. If she had a big freezer, she could buy more on sale, and freeze milk, cream, leftovers, and the veggies she planned to grow in her future garden. The Pioneer Woman used her freezer a lot, Jenny bet.

Making the run into town was time consuming. Later, maybe she'd buy a chest freezer, but where would she put it? She thought about that while she shopped, and it came to her. There was room for it in the laundry shed. Luke could make sure that they had the electrical set up to handle that. Then, maybe she'd get one of those meal-saving, vacuum-sealing doohickeys and freeze food she bought on sale. But as Jenny swung the canvas sacks of groceries from the back of the SUV and trudged toward her cabin, she remembered the tenuous state of her finances. A girl could dream.

The sun was slipping down in the sky, and Jenny was slicing a plump green avocado when she heard Luke's truck. Slipping off her favorite vintage apron, the one with the red and yellow dancing chickens, Jenny gave her hair a quick smooth. Flinging open the door, her heart flew up in her chest as she took in his cobalt blue eyes, even features, and dazzling smile that was meant just for her. This good-looking man in the red down jacket and jeans who smelled of fresh air and cedar was hers.

"Hey, you," Luke said in his deep buttery voice.

Jenny's eyes met his, and she stepped into his arms, feeling safe and cherished. Leaning her head on broad shoulders, she sighed with pleasure before he leaned in and gave her a kiss that left her weak-kneed. "I hated not seeing you for so long," she murmured.

"Right back at you." Luke hooked an arm around her neck and walked inside with her. "Supper smells good." Lifting the lid of the slow cooker, he inhaled and gave her a thumbs-up.

As they ate, the two caught up on what was happening in their lives. The green peppers stuffed with ground turkey, chickpeas and, yes, quinoa, tasted as savory and wonderful as they smelled.

"So, the doctor said your dad is better?" Jenny sipped a glass of crisp sauvignon blanc.

Luke swallowed a bite and patted his mouth with a napkin. "That's right. That accident was a blessing in disguise. If it hadn't happened, they'd never have run the tests and found the other problems. The hospital stay was hard enough, but getting a hard-headed man to get seen for follow-up was hard." Luke shook his head ruefully. "You know how my dad is about doctors. Mama said she'd hog-tie him if she had to."

Jenny took another a bite of spicy deliciousness and eyed him. "Women need to do that sometimes."

The corners of Luke's mouth turned up as he helped himself to seconds. "Daddy's new physician is sharp. She put him on new medication that's bringing his cholesterol down and getting his blood pressure where it needs to be. He may recover almost completely from the stroke." Luke winced. "He still smoked some. Snuck cigarettes down in the barn."

Jenny understood. No surprise that a man who still farmed some tobacco on his property would want a smoke every now and then.

"He's groused every step of the way about getting healthier, but the right medication, changes to his diet, and walking seem to be working," Luke said, relief in his voice.

"Is he going to back off on his schedule at the store and finally hire a manager?" Jenny fervently hoped the answer was yes. She'd not seen Luke much since the accident, and she'd missed him more than she'd thought was possible. Since his father's health had deteriorated, he'd been working at Frank's Friendly full time, waiting on customers, ordering inventory, doing billing and accounting and every other detail of a running busy hardware store. Luke was able to see her on some weekends, but when he did, he spent most of the time working on finishing projects he'd started at the resort. As Jenny's Christmas present, Luke had promised to fix up her beat up Airstream, the Silver Belle, and build the new laundry shed. She'd asked him several times to just stop doing any projects until he had more time, but he'd stubbornly refused. They'd fallen in love while working like plowmen. Maybe they should try to just have fun and date like normal people.

Jenny tuned back in just as Luke said, "...but the doctor says light duty or nothing. I'm interviewing managers now. Daddy's mad as a hornet, but that's just the way it is."

"Oh, dear." Jenny could only imagine how hard it would be for Frank to let someone else run the business he'd spent his whole life building.

Luke took a swallow of beer and looked grim. "Mama, Alice, the doctor, and I have all talked. He needs to cut way back at work or sell the store."

"Hard conversations, buddy." Jenny gave him a sympathetic look.

Luke nodded. "But necessary ones. I've got two good candidates for the manager job. If Daddy OKs it, we'll hire one of them this week and get him up to speed." He took a sip of beer and regarded her with those Paul Newman blue eyes of his. "I've been talking up a storm and haven't heard enough about you. What's going on?"

Jenny recapped her guests' departures, and their promises to come again. "That was exciting and just made me feel somehow *vindicated.* It confirmed for me that we built the right kind of getaway for a certain type of guest. I just need to figure out how to get more of them here."

Luke nodded, looking thoughtful.

Pushing up her sleeves, Jenny tried to decide how much to tell him about her anxieties. Yup. If he really was a keeper, she needed to go full speed ahead. "Was I crazy to try to take this on? I just don't know what I'm doing, and the responsibility, especially the money, keeps my nerves jangled." Looking down, she realized she was shredding the paper towel they'd used as napkins and didn't even know it.

Luke's gaze held hers. "I don't think you're crazy. Building the business is going to take time. Getting yourself all nervous about it isn't going to help fill cabins."

Jenny just eyed him, waiting. For such a smart man, sometimes he said the most lunkheaded things.

Luke caught her glance, froze, and put down the forkful of green beans he was about to put in his mouth. "Sorry. Being a guy. What I meant was, you probably should focus on what you can control. Get some ideas going for marketing, and try them out. You can see which ones work and which don't."

Jenny thought about it. "You're right." She cast at sideways glance at him, pretty sure he had no idea about how little she knew about business.

Pushing his chair back from the table, Luke stretched out his long legs and crossed his ankles. "The Lakeside Resort's going to be a success, Jenny. You need to make a plan for marketing and work the plan."

"I'll get going on it." Jenny gave him a crooked smile and pointed her fork at him. "Back to what you said. Does hiring a manager mean that things can get back to normal and we can see more of each other again?" She tried to keep her voice light, but being a good sport was wearing her down to the nub.

Luke gave her an apologetic look. "You've been understanding. I appreciate it."

"Thanks," Jenny said lightly. But, really, she'd had no choice.

Luke's dad was sick, his family needed him, and he was being a good son. Luke was doing what he should be doing. "Are we still on for Saturday morning?"

Luke leaned back in his chair. "Yes, ma'am. Alice and I will be here early. We'll knock out the shed and move in the washer and dryer, although it's been real convenient to have these babies here." Reaching behind him, Luke made a show of casually resting an elbow on the dryer and grinned at Jenny.

Jenny laughed. Reaching over, she took his hand, loving the strength of his fingers and the feel of calluses on his palms. "One of these days I want to have a real date with you. One where we go out to dinner at an actual restaurant and hold hands and stare at each other over candlelight."

"We'll get there, Jen. Just be patient." He gave her a regretful look. "I've got to get back. I need to swing by and check on Mama and Daddy, and open the store in the morning. I'll see you Saturday."

Jenny sighed inwardly but gave him a smile. The poor guy was going a hundred miles per hour trying to hold everything together. Of course she could be patient.

After Luke helped her clear and rinse dishes, he bade the boys farewell and put on his jacket. Enveloping her in a hug, he gave her an intent look. "It's hard not seeing you, Jenny."

"I feel the same." Jenny was a little breathless. Luke was not an expressive guy when it came to feelings, so on the rare occasions when he let her know how much he cared, her mouth went dry, her pulse went raucous, and her heart thudded with love and longing.

With a crooked smile and a wave, Luke stepped out into the cold, moonlit night.

As Jenny finished washing pots and pans, she thought about it. What was even better than all the internal fireworks was the secure feeling that she had with Luke. She knew with a hundred percent certainty he'd be there for her and would help her in any way he could. Jenny had dated some "all hat and no cattle" types in her past, big talkers who promised her the world but couldn't back it up. Her ex-fiancé, Douglas, came to mind. He'd called off their Christmas wedding last year because he'd found and ended up marrying his *soulmate*, the long-legged, brainy, dewy-skinned physical therapist, Aiden. Jenny closed her eyes and imagined erasing a chalkboard, a *Me Booster* tip her best friend Charlotte had taught her as a way to banish negative thoughts. That helped some, but then Jenny pictured throwing a bucket of icy lake water on the happy couple and smiled. That *did* help her feel better.

The next afternoon, Jenny blew out a sigh of relief when she got back from Wanda's Washeteria. A frizzy-haired, oddly dressed, possibly homeless woman had taken Jenny's sheets out of the dryer while they were still wet in order to put her clothes in on Jenny's quarters, and the manager had had to intervene. Rattled from that encounter, Jenny had accidentally splashed bleach on her newish J.Jill *corduroys* that fit perfectly even though she had plumped up over the winter. Jenny stepped on the gas a little too hard leaving the parking lot and her car threw gravel, but she didn't care. This was her last trip to that depressing place.

Back home, Jenny nosed her eleven-year-old SUV into the clearing and pulled up beside her cabin just as a fresh-faced brunette with tumbling curls approached, waved enthusiastically, and strode over to the car. "Hey, Jenny." She reached in the cargo area and nabbed a big laundry basket of freshly folded sheets and towels to carry in.

"Thanks, Lily." Jenny smiled gratefully at her as she grabbed two smaller laundry baskets, held one on her hips, and thunked shut the cargo door. "How are you? How's work?"

Though Jenny had initially had qualms about renting a cabin for a year to a twenty-three-year old, Lily was the model tenant and the year-round rent was a big help. The town librarian, her young tenant also taught meditation and yoga at the senior center.

"Fantastic," Lily said enthusiastically. "Our children's reading program is growing like kudzu, and I'm getting people on board for an adult literacy program." She followed Jenny inside, easily lifting the heaviest laundry basket onto the kitchen table. "I don't know if you've ever picked it up before, but we have a small regional paper here called the *Heron Lake Herald*. The editor,

Shandra Washington, comes into the library sometimes. She just had an interview fall through and was looking for story ideas, so I told her about you, and she wants to write a feature about the Lakeside Resort."

"Gosh, thanks for thinking of me." Jenny was thrilled but felt a clutching in her stomach at the thought of being interviewed.

"The circulation is small, but I thought you might like the publicity. Shandra needs to get the story by tomorrow, so you give her a call if you're interested." Lily pulled a scrap of paper from her pocket and handed it to Jenny. "She'll want to hear about the cabins and take a bunch of pictures. She said she wants to know how a city girl like you likes living in the country."

Jenny hid a smile. Shady Grove, the town she'd left to move to Heron Lake, had 2,076 residents, four traffic lights, two barbecue joints, and a second-run movie theater. Shady Grove was no Atlanta. "I'll call her. Thank you so much for thinking of me."

With a friendly wave, Lily headed out.

Jenny slung herself into a seat at the kitchen table, took her phone out of her purse, and eyed it. She'd never ever talked to a reporter or been interviewed. What if she choked up or came off as foolish or like a braggart? Her words would all be there forever in the archives in black and white. Jenny shuddered inwardly. Rubbing her sweaty palms on her jeans, Jenny thought about Luke's suggestions. *Get some ideas going and try them out.* Jenny sat up straighter, one of her father's favorite sayings popping into her mind. *Fortune favors the bold.* She could be bold. Her fingers trembling a little, Jenny dialed Shandra Washington.

The next morning, Jenny's heart was racing, but she was almost ready for her nine o'clock interview. In online searches she'd done last night, she'd read an article called, *How to Present Well in Newspaper Interviews*. Jenny had read *The key is to be yourself.* That one was a head scratcher. Not sure who else to be, Jenny decided she'd be even more real. Applying just minimal makeup, Jenny pulled her hair up in a high ponytail, and slipped on jeans, a chunky knit pullover sweater in a muted gold, and her most comfortable pair of brogans.

Hurriedly, she plumped pillows and ran a quick damp mop around the hardwoods to catch any tumbleweeds of animal hair she'd overlooked when vacuuming. Crossing her arms, Jenny glanced around her cabin, admiring her handiwork. She was going for a Magnolia-slash-Country-Living vibe, and she might have nailed it. The cabin and everything in it looked airy, warm, neat, and well-loved. Chewing a nail, Jenny wished her washer and dryer were in their new home instead of in the middle of her living room. Maybe artfully draping a patchwork quilt over them would help, but she doubted it.

She sniffed the enticing aroma of baking bread and smiled. In an old file box, she'd found her mama's famous recipe for Banana Pecan Bread. The two loaves she'd whipped up were baking, and smelling heavenly. By the time Shandra arrived, she'd have just pulled them from the oven to cool. The Dogwood would smell homey and welcoming.

It was 8:53. Jenny needed to corral up the animals. She didn't want the boys milling around the newswoman when she got out of her car. Stepping outside, she called, "Buddy, Bear, Levi. Come, boys." She'd settle the animals in the living room, distracting the dogs with peanut butter-filled KONG balls and Levi with a handful of carrots.

Instead of reluctantly responding when she called and sauntering in like they usually did, the three careened into the cabin panting, scattering rugs, and knocking over a plant. Bear dropped onto his front paws and began rubbing his nose in the rug. Buddy leapt onto the sofa and rolled around, his paws kicking in the air. If a miniature horse could look guilty, Levi did. He walked over to Jenny and leaned against her.

Her heart racing, Jenny stared. What had scared them? She hurried over to look more closely at Bear.

But Jenny stopped in her tracks and almost gagged when the pungent odor hit her. The intensity of it made her put her hands over her mouth and nose and try not to breathe. Burning rubber tire. Electrical fires. Stump dump fires. Jenny knew that all three of her animals had been sprayed by a skunk. She'd smelled the pungent odor of a skunk in the distance while driving down a highway, but had never smelled one so up close and personal. Eau de fresh skunk was an eye-watering, stomach-churning level of awfulness. Coughing, she breathed into her sleeve.

"Shoo, boys. Shoo!" Heart galloping, Jenny grabbed a broom and chased them out of the cabin, but the damage was done. The cabin reeked and so did she, just from that brief contact.

Throwing open the windows, Jenny hurriedly peeled off her sweater and jeans and pulled on the next clothes she laid her hands on, the bleach-splotched corduroys and a Carolina Mudcats sweatshirt that had shrunk in the wash. She sniffed herself. She still stank. Her hair. Desperate, Jenny grabbed a bottle of lemon room freshener, organic thank goodness, and sprayed her hair.

The oven timer dinged on the banana bread at the same time a knock sounded at the door. Jenny panicked and ducked under the counter. Could she pretend she wasn't home?

But glancing up, she saw a silver-haired woman in an African-inspired hair wrap outside her open window, peering in.

Pretending to be tying a shoe, Jenny bounced up, pasted a smile on her face, and called out cheerfully through the open window, "Good morning."

Shandra Washington put a hand to her mouth, but her eyes twinkled. "Oh, my word. Poor you. We've had a bumper crop of skunks this year. Isn't country life grand?"

Though the interview was conducted outside, sitting ten feet apart on Adirondack chairs with both women holding Kleenexes to their noses and talking to each other in loud voices, Jenny thought it went well. Shandra dug the whole woman over forty as a new entrepreneur angle and seemed fascinated by the family backstory, with Jenny fulfilling a dream that had been her daddy's but was now her own. With Jenny outside, standing the required eight to ten feet away and calling out highlights for Shandra to be sure not to miss, the newswoman took a self-guided tour of several cabins, declaring them, "So stinkin' cute."

Hurt by their banishment, the dogs and Levi lounged, sunning themselves over by the Silver Belle, trying to look innocent and pretending they didn't stink to high heaven. Keeping her distance, Shandra took pictures of them, using her long camera lens. "They are super cute."

After Shandra checked her small notepad to make sure she hadn't missed any questions, she looked at Jenny. "I'm going to write down a skunk remedy and leave it right here for you." She patted the arm of her Adirondack chair. "Tomato juice is old school. This peroxide, baking soda, and dish detergent recipe works better. You'll still end up needing to wash your critters at least twice. Gets it out of the animals' coats faster, but the real truth is you'll be smelling it until it decides to wear off." She gave an authoritative nod. "I'll email you copy of the article, and you can pick up a paper copy at Gus's Gas-N-Git. Best of luck to you, Jenny."

CHAPTER 3 — GREENHORNS BRAINSTORM

F OR ONCE, JENNY WAS GRATEFUL she had no guests arriving. For the next two days, she washed animals, did laundry, sprayed room freshener, and burned balsam-scented candles. Though it was cold out, Jenny kept the windows open and fires roaring in the woodstove. By the morning of day three, Jenny could pet the boys without keeping a paper towel under her hand and holding her breath.

At her computer, Jenny opened the attachment from Shandra, sat forward in her seat, and anxiously read the article the newswoman had written. The headline read: *Innkeeper Jenny Beckett Builds a Charming Rustic Getaway at Heron Lake, Though Sometimes Country Life Stinks.* Despite humorously detailing the boys' run-in with the skunk, Shandra's article included paragraph headers like *A rustic, homey haven; Family dreams come true;* and *Resort an economic boon to the county.*

Forwarding the article to Luke, Jenny sat back in her chair and smiled. In the masthead, she'd read that the circulation was 912. There were too many references to *city girl* and *former yuppie Jenny Beckett,* and the article under the story about the Lakeside Resort had a feature that read *Woman Pulled for DUI Found to Be Transporting Purloined Piglets,* but still, Jenny decided she'd count it as a win.

Luke responded almost immediately. *All publicity good publicity. Go, Jenny. XO*

The phone rang and Jenny smiled when she saw her best friend Charlotte's name on the screen. "Hey there, stranger."

"Hey, Shug." Charlotte sounded cheerful, as usual. "I'm on my way back from Ashe's house, and I need a dose of your good common sense. Can I come by for a visit? If you tell me you're too busy, you won't hurt my feeling one tiny bit."

"Never too busy for you," Jenny said. "Come see me. Where are you?"

"About thirty feet from your cabin. I'm just pulling in," Charlotte said mischievously.

Laughing, Jenny heard the crunch of gravel and ended the call. The boys began barking their manly *Halt Intruder!* barks. Levi looked like he wished he could bark and tossed his head around in a miniature horse's version of *Make my day!* Jenny slipped on a coat and stepped outside to greet her friend.

Charlotte stepped from her faded green four-door with the basketball-sized dent in the driver's side panel and a new crack that looked like the Blue Ridge mountain range running along the entire front windshield. Her raven black curls pulled into a high ponytail, her friend managed to look glamorous in lace-up work boots, jeans and a bright yellow down jacket she bragged about getting on sale for ten dollars at Old Navy. Her face radiating goodwill, she enthusiastically hugged Jenny, then Buddy, Bear, and Levi.

Jenny grinned as she watched Charlotte kiss the mini on his muzzle and wrinkle her nose. "What have you gotten into, little man? I love you anyway." Levi was her favorite, although she tried not to let the dogs know.

"We had a skunk incident. It'll go away eventually," Jenny said apologetically.

"My sinuses are acting up, and I can't smell much, so it's not too bad." From the trunk of the car, Charlotte pulled out several bolts of fabric and two gallons of paint. "Your interior design professional has arrived." She handed a paint can to Jenny. "I was hoping I could pop in and out of here over the next few weeks and get some work done." She hooked a thumb toward the Airstream.

"Luke texted me and said he finished his fixing up. It's time for me to do my fluffing up. I promise I'll stay out of your way. Luke told me he'd hooked up the water, septic and power in the Belle, so I'll bunk there if that's OK. I might float in and out for the next few days, so don't mind me."

"Sure. I'd love it." Jenny was glad for the company. Sometimes she got spooked being at the resort when no one else was around. They headed over to the camper, which stood less than ten feet from her tiny cabin, and Jenny unlocked the door. "The outside is still rough, but we'll get to that later. I do love the glimmer and shine of these Airstreams." She touched a hand to the dull and pockmarked exterior as they stepped inside. "But Luke's made the inside sound, clean, and comfortable." The two of them made quick work of stowing Charlotte's supplies and flowery overnight duffel on the pull-down jackknife sofa on the wall.

"This is amazing." Charlotte peered at Luke's handiwork. "He's done a fantastic job."

Jenny rubbed her chin, trying to remember what Luke had told her. "So, this is officially a renovation, not a restoration. A restoration is when you bring it back to exactly how it was in the prime of its life and stay true to every detail. That's what the purists want, he said."

Charlotte eyes were bright with interest. "Makes sense."

"We don't have the time or the money to do the complete restoration, and the goal was to make the Airstream function properly and safely, and be comfortable enough for us to get it back on the road." Jenny tapped the new flooring with the toe of her boot. "We went with vinyl, but I like it."

"Perfect." Charlotte gave an approving nod. "I'd go with saving money and being practical over expensive and first-class every time."

Luke and Charlotte's offer to redo the interior of the Silver Belle was the best Christmas present Jenny had ever gotten. "We found the cabinets and appliances at the Habitat for Humanity store. They were in a mobile home," Jenny said proudly.

"Smart. I love Habitat." For all Charlotte's wealth, she

frequented thrift shops and yard sales, carried an envelope of coupons in her purse, and always knew what station had the cheapest gas in town.

Jenny went on. "He patched the subflooring, shored up the frame, and put in new plumbing and electrical. He made the exterior watertight, repaired floors, replaced insulation, and put in a new shower enclosure and an actual toilet. Both are teeny-tiny, but better than having to walk to a public bathhouse in the campground to use the bathroom, especially in the middle of the night."

Charlotte grimaced. "So much better." She glanced around one more time. "The paint I've picked will be just perfect. The sofa will have clean guts and be extra-cushiony for sleeping, and wait until you see the fabric I've picked. So yummy and retro-looking."

"I can't wait." Jenny pictured how stripped down and dumpy the trailer had looked before Luke had gone to work. "This place has come so far. I can't wait to get it on the road one of these days."

"One of these days?" Charlotte gave Jenny a quizzical look. "Remember, we promised not to let falling in love with our guys get in the way of our spending quality time together. Are you and I still going on our camping adventure later this spring?"

Jenny felt a wave of guilt, hating to let her down. "I don't think I'll have the time or money. Plus, I'd need someone to run the resort while I was away, and I can't think of a soul who'd do it."

Charlotte's face fell, but she gave her a crooked smile. "I understand. The timing's bad. We'll do our all-gal shakedown trip in the Belle sometime soon."

But Jenny saw the clouds that had flitted across Charlotte's usually sunny face and knew she'd hurt her friend's feelings. Gazing at her intently, Jenny explained, "I'm like one of those ducks that looks calm on the surface but is paddling like crazy under the water. I've got money problems and so much to do to make this place a success. I'm overwhelmed."

"I understand." Charlotte's face cleared. "I'll help in any way I can. Can I give you money, or loan you money? I've got buckets and buckets of cash," she said airily.

"You're a good friend to offer, but I can't take your money. I'll figure this out." Jenny gave her a quick hug and put her hands on her hips. "I've got a project now. Want to help?"

"Love to."

"A lot of the guests who have visited so far seem into the birds. I love bluebirds, and I was just going to put up a bunch of nesting boxes to attract them," Jenny announced.

"Zion the serenity coach says bluebirds bring happiness, reassurance, and messages from loved ones in heaven." Charlotte zipped her coat and slipped on a wool hat she pulled from her pocket.

Though she teased Charlotte about the wacky-sounding motivational tips she got from the self-help blogs she followed with names like *My Phenomenal Fluffy Life, Curvy and Groovy,* and *Be Proud of Your Big Girl Build,* Jenny liked the idea of celestial messages from family and friends who'd gone before.

Outside, they headed to the shed. Jenny found her small stepladder and handed it to Charlotte. They loaded the wheelbarrow with a hammer, ten bird nesting boxes, mounting poles, and the non-drying automotive grease she'd had Luke bring her from the hardware store.

"What's that for?" Charlotte pointed at the grease.

"It's supposed to help keep snakes and critters away."

"Ugh." Charlotte gave a dainty shudder and hefted the ladder on a shoulder. The women set off for the spots Jenny had picked to mount the boxes.

"I've never done this but I've read up on it," Jenny explained. "At one point, the Eastern bluebirds were almost extinct. But bird groups helped educate the public, and people began reducing the use of certain pesticides and building bird boxes. The bluebirds are coming back."

"Yay." Charlotte gave an exultant skip and almost tripped on a root but caught herself.

Huffing a little from their pace, Jenny vowed she'd get more exercise one day soon. "From now to late June, the males, which are the deep blue ones, find nesting sites and sing to attract a mate and to tell other males to back off. Then, he finds the right girl and starts a family."

Charlotte sighed. "So romantic."

"We're putting the boxes in the open or on the edge of an open area. It's good if there are trees near it so the babies learning to fly can have a safe landing spot."

For the next hour, the two worked steadily. Jenny climbed the ladder to get a good hammer angle on the poles, and Charlotte steadied it with two leopard-print gloved hands. They took turns with tasks. The ground was hard and the boxes were heavy, but they made steady progress. "Break time," Jenny called. She'd worked up a sweat pushing the wheelbarrow up a small hill and over bumpy terrain. Handing Charlotte a bottle of water she'd wedged in her coat pocket, she pulled one out for herself, and they collapsed onto a small, mossy overlook.

Leaning on her elbow, Jenny panted slightly. She smiled when she saw that Charlotte had tucked a large osprey feather she'd found into the top of her wool cap. She looked like one of Robin Hood's merry band. "How are you? How about Ashe? How is that nice man?"

"I'm dandy and Ashe is extraordinary, kind, and good lookin' as all get out." Charlotte sounded as if she could scarcely believe her good fortune.

"He is," Jenny said. Charlotte's fiancé was a forty-eight-year-old gangly attorney with thinning red hair and gold-rimmed glasses, but he adored Charlotte. That made him a George Clooney-Brad Pitt combo to Jenny. Charlotte's cooking had filled him out so he wasn't so skinny, and she had him wearing clothes that made him look less like an academic and more like an outdoorsy guy who'd not think twice about stepping into a raging blizzard to get more wood for the fire.

"Have I thanked you for matchmaking us?" Charlotte took a slug of water and gave her a grateful look.

"About a million times." Jenny was still patting herself on the back for the fine job she'd done playing Cupid for Charlotte. Her friend had been afraid that her extra weight would mean she'd never find a good husband. Now she was engaged.

Charlotte stretched out all the way on the ground, propped herself on her elbows, and cast a sideways glance at Jenny. "How is that scrumptious Luke? How's his daddy's health, and how's his mama holding up?"

Jenny tried to sound upbeat. "His father's improving slowly. He wants to buck doctor's orders and go back to work and is mad that Luke's looking to hire a general manager for the hardware store." She winced as she thought about it. "His mama, Caroline, is trying to stay upbeat and keep him on the straight and narrow. Frank handled all the finances, and now she's having to take that on. Alice has her learning to do online banking." Jenny shook her head. "Frank's being sick has scared her to pieces."

"Of course it has." Charlotte studied her. "So Luke's still taking care of things at home and at the store and still hasn't had much time for you?"

"Alice is helping, but basically, yes," Jenny said glumly

"Any more talk about the engagement?" Charlotte asked quietly.

"None." Jenny felt blood thrumming in her ears. "Between my figuring out how to run this place and Luke's daddy getting sick, we haven't talked about it." She tried to think about what else worried her. "I keep thinking about the way that he proposed, and it's bugging me."

"The proposal being Luke kind of casually mentioning you all would travel once you got married," Charlotte clarified.

"Right. No ring, no one knee, no time frames." Jenny rolled her shoulders to try to loosen them. "Looking back on it, it's all a little free form, go-with-the-flow for me."

Charlotte, who had an annoyingly accurate way of knowing exactly what Jenny was thinking, lifted a brow. "But with all that Luke has on his plate, you don't want to be a burden by bringing up these concerns."

"Yup." Jenny raised a shoulder but then tried to get in the *think positive and positive things will happen* mode, another one of

Charlotte's *Me Booster* tips. "Things will settle down soon, though, and we'll have a chance to get back on track with this romance."

"They will."

Jenny regarded her friend. "How about you? Any talk of dates or rings?"

"No date yet, but we're getting the rings custom made. Mine will be nothing fancy, but his mama and mine put their heads together and decided to each give us a few small stones that we'll incorporate into the band." Charlotte sounded matter-of-fact about the ring, but her cheeks were pink with excitement.

"Sounds perfect." Though genuinely happy for her friend, Jenny felt a little stab of envy at the certainty Charlotte had in her life.

"I've got some scoop. The mayor of Celeste just got caught with his hand in the till. It seemed odd that the town barber bought a brand new Porsche and built a big swimming pool." Charlotte eyes gleamed at the scandal. "A developer who just moved to Celeste announced he wants to run for mayor. Word is, he wants to bulldoze the run-down historical homes downtown and build a bunch of ugly apartments. We can't let those precious pieces of history get gone forever. So, the small business crowd in town talked Ashe into running against him."

"Ashe would make a wonderful mayor."

"He would, but running a campaign takes time. I don't see much of Ashe unless I go to campaign headquarters, which is Ricky's Hot Dog Shop, and sit in the back booth folding mailings all night." Charlotte raised her eyes to heaven.

"So, we're both kind of sitting on the back burner," Jenny said wryly and considered her friend. "You seem to be taking it in stride."

"It's temporary, so I can handle it. Ashe would make a first-rate mayor." Charlotte faced her. "Here's my dilemma. I'm stalled on getting my designer-slash-interior decorator-slash-stager business going. I know lots of folks in Shady Grove, including Mama's and Daddy's friends who might hire me, but I don't want my business there. When Ashe and I get hitched, we'll live in Celeste. I don't want an hour-and-a-half commute to jobs."

"Right," Jenny said. "So, are you trying to get work going in Celeste?"

"I'm trying, but I've not gotten one bite there." Charlotte pressed her lips together.

Jenny tilted her head. "What's Celeste like?"

"Friendly. Decent folks. I'm surprised at how much I like it," Charlotte mused. "Do you know what the town motto is? *Celeste. A nice, quiet place to be.*" Her eyes sparkled with humor. "Ashe jokes that we should change it to, *Celeste. Pokey but nice, and we aim to keep it that way.*"

Jenny broke into a smile. "Catchy. These days, though, that message would be enough to cause a stampede of folks moving in trying to find Mayberry. Look at Waco. Lots of folks are looking for that friendly, small-town vibe."

Charlotte's brow furrowed. "And then they start complaining that we drive too slowly and that the roads don't get plowed fast enough when it snows."

Jenny knew Charlotte was still sore about almost getting run off the road last week by a car with out-of-state plates passing on a double line while going around a corner. "Maybe they could change the town motto to, *Celeste. Pokey and unfriendly.*"

Charlotte giggled. "*Celeste. Spiders and copperheads galore.*"

Jenny burst out laughing. "Or, *Celeste. Move along down the road.*"

"I could keep going to Chamber of Commerce meetings in Celeste and maybe try to drum up business in Morganton or Hickory," Charlotte said, sounding doubtful.

"How about drumming up business here on the lake?" Jenny suggested. "Target folks who've retired here or the ones with second homes here. Maybe you could meet with real estate agents here and in Celeste and see if you could help them with staging."

Charlotte looked intrigued. "Those are fab ideas. What if the realtors have listings that won't sell because the houses are so dated? I could shine up those Plain Janes and get them sold pronto."

Jenny bobbed her head enthusiastically. "Like you did with Daddy's house. And you've got the before and after photos and YouTube clips to prove it."

"I need to get the agent who listed his house for us to write a testimonial letter. I should have thought of that," she said sheepishly. "Sometimes I sound like I know more about business than I do." Charlotte shook her head ruefully, her osprey feather bobbing.

"I'm trying to figure business out as I go along, too." Jenny thought about it. "When I quit teaching to start my tutoring business, referrals came slowly." Grinning, she recalled her secret weapon. "Things took off when I brought warm Krispy Kreme donuts to staff meetings."

"Brilliant." Charlotte shook her head admiringly. "I'll drop off business cards and warm donuts to folks I want to work with. I can tell them I do good work on a budget."

"Smart. Everyone needs to keep an eye on the bottom line these days."

"So true," Charlotte said emphatically.

Jenny hid her smile. Charlotte's bottom line was gold-plated, since her parents had bought her Berkshire Hathaway stocks for each of her forty-five birthdays. But her friend wanted a career she cared about to feel good about herself, and design and staging were a natural fit.

"I'm having trouble filling the cabins," Jenny admitted, glancing over at Charlotte. "Kids are still in school so parents won't book. It's too chilly for lake activities."

"What about childless types or retired people? How could you get them here?"

"No clue," Jenny muttered.

A flock of geese flew over, and the two watched as they disappeared into low clouds.

Jenny sighed. "I love how they keep calling out to each other like friends checking in."

Tapping a finger on her mouth, Charlotte looked around. "The view on this bluff takes your breath away." She inhaled noisily. "The air is fresh and clean, and the only sound you hear is nature. If people who love this sort of thing could just experience this, they'd flock here."

"But how do I reach them?" Jenny stared moodily out at the lake.

Charlotte shrugged. "No clue. But let's brainstorm about how to grow our businesses."

"Sounds good." But Jenny wondered how the two greenhorns would have much to offer each other. Her donut tip had been her ace in the hole. Jenny rose stiffly, groaning at muscles that had already started to tighten. "Let's get those other bird boxes knocked out before we freeze like this." She reached out a hand to help Charlotte to her feet, and the two trudged off to help lovestruck bluebirds feather their nests.

CHAPTER 4 — EMBER AND THE CARAMEL CAKE

EARLY SATURDAY MORNING, JENNY HEARD Charlotte leave. She poked her head outside as she opened the door for the boys. The sun was shining, the lake was glittering, and Jenny was planning to finish a project with two of her favorite people in the world. Today was going to be a good day.

When Luke and Alice arrived about seven, Jenny felt happiness bubbling up inside her. The three of them got busy unloading supplies from the blue truck to take to the laundry shed. She couldn't help it: Jenny reached an arm around Alice's shoulders and one around Luke's and gave them a quick squeeze. "This feels like old times," she said. It had just been last fall when the three of them had worked like stevedores to get the cabins finished in time for arriving guests.

"Exactly, except I'm an old married lady now and my brother is googly-eyed over you." Alice grinned at her and did a little skipping step.

Luke rolled his eyes but gave Jenny's shoulder a pat. "Let me double-check my measurements. I'll meet you at the shed." Easily hefting two rolls of insulation from the truck bed, he trekked off.

"How are you?" Jenny hadn't seen nearly enough of her friend lately.

"Grad school is amazing. Being married is amazing." Alice grabbed a roll of drywall tape and some electrical wiring. "My mule of a daddy is making me crazy, but Luke and I are tag-teaming him."

"Thank goodness he's improving." Jenny staggered a bit as she hefted a five-gallon bucket of paint. She needed to step up her once every two week barbell-lifting regime.

Alice stopped for a moment. "Before I forget, I wanted to tell you I'm just about finished the updates to your website. I'll get it to you next week. Any changes, no problemo."

"I can't wait to see it." Alice's gorgeous and inviting winter website had been the reason that the first annual "Christmas at the Lakeside Resort" event had been such a smashing success.

"What's new in your world?" Alice paused to one-handedly adjust her fleece cap that had a fox face and ears on it.

Jenny gave her the highlights as they trudged over to join Luke.

"Anything new in y'all's baby endeavor?" Jenny asked cautiously.

"I've got endometriosis." Alice's tone was matter of fact. "Never had a symptom in my life, but after Mike and I started trying and had no luck, we got all the plumbing checked out."

"Oh, I'm sorry." Jenny snuck a quick glance at Alice's face to try to get a read on her reactions to the diagnosis, but she was blowing bangs out of her face and looked untroubled.

"So here's how they figured out the diagnosis. They examined my ovaries, Fallopian tubes, and the lining of my uterus..." Alice was saying just as Luke stepped outside of the shed.

He froze, eyes wide, and hastily retreated.

"You know how little I know about babies. So, does that mean that you have to go through special treatments?" Or can't conceive, Jenny edited, internally cringing at the thought.

Warily, Luke poked a head out the door just as Alice said, "My periods were always heavy..." Looking like a panicked prairie dog, he popped his head back inside.

Alice gave Jenny a devilish grin and went on. "But that's the only symptom I had. The good news is that lots of women with endometriosis get pregnant with no medical help." She put a hand to her chest. "I just have this feeling in my heart that this is going to happen for us. If it doesn't, we'll figure it out. Maybe we'll adopt or foster." She cracked a smile. "Or maybe we'll do neither and just get really selfish."

Jenny laughed. "That's such a good way to think about it."

Alice's eyes darted to the open door of the shed, where her brother had cautiously stepped back outside. "So, we're just trying to conceive at every possible moment. Yup. Mike and I are like little bunnies," she announced loudly.

"Gaack," Luke threw his hands over his ears and backpedaled inside.

Jenny burst out laughing. "You're a bad sister."

"I am." Alice nodded proudly. "Nothing grosses a brother out more than hearing about his sister's lady parts and married life."

"I'll remember that," Jenny promised.

Luke called out the door to them. "Let me know when the OB-GYN chitchat is over. We've got work to do, and we're burning daylight."

After they'd finished insulation and made short work of hanging the Sheetrock and mudding it, they began work outside while the joint compound dried.

Jenny and Alice were mounting frames for flower boxes they'd hang outside the windows of the laundry shed while Luke rolled paint around the back of the addition.

"This is going to be worth the extra work." Jenny took a step back and eyed their progress. "Flower boxes will make the laundry shed look cheery and tie it in to the other cabins."

Alice nodded her agreement as she lined up brackets and marked holes.

Feeling like an expert, Jenny drove in the screws Alice held in place. Last year at this time, she knew as much about using an electric screwdriver as she did about operating a jackhammer, but look at her now. She was a gal who knew her way around power tools.

Hearing car wheels on gravel, Jenny looked up and squinted. She wasn't expecting any new guests today, but maybe it was someone who'd seen the place online and wanted to have a look before they booked. A lipstick-red Mercedes purred into the driveway.

But Alice's eyes narrowed and she glowered. "Uh, oh. Here comes trouble."

Jenny gaped at the willowy, tawny-haired woman who unfolded elegantly from the sleek sedan. She looked like Ralph Lauren's glamorous wife, whom she'd seen in celebrity magazines at the Sassy Southern Gal Salon. Model thin, the woman wore a well-cut, bottle-green car coat, slim houndstooth-check trousers, and black leather boots. Tossing back her mane of shining hair, the woman walked toward them, her eyes locked on Luke. Though the blonde's look was classy, her hips swiveled like a Vegas showgirl. "Who is that?"

Alice rolled her eyes. "That's Chloe's sister Ember. She's always carried a torch for Luke."

"Huh. Yowsa." Luke's late wife Chloe had been a wholesome-looking, very pretty, girl-next-door type, the polar opposite of this foxy mama.

"Yup. Funny. One sister was so warmhearted, and the other turned out slick as an eel," Alice murmured while pretending to be working.

Luke glanced up, saw Ember, and walked toward her with a half-smile on his face.

"Luke!" Ember threw her arms around Luke's neck and fell into his arms, dislodging the sunglasses he'd lifted to his head. After a too long moment, she let go and smoothed her coat.

Luke took a step back, his brows raised and his eyes wide. He looked baffled.

"I heard your daddy's been real sick, so I baked him a get-well caramel cake." Ember gazed at him sympathetically. "And I think about you every October on the anniversary of Chloe's passing. How are you holding up, honey?"

Honey? Jenny watched the scene from behind her sunglasses, a hot flame of jealousy igniting in her stomach. Making herself get back to securing the brackets, she pressed so hard on the screwdriver that the screw flew off in the air.

And darned if Ralph Lauren's wife didn't go in for another heartfelt hug that lasted too long. Luke pulled away, unwrapped her arms, and held her shoulders. He said something to her, but Jenny couldn't hear what.

Alice met her eyes and nodded her head toward Luke and his former sister-in-law. "Let's get closer so we can hear what the she-devil is saying to him."

The flame of jealousy had turned into a bonfire. Jenny jerked her head in a quick nod. The two headed closer.

"Hey, Ember. How's tricks?" Without waiting for an answer, Alice began noisily loading Sheetrock scraps into the back of Luke's truck.

"Nice to see you," Ember said, her eyes never leaving Luke's.

Luke remembered his manners. "Ember, this is a friend, Jenny Beckett."

Jenny just stared at Luke and felt the blood rush to her face. A friend. Not *my friend* or *my girlfriend*? Not a woman he'd vaguely proposed to at Christmas? She felt like slapping Ember and Luke, or maybe spraying them with Eau de Skunk.

"Hello." Ember glanced at Jenny, but her eyes flicked away dismissively, seeing no threat from an unmade-up woman in dirt-colored, insulated overalls.

"How are you getting along, Ember?" Luke wiped his brow with his sleeve.

"Oh, I'm bumping along," she said with a wan smile.

"How's John Dale?" Luke stuck his hands in his pockets.

"He's in Atlanta with work again this week. He's busy, busy, busy, and never has time for little 'ole me, but that's nothing new." She shrugged helplessly.

"That means her third marriage is on the rocks," Alice translated sotto voce. "She's hoping to get Luke in the rotation as an emergency backup husband, especially if she thinks he has money."

Luke rocked back on his heels and nodded. "I think a lot of John Dale. Can't fault a man for working hard."

Ember gave a brave smile and touched Luke's forearm with a bejeweled hand. "You're looking well, Luke."

Jenny threw a large scrap of Sheetrock into the truck with unnecessary vigor, and it made a loud thud as it hit the truck bed.

"Even though the years have rolled on by, I'm still grieving poor Chloe. I think of her every day," Ember murmured sympathetically. "She's always in my heart, and I know she's still in your heart. Just remember, I'll always be here for you."

"OK." Luke looked slightly befuddled. "So you just stopped by to say hello?"

"It's been too long, and I was in the neighborhood." Ember gave him a coquettish smile.

Jenny scowled. Right. In the neighborhood, out in the middle of the country seventy miles from town and toting a freshly baked caramel cake to boot.

"Well, that's mighty kind of you," Luke said.

"You're staying at that little house on your parents' farm, right?" Ember batted dark lashes at him. "I'm going to start bringing supper some nights to you and your mama and daddy, just until your daddy gets back to his old self. I just love to cook, and John Dale is gone so much." She heaved a tragic sigh. "And there's hardly any point in cooking for one."

"There's no need to go to all that trouble." Shifting his weight from one foot to the other, Luke rubbed the back of his neck.

But Ember just held up a hand. "No trouble at all. I insist."

"He's caught like a rat in a trap," Alice hissed at Jenny.

Luke's cell rang and he glanced at it, looking relieved for the interruption. "Sorry. I've got to take this."

"I'll just go get the cake from the car," Ember called in a loud whisper and swished off.

Luke walked a few steps away to take his call. "Burt, I'm glad you called..." he began.

Jenny watched stony-faced, wishing Ember would accidentally step in remnants of the boys' morning constitutional.

"She is just a good-hearted woman," Alice said in a syrupy voice.

"She's an angel of mercy." Jenny found it was hard to talk

through gritted teeth. Looking at Alice, she threw up her hands. "And what about your brother? He didn't seem to *get* that she was trying to insinuate herself... all over him." Feeling boiling blood rush to her face, Jenny gave Alice an indignant look. "And Luke introduced me as a *friend*."

"He acted like he didn't have a lick of sense." Alice put her hands on Jenny's shoulders. "Breathe, girl."

And Jenny did, taking slow, deep, ragged breaths. Slowly, she begin to calm down.

"Jenny, think about it. First, Luke is a technical guy. He doesn't have the best social skills, and he's not the smoothest with the ladies, right? I doubt he knows how to handle a woman like that, and it might take him a minute to figure out that she's being so seductive."

Reluctantly, Jenny nodded her agreement.

"Second, Luke was married since he was twenty-three. He's sheltered. He's not good at recognizing..." She trailed off, trying to find the right word.

"Swivel-hipped, manipulative she-devils?" Jenny voice came out as a snarl.

"I was going to say scheming wenches, but I like yours better." Alice smirked. "I can tell you for sure, my brother is not a player. He may be naïve and he may need...um...guidance about how to handle certain situations, but he is just not the unfaithful type."

Jenny wanted to believe her.

Luke ended the call and recoiled when he caught the full brunt of their double-barreled critical glares.

Back from the car, Ember looked at Luke, dimpled, and proffered a cake carrier.

But Luke held up a hand. "Appreciate your going to all this trouble, Ember, but Daddy can't eat sugar anymore. I'm going to need to say no to the supper idea, too. Mama is working hard to keep him on a strict diet, and she won't let him eat a bite unless she's run it by the hospital dietician and cooked it herself."

Ember gave a twinkling smile. "Then, I'll bring *you* supper.

I know men living by their lonesome don't take good care of themselves." She wagged a finger at him playfully.

Jenny tensed, and Alice's grip on her arm was going to leave bruises.

"Much obliged, but if I'm not working, I'm out here with my girl." He walked over and put an arm around Jenny's shoulder. "She's an awfully good cook."

Jenny just nodded coolly at the woman.

"Well, bless her heart." But Ember's eyes were arctic. "Well, so good to see you all. I'd best be on my way."

As Ember swirled off, Luke called, "Tell John Dale I asked after him. Have a nice day."

Alice snorted and gave her brother a withering look. "Have a nice day? Sheesh." She strode off toward the laundry shed, shaking her head.

Jenny slid out from under his arm and glared. "That woman is awful, and she wants you."

Luke scrubbed his face with his hands and gave Jenny a hangdog look. "I didn't see it coming, so I was slow on the uptake."

"You were pitiful. Luke, she was hanging all over you." Jenny put a hand on her hip. "That should have been a clue."

"I got the message at that point." Luke held his hands palms up. "But when she was talking about Chloe, it kind of got to me."

"I get that," Jenny said grudgingly, but arched a brow. "And then she threw her arms around you and said she wanted to bring you supper." She swatted him on the arm with the back of her hand, but her indignation was fading. "We need some rules, buddy. One, no letting women hug you like that."

Luke held up three fingers in a Boy Scout salute. "I swear I won't ever let another woman hug me like that except you."

"Two, never accept cakes or meals from strange women."

He held up his forefinger. "Now, is that a *no* on caramel cakes specifically or just a *no* on cakes altogether?" Catching her icy stare, Luke hurriedly held up three fingers. "No accepting cakes or meals from strange women."

Jenny rolled her eyes. "And never, ever again talk to a

woman who walks like this." She did an exaggerated imitation of Ember's sashay.

"I swear I won't," Luke said solemnly. "I'm sorry, Jenny. I just kept thinking about her being Chloe's sister, and Ember's never acted that way before. Then I realized she was being overly friendly." With a beseeching look, he pulled her into his arms. "I was going to handle it."

Believing him, Jenny let herself be hugged, but then she pushed him away. She needed to let him suffer a little longer. "I'm watching you," she said, pointing two fingers to her eyes and then to his. But she hid a smile as she walked off to hang window boxes.

Their banter while they worked returned to their old mix of serious and silly. The three had a spirited debate about what they would do if they accidentally won a high political office. Alice would substitute all violent video games with Disney movies and make all Americans take a good manners course. Jenny would ban pajama pants in public and require citizens to regularly pick up roadside litter. Luke felt strongly about driverless cars. *Come on, people. You're driving!*

But although Jenny enjoyed their talk, she was still bothered by something. She believed Luke had not caught onto Ember's wiles until she became obvious. Because Jenny was so enamored with him, she'd never noticed his social ineptness that Alice had pointed out. She could see it now. A man who didn't notice other women flirting wasn't a bad thing, but it might get him in trouble.

Grabbing a water bottle, she took long swallows and watched him surreptitiously from behind her sunglasses. Another thing that annoyed her was that he had just described her as *his girl*. The term was so lacking in definition. This wasn't high school. What exactly did *his girl* mean? Were they getting married or not? If so, when? Jenny put back on her gloves and picked up a paintbrush, vowing she'd get answers to those questions, and soon.

CHAPTER 5 — 20K IN THE DEL MONTE CAN?

ARLY SUNDAY MORNING, JENNY WAS propped up in bed, sipping coffee and reading the latest Louise Miller novel when a text arrived that made her smile. Luke wrote:

Morning. Neighbors offered to take Mama and Daddy to church and to lunch at the cafeteria after. Got a spare sandwich for a hungry man?

Eagerly, she tapped out:

Two visits in two days? Bonanza! Love to see you. Come on.

In the kitchen, Jenny nibbled a sliver of the smoked turkey lunchmeat she'd just defrosted. After going online and checking out Smitten Kitchen, Gimme Some Oven, and a few other cooking sites, she'd decided to experiment with freezing the cold cuts she'd picked up on her last grocery store run. Yum. Delicious. Tonight, she'd google what else she could safely freeze so she didn't have to make the hour-and-a-half round trip to grocery shop so often.

Adding the water, honey, and olive oil to the dry ingredients, Jenny started a loaf of whole wheat in the bread-making machine. The bluegrass station was on the radio, and the fiddler and banjo players had to be having fun as they did a high-energy rendition of *Boudleaux and Felice Bryant's classic, Rocky Top*. The kitchen was sunny, the sky was blue, and Jenny hummed along the best she could as she sliced tomatoes and cleaned and dried lettuce.

At her computer, Jenny pulled up email. Slipping on reading glasses she'd just recently and reluctantly started wearing, she saw the email and attachment from Alice and shivered with anticipation. She'd finally get to see the updates to her website.

Jenny felt a fizz of excitement as she peered at the draft. The graphics were vivid and colorful, and the tableau Alice created made Jenny sigh with pleasure. It was a perfect depiction of how she hoped guests would experience summer at the lake.

On the landing page, Heron Lake was sky blue and sparkling just like it was today. Jenny glanced out the window at the glittering waves, the view that she still had to pinch herself to believe was hers. The website showed the rich brown of the log cabins with their cherry-red doors and dark green metal roofs. Crisp green-and-white striped awnings arched over the rocking chair front porches, and the small window boxes that hung on the porch railings had colorful flowers tumbling from them, purple verbena, coleus, bright yellow lantana, and trailing green sweet potato vines. The cabins looked so inviting. Jenny twirled a pen in her fingers, shaking her head in amazement.

Next, she clicked on the photos tab. A slideshow of images drifted across the screen. A balding man in a lawn chair sat on the dock reading, his legs white and skinny. Two preteen girls floated in kayaks, holding fishing poles. Two middle-aged and not-so-skinny women rode beach cruiser bikes on the dirt road behind the cabins. Guests wearing orange life jackets or blue water safety vests smiled as they loaded picnic baskets, coolers, and tubes into a pontoon boat, ready to embark on a day of cruising and water sports.

Good. Alice had stuck to Jenny's rule about not depicting too hip, unnaturally attractive, or envy-inspiring glamorous types featured in the upscale resort sites. The guests Jenny wanted to draw were regular folks. This was a place for guests to wear comfy clothes, not be productive, eat whatever they wanted to, escape the bustle of the world, and just relax.

As she gave the website mock-up one final admiring glance, Jenny's heart and breathing stopped as she saw the problem right in front of her, plain as day. Worry crashed down on her like a wave. Pressing her fingers to her forehead, Jenny made herself close the program. She'd jump in the shower, try to put what she noticed out of her mind, and talk to Luke about it over lunch.

"I'm trying not to wolf this down," Luke said apologetically after swallowing a bite of his turkey, bacon, and Havarti cheese sandwich with lettuce and tomato. "But the bread is still warm. You make the world's best sandwiches." Patting his mouth with a napkin, he took a bite of a crispy dill pickle. He tilted his head. "How's the marketing going?"

Jenny mustered a feeble smile. "It's going OK. My biggest success so far is the *former yuppie meets skunk* interview."

"I read the article, and it was good," Luke said staunchly. "You've just got to keep trying new ways of spreading the word and things will come together."

Though she nodded, Jenny was too distracted to let herself be reassured. Pushing her plate away, she gave him a level look. "So, I've got a problem. Alice sent me the updated website, and it's amazing. Take a look." Grabbing her laptop, she turned it so they could both see the screen as she scrolled through it.

"Huh." Luke peered at the screen. "Sis is good at this, no doubt about it."

"But don't you see what's wrong?" Jenny's voice was plaintive. "What's missing?"

Luke studied it more closely and looked chagrinned. "Ah. Got it. This features pictures of boats you do not currently own. Can't believe we didn't catch that detail."

"Exactly." Jenny hunched over, feeling stupid. "Summer will be here before we know it, and guests are expecting us to have kayaks, canoes, and a boat for excursions."

"Can't have a lakeside resort with no boats," Luke said mildly.

"How much would all those boats cost?" Jenny started to gnaw a nail and made herself stop. Her stomach gripped as she thought about the empty spaces on her reservation program, the cost of the materials she'd insisted she chip in on for the Silver Belle fix-up, the lumber for the laundry shed, and the payments on her beloved new washer and dryer.

"How about we go look at used boats next weekend?"

"Good." Jenny exhaled, her thoughts whirling. Maybe she'd luck into one of those bitter divorce scenarios where the revenge-seeking wife sells the cheating, soon-to-be ex-husband's prize boat for a ridiculously low price, like a dollar. She shook her head at her foolishness and tuned back in. "I don't know even know what kind we'd need."

Luke looked thoughtful. "For the resort boat, you'll probably want the space and stability of a pontoon. The boat sits level with the dock so it's easy to get in and out of, even for people with disabilities, older people, or the dogs and Levi."

Despite her worries, Jenny got tickled picturing the three boys standing majestically on the bow with the wind in their hair/fur, just like Rose in Titanic except their tongues might be hanging out of their mouths and no sinking was allowed.

"Let's look at boats that are about twenty-two or twenty-four feet long and that are about four years old. Boats with less than 200 engine hours on them would be best," Luke suggested.

Jenny tilted her head. "Engine hours are like mileage?"

"Yup. Lower is better. Let me take a look at Boats.com and check out some of the dealers and marinas that buy and sell or do consignment for people."

Jenny couldn't help but smile at the excitement in his voice. Boys and their toys. Closing her eyes, she tried to recall a conversation. "Lily said she bought her little VW Bug on an online buy-and-sell newspaper for the community. It's part of the *Heron Lake Herald,* and it's called the Frugal Heron or the Thrifty Osprey." The name eluded her but there was a penny-pinching water bird involved. She'd google it.

"Good thinking," Luke glanced at his watch and gave her a regretful look. "I told Mama and Daddy I'd pick them up at the K & W by one. Daddy wants me to run him by the store so he can check on things."

Jenny tried to hide her disappointment. Spending time with Luke led to wanting to spend more time with him. And she hadn't even had a chance to talk with him about the status of their relationship. She'd heard most men dreaded the *where is this relationship headed* talk, but it had to be done. Just not in two minutes while he was zipping up his coat and heading out the door.

"Bye, Jen." Luke gathered her in his arms and kissed her.

When he let go, she felt bereft. "I'll see you soon," Jenny managed to say.

He gave her a sideways grin, held up a hand, and was gone.

Jenny stayed busy the rest of the afternoon, adding final coats of sealant to the granite countertops in the cabins. Because she had renters arriving next weekend, she restocked goodies in the hospitality baskets she left for arriving guests.

This time, she was adding regional goodies, an idea she'd talked about with Charlotte. In the wicker baskets with the red calico tea towels she's bought at a Just a Buck store, Jenny arranged two bottles of Cheerwine, a small bag of Atkinson's Buttermilk Biscuit Mix, and a sampler of coffee from Smoky Mountain Roasters. Jenny liked the idea spreading the word about some of her favorite regional flavors.

Later, as she nuked a bean burrito for supper, Jenny got a text from Charlotte that read:

Visiting you tomorrow. Arriving in AM. Need to work more magic on the Belle. Glass of wine tomorrow night?

She could use a dose of Charlotte's optimism. Jenny texted back:

Come anytime, girl. Wine sounds great.

After scarfing down the burrito that tasted like the cardboard it came in, Jenny let the boys out for one final airing and slumped down at the computer. Though she was tired, she knew she'd never sleep unless she knew what she might be looking at money-wise for the new used boats. She found the website called the Thrifty Heron, scrolled through, and pulled up boats that met the criteria that she and Luke had discussed. When she saw the asking prices, she had a sick feeling in the pit of her stomach.

A pontoon boat like the one they'd talked about cost $20,000.

Jenny's thoughts started a panicky spiral. Where would she get the money? What if more unexpected expenses came up, say her eleven-year-old SUV died, or she got bedbugs in every cabin and had to have them treated? She was living closer to the edge money-wise than she ever had.

She put a finger on a spot on her temple that had started to throb. Jenny was fairly sure Luke didn't *get* how little money she had right now. This was going to take some creative financing, maybe even a groveling visit to Sterling Fairwood, the banker who'd signed off on her construction loan. If all else failed, she'd bite the bullet and dip into her small SEP-IRA, something she'd sworn to herself she'd never do. Maybe she should do what daddy had done when money was tight, buy a hundred dollars' worth of scratch-off lottery tickets with names like *Buck Up, Buddy* or *Hey, Big Spender*.

With a burn of resentment, Jenny wondered if Luke thought that she had a spare $20,000 on hand, just tucked in her jewelry box or in the Del Monte fruit cocktail can valuable hider she kept in her small pantry. And then another niggling thought. She knew nothing about his finances. They'd not talked much about money. They had just not had the time. For all she knew, he could be Bill Gates rich or maybe up to his neck in debt like Jax often was. She scrubbed her face with her hands. That was a nightmare of a thought. These were things they needed to discuss if they were going to have a future together.

Jenny tilted her chair back on two legs and thought about what she did know. She knew he felt terrible guilt about having been a workaholic during his marriage, especially because he'd lost his wife Chloe to cancer three and a half years ago and felt he'd let her down. After she'd passed away, he'd turned over operation of the business to Zander and sold him some of his stock, but kept enough to remain a silent partner. Luke had taken a sabbatical and moved from Athens, Georgia, back home to North Carolina, where he'd worked at his family's hardware store, done contracting work, and met her. She'd asked him if he'd been a big muckety-muck in his previous business, and he'd assured her he'd been just a small muckety-muck. That was all she knew. They needed to have that talk, whether the timing was good or not.

After pricing used canoes and kayaks, and checking all her

accounts for $20,000 she might have forgotten she had, Jenny put her elbow on the table and her chin in her hand. Clicking over to various banks' websites, she looked at interest rates and loan terms. Trying to come up with creative financing for the boats was giving her a headache. Closing all open sites, Jenny stretched and rose. She needed a break. Pouring herself a large Wilma Flintstone glass of table wine, Jenny crawled into her nightgown and went to bed. Things might look better in the morning, but she doubted it.

That night, sleep didn't come easy. The deep breathing and sheep counting didn't work, and the mental image of relaxing by the babbling brook had just made her need to pee. Giving up, she'd turned on the light and tried to read, but books couldn't keep her attention. Scrubbing her face with her hands, Jenny eyed Jax's bookshelf, remembering that beside his Zane Gray, Stuart Woods, and Lee Childs novels was a stack of business magazines that spanned decades. Maybe she could bore herself to sleep. Grabbing one, she blinked her gritty eyes and padded back to bed.

Slipping on her reading glasses, Jenny studied the cover of *The World of Southern Business*. The fellow on the cover of the September 1984 edition was Businessman of the Year Gavin Rogers, who rocked a Magnum P.I.-type thick moustache, a modified mullet, and a three-piece suit. His arms crossed, Gavin looked like a Captain of Industry as he leaned against a gleaming sports car, a Lamborghini Miura, according to the article.

Jenny flipped open the magazine and found the lead article. "From High School Dropout to Business Ace: Gavin Rogers Shares His Story about Making It Big in the Hospitality Industry! His Mantra: Get Real about Knowing Your Customer and Communicate to the Max!!!"

Jenny's interest ticked up. Such a coincidence that Gavin's tips related to hospitality, her field. Polishing her glasses on her nightie, Jenny had a fanciful thought. Though the article could be a bunch of dated silliness, maybe from his perch on a cloud Daddy wanted her to read it. That was a comforting thought. Adjusting the pillow behind her head, Jenny burrowed deeper under her coverlet and started to read.

The next morning, a bleary-eyed Jenny was scooping kibbles and regretting staying up so late reading when she saw Charlotte pull up in her sedan. She waved to her from the window and felt her worries lighten just at the thought of talking with Charlotte about Luke and money. Her friend pointed in the direction of the Dogwood and began toting boxes and canvas LL Bean bags into the Silver Belle.

As she took a life-affirming first sip of coffee, Jenny sat up straight, jolted by an idea that she suspected might be a good one. She had a funny feeling that it might have hatched after she'd read the business advice last night. Grabbing a pen, she scribbled down her thoughts before she forgot them.

- Know your customer inside and out.

- Communicate in a friendly way.

- No sales pitches. What do they expect from you?

- How can you deliver this and better yet, delight them?

Maybe Business Ace Gavin Rogers had ideas worth trying.

Jenny sat at the computer, scratching her head with a pen. She *did* need to post more on Facebook and communicate in a friendly way with the folks who'd signed up to receive her newsletter. She had about three hundred and sixty followers who were former guests, people who were considering staying at the cabins, internet lookie-loos, and friends and family who wished her well and wanted to keep up with her progress.

Though she'd written a few newsletters before Christmas, she'd slacked off, worried she might be bugging subscribers. Nibbling a nail, she thought about it. Remembering Charlotte's last visit and her comments about guests beating down the door if they understood the unique serenity and beauty of the lake, Jenny decided to write a breezy, cheery post that delivered the feel of a day on the lake to their living rooms. She'd include some new pictures and maybe a few short video clips of Heron Lake.

Starting to feel a fizzy excitement in her stomach, Jenny looked at her chicken scratch of ideas and made a To-Do list:

- Pic of bonfire

- Exterior shot of a cabin with smoke coming from chimney

- View of the lake from the bluff. A clip so people can hear the quiet, waves?

- Charlotte to take shot of me from behind reading book, feet in socks, flames of woodstove

- Pics of dogs and Levi

Jenny touched Bear's back with her bare foot and grinned. The dogs and Levi were her aces in the hole. Guests loved her guys. Adjusting the blinds, Jenny took a few photographs of Bear, Buddy, and Levi snoozing on her sofa. Grabbing her hat and coat, Jenny stepped outside to get some more pictures.

The lights were on in the Airstream and Jenny could hear country music, Charlotte's go-to tunes to listen to while she was working. Jenny felt reassured, glad for the company of a friend.

The morning sun was soft and golden and cast a warm glow on everything. Not wanting to waste a moment of this light that was an amateur photographer's friend, Jenny strode purposefully around, clicking away with the camera on her phone. She took shots of the cabins and of the Silver Belle. Building a small fire in her new firepit, she captured the flames of the campfire against the blue of the lake. The semicircle of white Adirondack chairs looked inviting. The new flagpole she'd had put in the clearing flew the North Carolina and American flags; they looked colorful and patriotic snapping in gusts of morning breeze. Though not a good photographer, she knew if she took enough photos and did some editing, three or four would turn out. As she headed in, Jenny caught a whiff of wood smoke. Too bad she couldn't bottle that and include it in the post. She'd have a full house.

Back in the cabin, Jenny picked the best shots and did her editing. When she'd finished, she clasped her hands together,

Susan Schild

scarcely believing how well they'd turned out. Those were some pretty shots she'd gotten.

Next, Jenny worked on a newsy, cheerful note.

> Good morning, friends! Hope you are all well and having a happy year. Late spring is a special time here at the Lakeside Resort. Lots of wildlife visit us regularly. At dusk, a mama deer and her two babies stroll through our clearing. The Canada geese call to one another as they fly over with their pals.

Jenny inserted the clip she'd caught of the geese flying overhead. The audio of their honking was clear, something she just knew followers would love.

> Temperatures are warming, but we still have plenty of chilly nights where you'll want to sleep under a down comforter. When you visit in spring, you may want to go on a hike, read in front of the fire, cook a pot of soup, and be cozy. If you're looking for a quiet, serene, and beautiful escape from the hustle and bustle of your life, come visit us. You'll also fall in love with summer here at the Lakeside Resort, with swimming, kayaking, and boating on stunning Heron Lake. Looking for rejuvenation, relaxation, and fun? Make your reservations at the Lakeside Resort!

Without one qualm of conscience, Jenny found a picture of a handsome boat on a dealer's website and cut and pasted it into the newsletter.

> Cabins are filling up fast and we'd love to see you. Returning guests, Buddy, Bear, and Levi send their best wishes!

Jenny inserted the pictures she'd taken of the boys snoozing on the couch with Buddy's head resting on Levi's flank. Adorable. Orvis dog catalog adorable. After proofreading and spellchecking it three times, Jenny held her breath and hit the send button.

CHAPTER 6 — SCRATCHING FOR IDEAS

THROUGHOUT THE DAY, JENNY ANXIOUSLY checked her mail to see if any readers had been inspired enough by her travelogue photos to book a cabin, but the only response she got was a newsy note from her Aunt Lottie from Wilmington, who wrote that her bursitis was better because she was drinking cherry juice, she'd met a *hotsy-totsy* widower with an almost full head of hair in her qigong class, and she was going on an indoor skydiving experience with her Senior Center pals. Jenny shook her head, smiling. She hoped she was just like Aunt Lottie when she was seventy-six.

But by late afternoon, her aunt was the only one who had responded in any way to her newsletter. Maybe she'd had a whole slew of folks who'd read her chirpy post and gotten irate with her spamming and strong-arm sales tactics. Jenny closed her eyes and rubbed them with her fingers. They'd probably jabbed the Delete key hard with their fingers as they'd unsubscribed. Jenny would check later, because she couldn't bear to look at all the *Unsubscribes* she probably had on her rapidly diminishing mailing list.

A knock sounded at her door, and Charlotte's voice caroled, "You-hoo, lovey. The sun's over the yardarm. Drinky time."

Jenny threw open the door and hugged her friend. "Glad you're here. You've been working hard."

"Busier than a moth in a mitten," Charlotte said gaily, her face speckled with small dots of cream-colored paint. "I used the roller on the ceiling and painted trim all day. I am completely exhausted, sore, and simply *parched*." She fanned her face dramatically and flung herself onto a kitchen chair.

Jenny smiled as she poured her a generous glass of wine in a Fred Flintstone glass and handed it to her. Charlotte's lustrous curls were tied back in a blue bandana, Rosie the Riveter style. "You look pretty."

"Thank you," Charlotte patted her do, looking pleased at the compliment. "So, what's new here? I need the full, unedited scoop."

Pouring herself a glass of wine, Jenny sat across from her and began by blurting out her worries about the boat. "My cabins are unrented and money is tight, but Luke and I have to go hunting for a $20,000 used boat on Saturday."

Charlotte's eyes widened. "Why?"

"Because we promised guests boating in the summer. Boat rides, tubing, picnics on the water, sunset cruises. We've got to have a boat and other water toys."

"Right. You have to have a boat." Charlotte took a large swallow of wine. She stared out the window, looking thoughtful. "It seems to me you just need to concentrate on what we've already talked about, getting more business."

"Right," Jenny agreed, but it just wasn't that simple.

"And you've been doing that. You had that amazing article in the newspaper. You came up with that idea for the gift basket promoting North Carolina brands, and you sent that newsletter today." Charlotte clasped her hands together. "I loved, loved, loved that post. I read it several times, forwarded it to friends, and listened to those calling geese about four times more." She sighed, remembering.

"Really? You liked it? I wasn't too pushy?" Jenny was afraid Charlotte was just trying to cheer her up.

"It was genuine and sweet and enticing," Charlotte said firmly. "And people who would be offended by that newsletter are curmudgeons you don't want on your mailing list."

Jenny considered it and nodded. "True. And I haven't done a mailing since before Christmas."

"You see?" Charlotte held out a hand, palm up. "I think you're on the right track and that the bookings and the money will come. You just need to keep on with what you're doing."

Suddenly it clicked for her, and Jenny started to smile. "Luke said make a plan for the marketing and work the plan. I wasn't sure what he meant initially, but I'm getting it now."

Charlotte grinned, and raised Fred Flintstone in a toast. "To working our plan."

Jenny raised Wilma Flintstone, and the two women sipped.

Buddy and Bear jumped up from the couch and ran to the front window. They stood rigidly, in eye-staring, tail-furling full alert. But then they began the happy whining they used when someone they knew and liked approached. Lily strode by in exercise gear and a puffy jacket, with a yoga mat slung across her back with a strap.

Seeing the light in Jenny's cabin, she approached. Jenny opened the door, smiling. "Hey, Lily. You going up for your evening yoga and meditation?"

"I am," the young woman said brightly.

Jenny gestured toward Charlotte. "Not sure if you all have met, but Lily, this is my good friend, Charlotte. Charlotte, Lily is my one, wonderful, year-round tenant who is the librarian in town."

The two exchanged pleasantries.

Lily tilted her head. "Mind if I take your dogs with me? Buddy and Bear are so incredibly smart. Both have almost gotten the hang of downward dog and their stretching is superior." As Lily shook her head in wonder at their cleverness, Bear's tail swept Jenny's phone charging station off the end table and sent it crashing to the floor, and Buddy took a moment to fastidiously groom his nether area.

"Sure." Jenny rummaged in the cubby under the stairwell for their retractable leashes. "What's new with you?"

"Well, we had exciting news today. We got a bequest from a wealthy patron to expand the library. With all the dust and construction mess, I'll be out of work for a month later this fall, but the patron provided for paid leave for the librarians and staff while the renovation went on. What a fine lady." She shook her head admiringly.

"That's amazing." With all the bad news blaring from out there in the world, it was nice to hear about a kind person acting generously. Smiling, Jenny handed the dogs' leads to Lily.

"Come on, fellas. Let's go mellow out." Lily and the dogs headed for the door.

Noting Lily's erect posture, Jenny stood up straighter but felt a twinge in her sacrum. Boy, was she out of shape. "Maybe I'll join you and do yoga one evening," she called.

"I'd love it." Lily gave a twinkling smile and waved with a mittened hand. "I'll have these boys back home soon."

"Take your time." Jenny closed the door.

Charlotte sighed. "She's adorbs."

"She's is, and smart as all get out, too."

"Were we ever that lovely when we were young?" Charlotte asked wistfully.

"We were." Jenny said staunchly. "Every woman is in her twenties and thirties. All that collagen, carefree existence, and youthful exuberance." She rested her glass in her palm. "I miss my younger, prettier self."

"Some days I look in the mirror and can't believe how old I am. On my fattest days, I used to not look in the mirror at all." Charlotte grimaced but then smiled. "Ashe has helped with that, though. He thinks I'm just perfect the way I am." She shook her head, fighting a smile. "That crazy man with bad vision."

"That prince of a man who sees 20-20," Jenny corrected. "We're our own worst critics, but older women are lovely, too, especially the kind ones. That shines through."

"I think that's true. Pretty is as pretty does," Charlotte agreed and began absentmindedly braiding Levi's mane. "So, Lily teaches yoga and meditation?"

"Yes." Jenny sat up straight, her thoughts racing. "What if we got Lily to offer a weeklong yoga and meditation experience in the fall here at the Resort? We could hold it during the weeks she's free. She'd make money and grow her group of private yoga clients, which is what she's talked about wanting to do. We'd draw new guests looking for that kind of getaway."

Eyes wide with excitement, Charlotte swallowed her wine wrong and coughed a bit. "I adore that idea."

Jenny did too. "I want to run out there right now and interrupt her meditating to ask her about it, but I'll make myself wait."

Charlotte touched her thumb to her forefinger and made a circle. "Restraint is a virtue, my child." She giggled. "That was my imitation of Zion the Serenity Coach."

Jenny laughed. "I'll run the idea by Lily when she drops off the dogs."

"Good." Charlotte gently stroked Levi's muzzle, and the two of them gazed at each other soulfully. "Precious boy, your little nose is like velvet."

Jenny looked at Charlotte, her mind speeding again as she remembered ace businessman Gavin Roger's anecdote about creating unique and memorable connections with guests. "You know, I was reading this article about a guy who made it big in the hospitality industry. He started leaving his grandmother's red velvet cake cookies for guests in their rooms when they checked in, and guests went wild for them. He had so much demand, he started selling the cookies, too, so he had more money coming in during slower times at the hotels. Memorable calling cards, he called them." She pointed at Charlotte. "You know those little grapevine wreaths with the cotton stems and bolls that you made for each of the cabins? So many guests have said they loved them. Maybe you could make some and give them to the realtors and other folks you visit to drum up business as little hello presents."

Charlotte brightened. "I love that idea. Those wreaths are easy to make and the cotton and vines are free. I just pick them up from the field right outside Mama and Daddy's house."

"Maybe down the road, we could start selling them here," Jenny mused aloud.

"Excellent idea. Memorable." The two grinned at each other. Charlotte rose and put her glass in the sink. "Ashe will be calling soon, and I think I'll go slather myself with Ben Gay so my muscles won't freeze up on me like the tin man. I'm leaving crack of dawn tomorrow. Well, at least by nine." With a quick peck on Jenny's cheek, she was out the door.

Tidying up, Jenny hand-washed the glasses, sponged counters, and wiped down the refrigerator, trying to keep busy while she waited anxiously for Lily to stop back by with the dogs.

Intent on her busywork tasks, Jenny jumped when a soft knock sounded at the door. Smiling, she opened the door to Lily and the dogs. As Bear and Buddy surged inside, Jenny cocked her head. "Lily, do you have a minute? I have an idea I want to run by you." And she detailed their plan.

Lily was on board for the fall and excited, promising to make flyers and spread the word in her online yoga community. As they talked, Jenny felt hopeful and light. Though the program might not fill and was months away, she had a feeling that it could be a good fit for the Lakeside Resort. The Yoga and Meditation Retreat might be a winner.

After Lily left, Jenny practically floated up to her bedroom, buoyed by exciting ideas.

Maybe they could do sunrise yoga out in the clearing in front of the cabins. Graceful yoginis gazing out at a peach-colored ball of sun rising out of the dark blue water of the lake would be a sight. Maybe Jenny could learn to be more serene and deal with adversity with Zen-like calm. Jenny grinned. Nah. She could learn to dial it down a bit, but it seemed unlikely she'd ever get too calm.

Jenny just had to tell Charlotte. She texted her.

Lily said yes. The first Fall Yoga and Meditation Retreat at the Lakeside Resort is a go!

Charlotte replied almost instantly.

Oh, yay! Stellar!

Still smiling, Jenny locked up and turned off the lights. As she headed to the bathroom to brush her teeth, she paused, studying the computer. She just had to check one more time to see if her newsletter had shaken loose any inquiries. Bracing herself for disappointment, Jenny pulled up her social media and gasped quietly. Two couples and a family had inquired about bookings.

"Thank you, Gavin Rogers, and bless you, Daddy." She tapped out responses as fast as her fingers would fly.

In bed, Jenny tried to get into her book but kept reading the same paragraph over and over again. She was too revved up for reading. Flipping on her secret TV, she clicked through the shows that she'd DVR'd. The amiable, down-to-earth crew from *Maine Cabin Masters* — Chase, Ashley, Ryan, Dixie, and Jedi — arrived at a neglected lakeside camp they were going to restore in a graceful, speedy-looking pontoon boat, just like the one Jenny would soon own whether she liked it or not. Later, those nice men Frank and Mike from *American Pickers* wore pointy-toed boots and cowboy hats as they picked West Texas. Both shows were interesting and somehow soothing. Just as Jenny eased back on her pillows ready to watch, her phone rang. It was nine, late for a lot of callers.

Grabbing her cell, she blinked at the brightness of the screen. Mama. Tensing, Jenny fumbled the cell, worried that this was a bad news call. "Hey, Mama. What's up?"

"Hello, honeybun. Oh, my stars, I just looked at the time and realized I'm calling you so late. Everything is just fine," Claire reassured her. "I think about you so much and just wanted to catch up."

"Good to hear your voice, Mama." Jenny relaxed. They hadn't talked much over the past few months. She'd been so busy with the resort, and Mama and her husband Landis stayed busy with their bucket list trips. Jenny remembered their latest adventure had been a river journey down the Mississippi in a steamboat. "How was rolling on the river?"

"Oh, so fascinating. All that American history, antebellum mansions, charming small towns, and Civil War sites. I wished I'd brought my paints because the colors were..."

Jenny tuned out a bit, enjoying the girlish excitement in Mama's voice.

Claire was wrapping up her travelogue. "...and New Orleans was a festive town."

Jenny grinned. Mama had probably caught a glimpse of the

bawdier part of the Big Easy, but she'd put a polite spin on it. "Sounds nice, Mama."

"It was. Now, listen to me, just yammering away about myself. How are things with you, sugar?" her mother asked.

Jenny hesitated, not wanting to burden her mother with worries. But after the divorce, Mama had opened up about the seismic problems she'd had being married to Jax, ones she'd hidden from Jenny. The two had grown closer and vowed to always be truthful with one another.

"I've got typical small business growing pains," Jenny admitted, reaching down to scratch Buddy, who'd jumped up on the bed. "I've got too many empty cabins and a lot of expenses, but I'm working on it."

"Oh, I'm so glad to hear you say that. I mean not about the money problems, but about the vacancies," Claire said fervently. "We've got a big problem, and you might be able to help us." She lowered her voice and spoke in a confidential tone. "You know how smart Landis is. He's the smartest businessman I ever knew."

"Yes." The son of a tenant farmer, Landis had become a successful banker.

"Well, I'm fit to be tied about the *not smart* thing he's done," her mother said plaintively. "He's sold this house right out from under us."

"Yikes." This was big.

"Landis and I planned on putting the house on the market in midsummer and downsizing to a smaller place at a senior community in Asheville."

"Right," Jenny said, puzzled. They'd talked about this downsizing idea before. Landis's home in Summerville, South Carolina, was 5,000 square feet, way too big for two people. When Mama had married him, she'd confided to Jenny that she'd actually gotten lost in the middle of the night on the way back from the bathroom and had to call out to Landis to help find her.

"Here's the problem," Claire said, a touch of flint in her voice. "On a whim, Landis put the house on the market two weeks ago with a pretty good price tag on it, just to test the waters, he said. But of all things, two couples got into a bidding war over it."

"That's tremendous Mama." A sudden windfall sounded like a fine problem to her.

"Landis got caught up in the excitement, and we accepted an offer, but the new owners want us out by May 10. That's just over a month away!" she said, the wobble in her voice betraying her anxiety. "The Over-55 place we like isn't completely built yet. We put a deposit on a home, but it'll be mid-July before it's completed if the weather holds," Mama said with a voice that shook.

"Ah." Jenny heart went out to them. Though she wasn't proud of herself, she was mildly reassured that the intimidatingly accomplished Landis had made a somewhat boneheaded decision. Jenny had sure made enough of them in her life. "Come stay at one of the cabins," she said. Landis and Mama had never even seen the cabins. She couldn't wait to see the expressions on their faces when they first glimpsed Heron Lake.

"Oh, you are the answer to my prayers. I was afraid to even ask," Claire said, relief in her voice. "We looked at short-term rentals but it's all so depressing. I couldn't stand the chaos, and I would feel so...unrooted."

"I completely understand." When she'd been evicted from the chicken coop cottage that she'd called home for years, she'd felt bereft until she'd made a new home at the Lakeside Cabins. "Stay here. I mean it."

"We'd be so, so grateful," her mother said, relief in her voice. "We'd pay you, of course, and it would give us practice in living in a smaller space."

"A much, much smaller space. Three hundred square feet," Jenny reminded her.

Claire hesitated. "I don't want us to impose or you to regret your invitation when you get sick of having your mama around."

For the most part, she'd always gotten along well with her mother, even during the turbulent teen years. The two of them had weathered the same storms caused by Jax, and learned to look out for each other. Mama used to be a world-class worrier and a constant tidier with spotless kitchen floors and a compulsion for spraying everything with Lysol. But she'd let so much of that go when she married Landis. The only friction: Jenny's back got up when Mama gave her not-so-subtle hints about getting married again and having the security of a husband, but she had eased up on that since the Douglas debacle. These days, with her newly discovered passion for art, her swirling Stevie Nicks-inspired outfits, and her determination to embrace and enjoy all life had to offer, she was a happier, more relaxed version of her old self. "I don't think we'd get on each other's nerves living so close. Do you?"

"I hope not. We'll only come under one condition. If there's any friction at all because of us living so close, we'll move right out with no hard feelings. Not a one," Mama promised.

"You got a deal." Jenny smiled, imagining coffee, conversation, and walks with Mama.

"Oh, how delightful! This will be a grand adventure, and I'll get to spend time with you and those grand dogs and horse of mine. We'll stay out of your hair, but I'll help you out in any way I can; folding laundry, walking the animals, manning the front desk." She paused a beat. "I can't wait to get to know your new fellow, Luke, better, too."

Jenny groaned internally. She'd best ask Luke what his intentions were before Mama beat her to the punch and gave him a polite but pointed third degree about that very topic.

CHAPTER 7 — DIALING FOR DOLLARS

J UST AFTER DAYLIGHT FRIDAY MORNING, Jenny gave up pretending she could go back to sleep and dragged herself to the kitchen for coffee. The boat-buying trip was tomorrow morning, and she had just $700 and change in her business account. Jenny needed to get out of her wishful thinking mode and start scratching up some cash.

During last night's restless sleep, she'd had dreams of her father earnestly reading business magazines and working his hardest to be successful, despite the cards being stacked against him with his bipolar disorder. Remembering those hazy dreams as she sipped her freshly brewed java, Jenny felt a wave of poignant sadness for him and blinked back tears. She thought about how hard he'd tried, and maybe bits and pieces from Gavin Rogers' story about how he'd grown a business from nothing had seeped into her unconscious. Jenny sat stock still for a moment, and suddenly knew exactly what she had to do. Pulling her robe around her tighter, she knocked back her coffee, poured herself another cup, and headed to shower. When the banks and businesses opened, she'd be dialing for dollars.

Jenny felt marginally more confident about money since she now knew Mama and Landis would be paying rent for two whole months. She'd love to be in a position to insist the two stay at her cabin for free, but she wasn't, and she knew Landis and Mama would only agree to stay if they could be paying guests.

Giving herself a quick pep talk, at 9:01 Jenny called Sterling

Fairwood, the senior loan officer at Goodlife Bank who had given her the original construction loan that had enabled Jenny to complete the cabins last fall. After asking for an increase in the loan amount, getting stonewalled, and then finagling with him, Sterling seemed disinclined to budge with more money until Jenny mentioned her *mama and darlin' stepdaddy, Landis Collins*. Landis had been Chairman of the Board at Goodlife until he retired at the end of last year. Sterling must have suddenly remembered that family connection, because he sounded positively cheerful as he offered to loan her more money.

But not enough. Bracing herself, Jenny called her investment firm and cracked her SEP-IRA. When the financial advisor told her what the penalty and tax implications would be, Jenny swallowed hard but agreed to it. Many of the successful business types she'd read about in those thirty-year-old *World of Southern Business* magazines had maxed out their credit cards to get their first businesses up and running. *Fortune favors the bold*, she reminded herself. This had to be done.

Then Jenny had another idea. Last night on television she'd seen a public service type of commercial about the North Carolina Department of State Treasurer site for recovering unclaimed money. Could there be the tiniest chance that she had some security deposit, state income tax refund, or bank account she'd completely lost track of? Some people were losing track of their money, because the site said North Carolinians had left more than $700,000,000 of unclaimed property and cash. She found the site, sent up a prayer, and tapped in her name. Jenny gasped quietly when she found a security deposit for a utility company and a $260 balance in a savings account she now vaguely remembered opening at a bank she hadn't banked at in years. Jenny bounced in her chair as she printed the form. Four hundred and twelve dollars would be on its way to her as soon as the good folks in state government processed the claim. This was no windfall in the scheme of things, but she'd gladly take it.

Her worries lightened about the outlay for boats, Jenny found herself whistling as she poached an egg and made avocado toast. Though broker than she'd been in a long while, Jenny felt optimistic and was excited about hunting for a boat Saturday.

"Boys, time to get some fresh air." Jenny shrugged on her coat and scarf and threw open the door to her cabin. Buddy and Bear cavorted like pups, fake fighting and chasing each other around in circles. Levi was feeling his oats, too, and did a little bucking shimmy and then kicked as he circled around the periphery of the wild dogs. Jenny smiled, watching them until they wound down, walked down the lake bank, and lapped up sips of cold water.

Striding to the dock, Jenny checked to make sure the frosty weeks of January and February hadn't pushed up any pilings from the muddy lake bottom, something she'd read about in an article in the *Heron Lake Herald*. But all of the pilings looked like they had in the fall, even and sturdy. Spotting a fishing rod that lay partially hidden under a pile of leaves, Jenny picked it up to put it in the boathouse for spring. Though she'd never fished in her life, she thought about the fishermen she'd seen on the lake and the graceful arc of line they cast. She'd give it a try.

Though her rod bounced with her enthusiastic toss, the line did not leave the end of the pole. Oops. She needed to release that little button on the handle. Her second cast caught the side of the dock and took several minutes to unhook. But her third toss made a whizzing sound as it flew gracefully thought the air and plopped in the water. Pretty darned professional looking.

Proud of herself, Jenny reeled in her line, but it jerked taut and pulled so hard that she almost let the rod slip through her fingers. Snap. She had a fish on the line, and a big one. Why hadn't she brought her phone? If she had it, she could one-handedly google how to get a giant fish off a hook without hurting him or possibly without handling him. The rod bobbed like in a *National Geographic* special she'd seen the other night about people with dowsing rods finding water. Her thoughts racing, Jenny gritted her teeth and reeled in the first fish she'd ever caught in her life.

Slowly, the fish's thrashing and underwater zigzagging slowed. Jenny gasped as the whiskery, tentacle head of a fish rose from the water. Resting the flopping fish as carefully as she could on the dock, Jenny racked her brain trying to remember any tips she'd seen on *Carolina Outdoor Journal*, the fishing show that Luke liked to watch. Though she was not riveted watching men in boats fishing, Luke was, so she'd paid some attention to the show. Jenny remembered the knowledgeable fishermen using towels or gloves to take fish off hooks and using needle-nose pliers to remove hooks from the mouths of bigger fish. Glancing around wildly, she saw no fish towels or pliers lying around. But she couldn't leave the guy hooked and flailing on the dock. With trembling hands, Jenny took off her wool scarf and wrapped it around the fish. Grasping the fish's body and head, she slowly worked the hook out of its mouth. "Please, please, please," she murmured. Freeing the hook, she gave the fish an awkward pat as she slipped him back in the lake. The fish swam away, looking none the worse for the wear. Her heart still drumming a staccato beat, Jenny stowed the fishing rod, held the fishy scarf between two fingers, and reminded herself to get fishing lessons from Luke. The owner of a lakeside resort needed to know how to catch and release a fish without having a case of the jumps.

When she got back to the cabin, she left her fishy scarf outside and went inside to energetically wash her hands when she heard the ping of a text. Charlotte wrote:

Headed your way early Saturday AM. Need a titch of paint touch-up, but at nine when Luke gets there, IT'S TIME FOR THE BIG REVEAL, i.e., you get to see the final work I've done on the Silver Belle. Promise no peeking 'til then. Kiss the boys for me.

Jenny grinned. She was dying to see the inside of the Belle. Though sorely tempted, she'd summoned all of her willpower and not peeked at the final product. The camper being comfortable and functional meant that they could go camping as soon as she found a babysitter for the resort.

Saturday morning, Jenny took extra care with her appearance. She blew out her hair until it was shiny and swingy and slipped on black jeans, boots, and a blue cashmere turtleneck sweater she'd found at the Fire Department Rummage Sale. Applying light makeup, she was slicking on a peach lip gloss when she heard car wheels on gravel. Charlotte and Luke had arrived.

Outside, Jenny waved, and hugged them both. "I'm so excited to see the inside of the new and improved Belle that I can't stand it."

Luke smiled indulgently, and put an arm around her shoulder as the three of them headed over to the Airstream.

Charlotte cleared her throat. "Before we get to the Big Reveal," she began, pointing at the camper and then putting a hand on her chest, "I want to tell you how much this has meant to me. I put before and after pics on my website." Eyes sparkling, she put her hands on her cheeks.

Jenny wondered at all the hand-waving and pointing, and decided Charlotte was just excited. But then the morning sun caught the sparkler on Charlotte's ring finger, and Jenny whooped with excitement. Grabbing her hand, Jenny grinned and pulled it toward her to get a better look. "Let's see that rock."

Charlotte's face was pink, and she radiated happiness as she held out her hand for Jenny and Luke to see. The engagement ring was a simple but lovely round solitaire. "I'm not sure I'm supposed to show this to anyone or not, but I just have to," Charlotte said as she pulled a black velvet box from her purse and opened it toward them. "Here's the wedding ring."

Two glittering curved bands were made to fit snugly around the solitaire, enhancing its shine. In the channels of the two rings were small jewels, sapphires, rubies, and emeralds. "These are the smaller stones from the two mamas."

"I love that idea, and this is the prettiest set I've ever seen," Jenny said, meaning it.

"It's real nice," Luke said, looking bemused. He looked pleased that Charlotte was happy but not so sure of what all the fuss was about.

Charlotte clutched the box to her chest and bounced on her toes. "I love it. It's so *us*."

The set *was* just made for Charlotte and Ashe, fine quality, understated, and meaningful without breaking the bank. Jenny had a moment of envy and gave herself a quick talking to. One of these days, her time would come.

"I need to be in Celeste by ten-thirty for a "Meet and Greet the Candidate" pancake breakfast, so let's get on with the show." Tucking the velvet box back into her purse, Charlotte looked at them both. "This fresh and pretty Silver Belle represents a ton of hard work by Luke. He took a dumpy, sad, dated trailer and made it functional, clean, and airtight. All I did was pretty it up." She gazed at Jenny, her eyes dark with emotion. "But we both did this because we love you, Jenny." Charlotte paused and took her phone from her purse.

Touched, Jenny leaned her head on Luke's shoulder. "I love y'all back."

Grinning, Charlotte hit a button on her phone and a loud drum roll sounded. "Ta-da!" She swung open the door to the Silver Belle.

When they stepped inside, Jenny gasped and looked around, delighted. The whole interior was warm, inviting, and comfortable. Charlotte had painted the interior a creamy white and added a patterned accent of wallpaper that looked like thin strands of bamboo in shades of earthy brown and a soft, sea glass blue-green. She'd covered the fluffy cushions of the small couch with a subtly striped duck cloth fabric that incorporated those brown and blue colors. "Won't get ripped by the dogs' nails," she pointed out.

"You put that backsplash behind the sink. Looks sharp," Luke commented, peering at her handiwork.

"And I added three-inch-thick memory foam padding to the pull-down sofa, too. That'll make it as comfortable sleeping on the couch as it is on the bed," Charlotte said. "I got those amazing pendant lights at Habitat."

"So smart." Jenny spied the curtains and sighed softly, remembering happy afternoons watching videos of *The Roy Rogers Show* with her grandmother and grandfather. The curtain fabric featured a smiling, square-jawed Roy Rogers in his fringed shirt riding Trigger and Dale Evans in a full skirt riding Buttermilk. Bullet, their faithful German shepherd, bounded along beside them. "You remembered how much I loved Roy Rogers because it was my granddaddy's favorite show. I just love it. Where did you find this amazing fabric?"

"Etsy," Charlotte said proudly. "I couldn't believe the colors of the print tied in so well with what I had going in here."

"You kept that Formica table and chairs. Looks like you did a nice patch job on the seats." Luke stooped to examine the chairs. "I can't even see the tears that were there."

Jenny put an arm around Charlotte's shoulders. "It looks amazing and you did this whole thing on a shoestring budget.

Charlotte gave a curtsy. "I'm the queen of doing things well but on the cheap."

"Fine trait in a woman," Luke said gravely.

Jenny thought so, too.

Charlotte glanced at her phone. "I need to skedaddle." She clasped her hands together and looked at them. "All right. So you two are off to find a used powerboat. How about Jenny and I try to find some gently used canoes and kayaks on the Thrifty Heron and Craigslist?"

"Good," Luke said with a grateful nod. "I know you're a pro, so if you'd help Jenny with that shopping, it would be a big help to us."

To *us*. Jenny heard it, and flushed with pleasure. There was an *us*. There was a future. She might not have the ring yet or the wedding plans, but they'd get there.

With hugs all round, Charlotte motored off, a bejeweled hand out the window waving madly.

Jenny and Luke headed off to look at boats. The sun dappled yellow on the bright green growth of spring leaves. The redbuds had pinked up and the forsythia's yellow buds were about to burst open. Jenny cracked the window to let in some fresh morning air and just felt happy at the prospect of riding around back roads in the truck with Luke.

Jenny felt the wind blow back her hair and closed her eyes for moment. "Yesterday, I scared up some money for the boat."

Luke frowned. "I was going to suggest I buy the boat. You can buy the kayaks and canoes."

And he was springing that bit of news on her now? Though exasperated at his lack of communication, Jenny was thrilled that he'd offered. But she picked at a fingernail, not sure how she felt about co-mingling funds when she didn't have a ring on her finger. She gave him a level look. "I'd feel better if I just bought them myself."

The muscle in his jaw worked as he flipped on the signal and changed lanes. "I wish you'd let me help."

"It's fine," Jenny said, though the money-finding had been hard. She wanted to lighten the mood. "I accidentally caught a giant fish yesterday and had to get him off the hook by myself. That was my first-ever fish, and I wasn't even using any bait."

"Impressive." Luke glanced at her. "Generally, the rule is no bait, no bite. Was there a lure on the line?"

Jenny rubbed the spot between her eyebrows as she recalled that shiny bit near the hook.

"There was a lure," she admitted. "Do you think I hurt his mouth?"

"I think he'll be fine," he said lowering the visor to block some morning sun. "So, the fish was giant, like five pounds or eight pounds maybe?"

Jenny had no idea. "Probably fifty," she said vaguely.

Luke chuckled. "Your first fish and you're already telling fish stories."

"Yep." Jenny took a sip of coffee. "I need some fishing lessons when it warms up, and I need you to teach me how to drive a boat."

"Done."

At the boat dealer's lot, a mustached man in salmon-colored pants and sockless boat shoes slapped the hull of the boat and smiled the proud smile of a parent whose first child has just graduated from college. "This little baby is a peach with only 132 hours on it. The couple who bought it got divorced." He shrugged and gestured to other boats on the lot. "Most of our inventory comes from folks trading up to bigger boats, but we also get a lot of older residents downsizing to move closer to their children, people who got into money trouble, or couples splitting up. As soon as one spouse calls the attorney, the toys go just like that." He snapped his fingers and chuckled.

But Jenny didn't find divorce or financial trouble the least bit funny. She shot Luke a doubtful look, but he just took her hand and gave it a reassuring *It's going to be OK* squeeze.

As they climbed into the boat, Jenny thought about seaside fishing towns where clergy did a blessing of the fleet. Maybe Ella's Episcopal clergyman husband would bless the boats they bought, warding off divorce and money woes.

But Luke was scowling. While the salesman answered a question from another customer, Luke spoke quietly to Jenny as he pointed out his concerns. "The exterior is shined up and the engine hours are low. But look at the dents in the pontoons. There's corrosion on the engine mounts. There's fishing line wrapped around the prop." He tapped the carpet with his foot and sniffed. "What do you smell?"

Jenny breathed in and grimaced. "Stale beer?"

"Yup. The owner didn't take care of this boat, and that's a shame. I don't want you buying someone else's problems." He shook his head. "This isn't the boat for you."

Several dealers and marinas later, Jenny and Luke arrived at the house of a woman who'd advertised a boat for sale on the Thrifty Heron website.

"I'm Mary Parsons," the women said. After introductions, the woman walked them toward the boat in the back yard. "I'm buying my husband, Jim, an even bigger, faster pontoon for his sixty-fifth birthday. I'm having it specially built for him. He'll be in hog heaven," she said, sounding delighted. "He thinks he's getting old, but I keep telling him he's just coming into his prime. And I mean it. Since he retired, he's got a sparkle in his eye, he's more fun, and he chases me around the house. Oops, that was too much information." Mary giggled and put a hand up to her mouth. "This is the first time I've ever been able to pull off a surprise like this, and I can't wait."

The woman gave them the details on the boat, and they stepped aboard to examine it more closely. Mary's cell rang and she stepped away to take the call. "Sure, sugar," she trilled. "Come up here as soon as it warms up. We'd love to see the grands..."

Luke spoke quietly. "This boat is a cream puff. Well taken care of. All the service records. Low engine hours. Interior's in good shape." He pulled out his phone and tapped away.

"What are you looking at?" she hissed, her nervousness making her grouchy.

"The *NADA Guide* is a blue book for boats." Luke squinted at the screen. "The price is fair."

Mary walked over, and Jenny stood up straighter, steeled herself, and made an offer for the boat and the trailer.

"Sugar, you've got yourself a deal. I'll need you to wait until May 24 to pick up the boat so Jim won't get suspicious. We pick up his new boat at the dealer on the 22nd."

Jenny couldn't help but worry. "How are you sure your husband will like the boat you're buying him? I don't want either of you to regret selling this one."

The woman winked. "I pay attention when he reads the boating magazines. I also quizzed his best friend, Bill. Those two men talk about and drool over dream boats like teenaged boys used do about dream cars and dream girls."

After agreeing on the details, Jenny and Luke got back in the truck.

"You did well," Luke said.

"Thanks." She gazed at him. "I couldn't have done it without you."

He gave her a crooked smile and took her hand. "You don't have to, Jenny."

CHAPTER 8 — LUKE'S WALKABOUT

ON THE DRIVE HOME, THEY stopped at an outdoor store and bought three kayaks from the 2018 inventory. The price was right, and Jenny helped Luke tie them down into the bed of his truck with fastening straps. "We got so much done," Jenny marveled, as she rubbed her sandy palms on the legs of her jeans and swung back into the truck.

Luke turned over the engine. "Your next job is finding used canoes and a few more kayaks. You and Charlotte do your yard sale thing, and keep your eye on the Thrifty Heron and any other buy-and-sell websites. We can go online and order accessories for the boats: safety vests and life jackets, paddles, floats, tubes, and skis. Get a list started."

"I will." Jenny's stomach rumbled. "Can we stop on the way back and eat?"

"Let's do. How about Slowpoke's Diner, that new place in Jamison?"

"Let's do it." This was as close to a real dinner date with Luke as she'd ever had.

Luke took a large bite of his grass-fed beef hamburger with bacon and smoked Gouda while Jenny devoured a fried green tomato sandwich topped with smoky pimiento cheese on toasted *ciabatta*. "*This is so good. Not everyone knows how to make pimiento cheese,*" Jenny mumbled, her mouth still full.

Luke swallowed and took a long pull of iced tea, patted his mouth with a napkin, and gazed at her with his mesmerizing navy blue eyes. "So, when are we getting hitched?"

A piece of lettuce she'd been chewing went down wrong, and Jenny had to take a long swallow of her ice water to stop the coughing. Red-faced and watery-eyed, she cleared her throat. This was exactly what she'd been longing for, and now that Luke wanted to get a date nailed down, she wasn't sure how she felt about it. Luke was kind, steady, caring, and he seemed crazy about her. She really did want to marry him.

Pretending to cough a little more to buy time, Jenny's thoughts raced. Though they'd not gotten into specifics after his casual, free-form proposal in December, the general plan was that they'd marry, Luke would move in, and they'd run the Lakeside Resort together. He might pick up a few more contracting jobs here and there, but they'd be all-in together on the resort.

Luke cocked his head, his eyes kind. "You getting a mild case of cold feet, darlin'?"

Jenny eyed him and just blurted it out. "We'll be together twenty-four hours a day, seven days a week. What if we get on each other's nerves? What if you start bossing me around?"

He shrugged and poured more ketchup on his fries. "You'll just have to tell me to back off."

Jenny nodded, took another, smaller bite of sandwich, and chewed contemplatively.

Here's what she was really worried about. What if Luke met a lithe and exquisite smart woman like Aiden, whom her ex, Douglas, sappily called *the love of my life?* And what about her pathetic ex-husband who'd left her for his skinny, intense, Vape-smoking boss, Natalie?

Jenny took a long sip of water, remembering all the wrong men she'd found so attractive over the years. She eyed Luke. His love for her seemed so steady and intense but, in the long run, could she trust him with her heart? Avoiding eye contact, she murmured, "What if you change? What if you fall out of love with me and in love with a woman who is way smarter, prettier, and more accomplished than I am?" She hated sounding so insecure, but she had to ask.

Luke reached for her hand, which was icy because of her fears. "Jenny, I will never leave you. I have never been so sure of anything in my life. No woman will ever come between us."

Jenny stopped examining the salt and pepper shaker and met his eyes, feeling a wave of relief and tenderness. She believed him. With a shaky smile, she took her napkin and dabbed at brimming tears. "Then we'd best get out our calendars and pick a date."

Luke's phone dinged the arrival of a text, but he ignored it. A moment later, another text dinged, and then another. He sent her an apologetic look. "I need to make sure it's not about my dad." Pulling his phone from his pocket, Luke glanced at it, his brows furrowed. "It's Zander. My business partner."

Sensing trouble, Jenny gave an involuntary shiver.

Luke's eyes were lit with worry as he looked at the screen. Looking grim, he held up the phone. "He's had an accident, a bad one. He's in the hospital. I need to call him." Striding to the lobby of the restaurant, Luke made the call.

A cold knot formed in Jenny's stomach as she watched him talk and pace, his face tight and his shoulders high. Appetite gone, she pushed away her plate and waited anxiously. Though she'd never met Zander, she knew he was not only a business partner but a longtime and dear friend of Luke's. They'd met in college, started a business together, and worked tirelessly to make the business a success.

A few moments later, Luke slid into the seat, his chin set and anguish in his eyes. "Zander banged himself up badly. He's broken his hip, his femur, an arm, and his wrists."

Jenny drew in a breath sharply, wincing as she pictured those injuries. "He's OK though. I mean he's going to live, right?"

"He'll live." Luke's rubbed the spot between his eyebrows.

"What happened?" Jenny didn't want to be ghoulish but wondered how Zander had busted himself up so thoroughly.

"A car accident." Luke suddenly looked tired and shook his head. "His recovery's going to be long and tough. He'd looking at rehab and then months of physical therapy, and he's got no one to help him." He grimaced. "Zander's always dated glamorous, much younger women who are models and actresses. The flake he'd been dating left when she heard he had been hurt, cleared her stuff out of his place and won't take his calls."

Serves him right for not dating a grown-up, kind woman closer to his age, Jenny thought meanly but said nothing.

Luke rubbed the back of his neck. "And we're right in the midst of a negotiation to acquire a company in Melbourne, Australia. It's a huge deal that will bring the company to the international forefront, and he can't even get out of bed by himself." He shook his head. "No one else can handle it."

Jenny had a sinking feeling in her stomach. "No one else but you, right? He wants you to go to Melbourne for him," she guessed, her voice flat.

His eyes pleading, Luke took both of her hands in his. "Jen, I've got to help. He's not just a good friend, but I've got a big stake in the financial success of the company. My stock is my nest egg and my financial security. We bought another outfit in January, so now we've got three hundred employees. If the deal goes south, we all stand to lose a lot."

Jenny nodded wordlessly as it all sank in.

Luke was leaving her. He'd be time zones away. Worlds away. While Luke settled the bill, Jenny surreptitiously grabbed her phone and mapped it. Melbourne was half a globe and a wide ocean away from Heron Lake. It was 9,853 miles away. Twenty-three hours. Her heart sank. There would be no coming home for weekends. The distance was daunting. Would they even be able to talk on the phone? Her cell service to Hickory and Charlotte were bad enough.

Jenny speedily read more. Melbourne is emerging as a hub of innovation not only for Australia, but for the United States and Asia-Pacific regions. More and more global companies are establishing headquarters there. Top talent is migrating to the city being called tech's new golden Shangri-la.

Good grief. She had no idea Melbourne was such a big deal, though, to be fair, the only news Jenny had read lately was the

Heron Lake Herald and a *People* magazine that one of the guests had left in their cabin.

In the truck, while Luke made one more call to Zander, Jenny googled facts about Australia. Snap. That whole country was kind of intimidating. Australians had been credited with inventing the black box flight recorder, the cochlear implant, and the electronic pacemaker. She groaned internally as she read on. Son of a biscuit. They'd also invented box wine. That *was* genius.

"I'll stop by the hospital, and you can brief me before I head out. Yes. Yes. I'll text you my travel itinerary tonight," Luke went on, still hammering out details with Zander.

Quickly, Jenny tapped in *famous Australians* and gasped quietly. Something had to be in the water because that country grew beauties like Rose Byrne and Naomi Watts. The men probably all looked like Hugh Jackman, Keith Urban, or those handsome Hemsworth brothers. Australia made especially attractive people, and they had the charming accents and that joie de vivre that she knew about mainly from Steve Irwin reruns and old Crocodile Dundee movies.

Both of them were quiet on the drive home. Jenny gave herself a mental shake. She'd let her old insecurities flare up into a fire, and she needed to stop it. In her heart, she knew Luke would never fall for an Australian beauty or become so enamored of another country that he wouldn't come home. But with him being so very far away, she'd miss him so that she wasn't sure she could bear it. Fighting tears, she reached over and squeezed his hand. "You have no idea how badly I'm going to miss you," she said in a shaky voice.

"I think I might, Jenny." Luke pulled her hand to his mouth and kissed it.

So at five o'clock on a still dark Sunday morning, Jenny heard Luke pull up in the driveway. What felt like a hive of bees buzzed in her stomach. She couldn't believe he was leaving. Last night he'd called her when he got home and told her he might be gone for two and a half months. Jenny had tried to sound like a matter-of-fact good sport, but when she'd ended the call, she'd closed her eyes, feeling bleak and lonesome. Since the first of the year, having a romance with Luke had been like being in a long-distance relationship, except he lived just over an hour away. She'd just have to soldier through this.

This morning, she was taking him to Charlotte Douglas Airport. He'd see Zander in the hospital in Athens, Georgia, get briefed on the ins and outs of the possible acquisition, and head out to Melbourne on the red eye tonight.

Hurriedly, she slicked on claret-colored lip gloss and smoothed her hair one last time. Jenny had risen before dawn to shower, blow out her hair, and apply makeup. She'd slipped on jeans, a scarlet cashmere boat neck sweater, and her good wool walker coat instead of her puffy down coat. She knew it was silly, but before he flew off she wanted Luke's last memory of her to be of her looking as pretty as she could muster.

He gave a soft rap on the door, and she swung it open, her heart tripping as she saw him standing there. "Hey, there." She gazed at him intently, trying to memorize his indigo-eyed, broad-shouldered handsomeness.

"Morning." Luke leaned in for a quick but scorching kiss. With a heart-melting slow smile, he tipped her chin up with a finger and looked into her eyes. "You going to be all right, baby girl?"

"I am," she said, with more confidence than she felt. Jenny poured hot coffee into two stainless steel to-go cups and plucked several sausage biscuits wrapped in foil from the still-warm oven. "I've got breakfast, and I'm ready if you are."

Luke squatted, giving scrubbing pats to Buddy, Bear, and Levi. "All right, guys. You're the men of the house while I'm gone. Keep an eye on things and especially on your mama. I'm counting on you."

Holding the passenger door open for Jenny, Luke stepped into the driver's seat of her SUV. As their headlights bounced down the rutted road and onto the main road, Jenny partially unwrapped a biscuit and handed it to him. Luke took a bite, sighed with pleasure, and began rattling off a list of reminders and instructions.

"My truck stays outside the Dogwood. It's always good to look like a person driving a truck lives in the house. When I get home, we're going to look into a security system and cameras." He paused for a sip of coffee. "If you and Charlotte decide to take the Airstream on a trip, tow it with my truck. You've got more towing power and stability than with your SUV, plus it's newer. Remember to set the brake and set the chocks."

"OK." She wasn't sure what chocks were, but she'd sure set them.

"Remember to enforce your cancellation policy. Those no shows or people who call late to cancel directly affect your bottom line. It's not good business to let them slide."

"OK." This reminder list meant Luke was worried about keeping her safe.

"We should be done with the coldest part of winter, but if you get a real cold snap, make sure to keep the heat on low in the cabins. We don't want the pipes to freeze." Luke took one last bite of biscuit and crumpled up the foil. "Daddy says to just pick up the phone if you need a handyman. He knows he's on light duty but says he'd be glad to do what he can. Alice and Mike have said the same thing."

"Couldn't Zander have done this deal in Charlotte or Raleigh?" She knew she sounded petulant but didn't care.

"He wants access to international markets." Luke sent her a *buck up, now* kind of smile. "I'll be home before you know it."

She looked over at his chiseled profile illuminated by the dashboard lights. He was so handsome it made her heart ache. "Did you know an Australian invented google maps?

A smile played at the corners of his mouth. "I didn't know that."

"Yes, indeed." Jenny looked out the window at the dark landscape, and tried to decide whether to air this other worry. "Luke, promise me you won't go falling for any of those famously attractive Australian women. Elle McPherson is from Australia, you know."

"You've done your research." Luke gave her a crooked smile. "I only care about you, Jen. Plus, I'll be so busy, I wouldn't notice if I sat across from Elle at a meeting."

"I would hope not," Jenny said primly. Her heat sank when she saw the sign for the airport. They were just seven miles away.

Luke gave her hand a reassuring squeeze. "Reach into the back seat and get my backpack. I've got something for you."

Jenny retrieved the bag, put it on her lap, and pulled out a square package wrapped with newspaper and tied with kitchen twine. She glanced over at him questioningly.

"That's it. Open it." Luke flipped on his turn signal and took the exit for the airport.

Jenny carefully pulled off the paper and put a hand to her mouth. "I can't believe you thought to do this." He'd taken her daddy's colorful, detailed, hand-drawn rendering of his vision for the Lakeside Resort and had it made into a 3D canvas print. In the pale morning light, she could make out Daddy's dream, including the vintage RVs, the eight tiny cabins in a semicircle facing Heron Lake, red canoes pulled up on the lawn waterside, a rope swing hanging over the water, and a power boat zooming by towing children on tubes.

Luke broke into a grin. "You like it?"

"I adore it." Jenny held the canvas to her chest, blinking back tears. "This is the most thoughtful present anyone has ever given me."

"Glad you like it." Luke looked pleased. "The Resort was your daddy's dream, now it's your dream, and one of these days, it will be the next chapter in our lives." Pulling into the Kiss and Go Lane, he put the SUV in park. Turning, he held her face in his hands and his eyes searched her face. "I know these past few months haven't been easy but, believe me, when I get home and we get some of this duty and work and mess behind us, we're going to have an amazing life together. I love you, Jenny." With that, he leaned in and gave her a kiss that made her melt.

Happiness flooded in. The loneliness and doubts of the past

few months flew away, and Jenny felt a rush of elation. "I love you."

A yellow-vested TSA agent tapped at the window, giving them a grin and *time to move a*long whirl of the finger.

Luke gave her a quick scorcher of a kiss, grabbed his gear from the back seat, and stepped out of the car. With a crooked smile, he raised a hand and strode off toward the automatic sliding doors of the airport.

Jenny slid out of her seat and went around to the driver's seat. Taking a few slow breaths, she tried to calm the wild beating of her heart. She already longed for him so much it hurt, but his words had reassured her so. On lonely days, she'd sometime wondered if she'd imagined his love and his promise of a future together. Now, all she had to do was make it through the next few months without him.

Swallowing the lump in her throat, Jenny put the car in gear and slowly headed home.

Back at the cabin, Jenny felt empty, ephemeral. Drifting around, she did chores, anything to not think or feel. She emptied the dishwasher, cleaned out the refrigerator, shook out the boys' blankets, and started a load of wash. Outside, she groomed Levi, giving him a once over with the soft brush that he loved.

Jenny fixed herself a cup of tea, slid behind the computer, and made herself face reality. She pulled up the time zone converter. Melbourne was fourteen hours ahead of her in North Carolina. She glanced at the time. So it was eleven-thirty in the morning on Heron Lake, and that would mean it would be one-thirty AM *tomorrow* in Melbourne. The best time to talk with Luke, or better yet, video chat with him, would be four-thirty in the afternoon her time and six-thirty AM his time, before he went to work. Though she'd be heading into the homestretch of her work day, that might work. Jenny pinched her bottom lip. She didn't want to try to call him during his work day. They could talk after he finished work if she called him at two-thirty in the morning her time the day before. Jenny smiled wryly, imagining how coherent she'd be at that hour. If she tried for ten PM his time, she could call at eight

AM her time the day before, but by then her work day was in full swing. That could work too, though. Whoa. This would take some getting used to. Taking orange sticky notes, Jenny wrote in bold the best times to call, morning and evening, and put them on the wall behind the computer.

The next two nights, Luke didn't call. They usually talked several times a day, and Jenny was always reassured by hearing his voice. But, with jet lag, the time difference, and him hitting the ground running with work, she knew she'd have to get used to less connection with him. But still, she felt restless and lonely throughout the day and found it hard to sleep at night. Jenny decided she'd call him at five the next morning.

"Hey, there," she said, trying to sound upbeat and normal, not consumed with missing him.

"Hey, yourself." Luke's voice was warm, affectionate.

"How are you? How were the flights? Are you doing OK?" Her words came out in a rush.

"Everything is fine, though this flying around is for a much younger man," he said with a chuckle. "I'm in this little hotel room and can walk to the office. The people seem nice. I'm still too tired to be with it, but I'll get there."

"You will," Jenny said. "How's Zander's recuperation coming?"

"He's improving. He'll be released from the hospital in a few days. Then he's off to rehab. After that, he'll go back home, but he's got to hire caregivers to help out. Physical therapists and occupational therapists will visit regularly."

But Jenny heard the clicking of keys. This was the first time they'd talked in two and a half days, and Luke was typing while he was talking with her. The hair on the back of her neck stood up as she felt her blood pressure rise. "You sound busy, so I'll get going. I have a million things to do," she said brightly.

"Don't go, Jenny," Luke said.

"Why are you typing while we're talking?" she asked bluntly.

"I'm sorry." Luke sounded contrite. "Work is wide open, and I need to get this done so I can get back home to you."

They talked a few more minutes, but Jenny felt deflated. It

wasn't as though she expected ardor and poetry from Luke. He wasn't that kind of guy. But typing while talking was just plain rude.

Over the next few days, they talked briefly most mornings. Video chats didn't work, they discovered. Jenny found their conversations only vaguely satisfying. It was so good to hear Luke's voice and to have a few minutes of catch up, but the connection often skipped in and out and Luke wasn't a big talker on the telephone. Once they got beyond pleasantries, he responded to questions about his day with just a few words, and then petered out of things to say. Jenny reminded herself that he'd been that way when he'd lived in the same area code, but she found it frustrating now because those conversations were like lifelines to her. Still, though he might not have a lot to say, she could listen to his voice, hear his breath, and relish that warm chuckle of his.

After their last call, Jenny felt oddly let down. She tried to give herself a pep talk. Luke being so far away is just temporary. He'll be home before I know it. He's stiff on the phone because that's how he is, not because he doesn't care about me.

Sometimes the pep talks worked and sometimes, they just didn't.

CHAPTER 9 — TREE FORTS, TEEPEES, AND LIGHTHOUSES

WHEN A BLEARY-EYED JENNY LET the boys out the next morning, she saw Charlotte's faded green four-door parked beside the Belle and her mood lifted. Good. She was glad for Charlotte's company. Her friend must have come in early this morning when Jenny had finally fallen asleep. She was becoming an insomniac, and she didn't like it.

As the last of the mist burned off the lake and the sun began to shine, a bright-eyed Charlotte popped by, clutching a stainless steel coffee cup. "I'm here. Hope you don't mind."

"Not one bit." Jenny hugged her.

"Come for a walk with me. I came to talk with you about a sensational idea I had."

"I'll be ready in a jiff." Jenny swallowed down the last of a protein and fruit smoothie, pulled on her coat, and grabbed her own steel cup of coffee. The two strode off down the dirt road that led away from the cabin.

"First off, how are you doing with Luke gone? Are you missing him something fierce?" Charlotte asked tentatively.

"Like crazy." Jenny slipped on sunglasses.

"Are you doing OK communicating across time zones?" Charlotte persisted.

"So-so. We're way off-kilter, but we're trying to make the best of it." Jenny raised her chin. "I made a decision last night. I refuse to pine for two and a half months." She stood up taller. "Luke always tells me to focus on what I can control. I'm just going to do the best I can with the distance and focus on growing the business." She'd made that vow at two AM this morning after spinning like a top for hours trying to sleep. The plan hadn't stuck yet, but she'd work on it.

"That's exactly what you should do," Charlotte said encouragingly. "And my idea ties right in with that."

"So tell me." Jenny tried to drink coffee and walk but it was hard. Stopping, she took a pull of a bold medium roast. Aaah.

Charlotte retied her boot, and they resumed walking at a good clip. Her expression grew solemn. "You know my weight has always been...an issue for me."

Jenny zipped her lip. If she said something that she meant, like, *You're perfect as far as I'm concerned*, Charlotte would either bite her head off or launch into a long and detailed description of the ideal American woman's proportions according to some poorly researched, junk science, sample-size-of-five survey she'd read on the net.

"At the gym where I used to belong, a lot of people were nice, but just as many people were subtly mean. It was usually the extra-skinny girls who wore makeup when they worked out and the men who grunted when they lifted free weights. They'd stare at me, and not in a *You go, girl!* encouraging way. In a disgusted way." Charlotte frowned and kicked a rock down the road.

Jenny's face burned, her temper burning. What gave anyone the right to be mean to someone because of their size or looks? Sometimes she just couldn't stand people.

Charlotte went on. "Some averted their eyes like size fourteen or sixteen could be contagious. Some of them offered tips on weight loss. But it was the disdain, the repulsion in some people's eyes, that finally got to me and made me decide to join an all-women's gym that's body positive. They push body acceptance and encourage members to focus on fit and not thin."

"I'm glad you did." Jenny still was hot about the stupid people at that other gym.

"So, I've met a lot of good folks there. I like the gym, even though we do barre with thousands of squats and pliés and use those heavy ropes and toss around tires and jump over boxes." Charlotte gave a rueful smile. "But a few of us have been talking about how nice it would be to get out of our normal routine and just focus on getting healthier. We talked about a spa, but they can be pricey, and the theme seems to be that the women want a low-key getaway where they can relax and focus on feeling good." She turned to Jenny, her eyes dancing with excitement. "What if we did that here? We could fill those cabins. We could call it the *Fabulous You Fit and Healthy Week.*"

"The name is kind of a mouthful, but I love the idea. What could we offer them, though? How would they get fit and healthy here at the resort?" Jenny racked her brain for ideas.

"We could take long hikes in the morning and evening. We could go to the state park and get that hunky ranger Emory to lead nature or bird-watching walks," Charlotte said excitedly. "So much more pleasant than throwing dirty old tires." She shuddered prettily.

"We could get a caterer from Celeste or Shady Grove to cook and deliver food. We could roll the meals into the costs and make the whole thing more of a package." Jenny thought about them wanting a low-key, cost-effective experience. "Or how about a healthy, rotating kind of deal where each cabin or camper takes a turn making the others a healthy supper. They could do breakfast and lunches on their own."

"Now you're talking." Charlotte beamed. "Most of the women at the gym are not fussy, and the ones that are, we'll give ground rules to up front about no persnickety behavior allowed," she said firmly. "Gals watching their budgets can double up in cabins. If I can stay with you in the Dogwood, we can put a camper in the Silver Belle and you'd have six places to rent out."

Jenny gave her friend an admiring look. "You *are* a brainiac."

"Nope, just an entrepreneur." Charlotte gave her a cheeky grin. "Could we do it as soon as next month on May 4? I talked to the women about dates, and that's one they came up with."

"I don't see why not. I have the vacancies, as long as you think we can get it all organized by then."

"We can. Let's do it." Charlotte sounded as perky as a junior varsity cheerleader. "I still want us to do a weekend for people with developmental disabilities and their parents. That will take longer to organize, so let's think about scheduling that for fall or early winter."

"We'll do that, I promise." Jenny made a mental note

"If we can get this *Fabulous You* weekend on the books soon, do the yoga retreat and the disability-friendly weekend in the fall, and slowly get other reservations, your weeks are filling up fast. We need to figure out where we're going to put people for the special events and what weeks are reserved for what crowd."

"Good. But it's more than getting people here. We've got to help guests love it when they're here," she reminded Charlotte. She'd looked at small inn ratings online and seen how a one-star rating could negate eight or ten five-star ratings. "One misstep or oversight or wrong assumption about what the guests want, and we could get a slew of bad reviews."

"We'll plan it meticulously," Charlotte said with a steely-eyed look. "I'm going to the Just a Buck store and get big calendars and colored markers. We need to plan it out in detail so we can see it big and plain instead of in Outlook."

"Good." They stepped around a gully. "I've got a piece of big news."

Charlotte looked intrigued. "This place looks quiet, but it's a hotbed of activity. Tell me."

"Mama and Landis are going to rent one of the cabins for two whole months starting on May 18. Landis accidentally sold their house out from under them, and they're coming here."

"Oh, wow." Charlotte was quiet for a moment, taking it in. "I love your mama even though I don't know her all that well. So, it's nice you'll get time together, plus you'll get two solid months of income from that cabin. Ka-ching."

True. "That's not all. They're moving up to Asheville, so we should be able to see each other a lot more."

"Watch out, world. The Beckett women are back together again."

Jenny gave her a sideways glance. "Do you think she'll drive me crazy?"

"Possibly." Charlotte sipped her coffee and shook her head slowly. "I know she's keen on your getting married again and that she worries about you on your own, but that's all I know about your dynamic. Do you two talk well together?"

Jenny bobbed her head. "We do. And it's not like she'll be hanging around the cabin all day with me. She and Landis are joined at the hip. After being lonesome with Daddy, she doesn't seem to want to let Landis out of her sight, and he's the same with her." She shook her head. "Mama goes with him to each of his doctors' appointment. He pushes the cart when she grocery shops. While she tries on clothes at Belk's or Talbot's, he sits outside the dressing rooms in the comfy chairs with the other husbands."

Charlotte shuddered dramatically. "If Ashe and I spent that much time together, we'd come to blows." Taking a deep breath, she rolled her hands toward her face in a wafting movement. "I think relationships do well with fresh air."

Jenny grinned, and the two headed home.

At 3:03 AM the next morning, Jenny was wide awake. She wasn't dwelling on Luke being gone, but just couldn't relax. She'd slept a few hours, but her trick of reading Daddy's dated business magazines to fight insomnia wasn't working. Pulling a comforter around her for warmth, Jenny shuffled over to the laptop and started searching for marketing tips for hotels, but soon got discouraged. She was small potatoes and couldn't glean much from reading about best practices at the Marriotts, Hiltons, or Wyndhams. A frustrating hour later, Jenny's eyes began to droop as she skimmed articles on *How Business Conferences Can Skyrocket Your Bottom Line* and *Retaining First-Class Housekeeping Staff.*

At five-thirty, just as she decided to try to sleep again, she happened upon a site called *Small Hoteliers and Innkeepers Forum* that was geared to the owners of small independent hotels, motels, inns, cabins, and specialty properties. As she read some of the topics and posts, Jenny felt a buzz of excitement. She might have found her people. Eagerly, she looked at the pictures. One couple in Texas owned a motel that consisted of twenty teepees. A fellow had ten tree houses he rented. A woman and her sister owned and rented two converted lighthouses, and a lady named Bertha had made a motor court of vintage RVs. Holding her breath, Jenny signed in to the forum as CabinGal. Her fingers shook as she introduced herself.

Brand new in this biz. I own eight small cabins on a lake in North Carolina, she wrote.

Welcome, sister. Pleased to meetcha, Bertha the vintage RV motor court owner wrote.

Ahoy! Glad to have you on board, was the missive from the lighthouse keepers.

In minutes, seven hoteliers had introduced themselves and offered their help.

Mulling it over, she started typing before she chickened out. *Need advice from you about filling the cabins in nonpeak seasons, drawing small groups, building a regular clientele.*

Jenny held her breath as the faint dots bounced and smiled delightedly as people began responding to her post. The theme seemed to be to look for subject matter experts and offer themed events or to hold a gathering with people that had similar interests. The other hoteliers had some success filling rooms with:

...an organizer who talked about paring down and simplifying.

...healthy cooking classes.

...a Scrabble tournament.

...a quilting group that comes for a week every winter.

Zig, the owner of an old-timey motor court of chalet-style rooms near Yellowstone wrote: *Got a geologist that comes in for a week twice a year. Gives talks and leads tours of Old Faithful and the other geysers of Yellowstone. Draws both geyser enthusiasts and rock hounds.*

One of the lighthouse sisters wrote: *We highlight the seafaring theme: history of pirates on the coast, the life of a lighthouse keeper, scrimshaw enthusiasts, WWII history buffs.*

The last post was from Bertha, whom Jenny already liked for

calling her *sister* and for her vintage RV motor court property. She wrote, *Think about what's unique about your property. Capitalize on that in your marketing, and your people will find you!*

Exhilarated, Jenny hugged the comforter around her. She'd stumbled across such a treasure trove of wise and friendly compatriots. Knowing she could call on them made her feel less alone. She tapped out her final post for the early morning:

You are the best. I am so grateful for your help to me. I'll keep you posted.

Tenting her fingers, Jenny thought about it. What was unique about the Lakeside Resort was the inspiring lake setting, the serenity, the wildlife, and the uniqueness of the cabins. The low key *Fabulous You* week Charlotte was spearheading was the right fit for the resort, as was the Yoga Retreat, if they could fill them. Maybe kayaking clinics? A birding weekend? Jenny didn't want to pursue groups at the expense of the regular guests looking for a getaway, though. She needed to let the ideas simmer and see what she came up with.

Tuesday midmorning, Jenny wiped her brow with her sleeve and thirstily drank a tall glass of cold water after finishing her chores. She'd wheel-barrowed several loads of firewood from the woodpile to the firepit and rolled a coat of stain on the dock to keep the boards from giving splinters to bare feet. All morning, Jenny had been thinking about Luke, wondering how his work was going and how he was managing.

The phone rang and Jenny smiled when she saw Alice's name. It had been way too long.

"Hey, Jen," Alice said warmly. "I've missed you!"

"And I've missed you more than you know," Jenny said.

"I can't talk now. I'm on my way back from Mama and Daddy's, and traffic's getting heavy. But can you meet me for lunch at Slowpoke's Diner in about an hour?"

Jenny reviewed her long mental to-do list and decided to chuck it. Seeing Alice was more important than putting a second coat of stain on the dock. "I'll be there."

As she stepped inside the diner, Jenny felt a twinge of sadness as she remembered her dinner with Luke. The place smelled delicious, and Jenny's mouth watered as she remembered how tasty the food had been last time. Man, the place was jumping at lunchtime. Glancing around, she saw young guys in power company shirts chowing down, a group of retired women chatting, and several older couples having lunch. Jenny slid into a booth.

She was perusing the menu when she heard the distinctive roar of a powerful engine. A combat-worthy black truck with extra-brawny tires and a frame that was jacked up high wheeled into the parking lot. Jenny grinned as she watched Alice slide down from the truck and smooth the wrinkles from her pink-and-white seersucker shorts.

Alice spied her, hurrying over to the booth. They hugged each other warmly.

"You look good in Mike's truck," Jenny said.

"I look like a very macho chick. I like it." Alice grinned. "Mike had a teacher development day over in Raleigh and wanted to save on gas, so he took my car."

"You're so busy with graduate school that I hardly ever see you," Jenny groused.

"Plus taking care of Mama and Daddy and trying to impress my new husband with my cooking and housekeeping skills. I'll lull him into thinking that he's married Martha Stewart, and he'll be mine forever." Alice gave a maniacal laugh that ended in a giggle.

Jenny chuckled. "I don't think Mike's going anywhere."

After the waitress left with their orders, Jenny examined her friend suspiciously. Alice had ordered fresh fruit instead of fries, had not asked for a bottle of Texas Pete to douse on her burger, and had asked for ice water when her usual order at restaurants was *a large diet Pepsi and keep 'em coming*. "You're eating clean. Is this some new health kick?"

"Guess what?" Alice broke into a slow smile and put a hand on her flat stomach.

Jenny gave a happy yelp. Standing, she leaned across the table to hug her friend, blinking back tears. "Mike must be over the moon, and your mama's probably ecstatic."

"Everybody's thrilled to pieces."

As her friend excitedly detailed the plans they were making for the arrival of their baby, Jenny felt a powerful mix of joy, longing...and a sense of being left behind. It wasn't the baby, she decided. Maybe she was missing some female DNA, but she sure didn't want a baby at this age. Here was the hitch. After drifting along with no wedding date set, Alice and Mike had finally married and started this happy, homey new chapter of their lives. Jenny wanted a chapter like that, too, but her man was so far away he was already in tomorrow.

As Alice wound down, she dug into a piece of coconut cream pie and Jenny forked into her apple pie with a large scoop of melting vanilla on top. "Have you told Luke the good news?"

Frowning, Alice dabbed a bit of whipped topping from her lip. "I had to text him about the baby. I tried to call him a bunch of times and either got voice mail or couldn't get through."

"I can relate," Jenny grumbled as she took an extra-large forkful of the pie. Who was she trying to stay somewhat skinny for? No one. Maybe she'd have a second slice.

Alice gazed at her knowingly. "How are you doing with this separation?"

Jenny raised a shoulder. "I miss your brother terribly. I didn't know it would be this hard," she admitted. "It's hard to stay connected, especially with the time zone situation."

Alice patted her hand. "That's tough." She raised her eyes to heaven. "And I know how Luke is on the phone. He gives the bare details and sounds like he can't wait to end the call."

"Exactly." It was a relief to be understood. But it was more than Luke not liking phones. Jenny slumped, remembering Luke admitting that his workaholic ways had wreaked havoc on his marriage to his late wife. "When he gets to working flat out, he's a remote guy."

"I know. It's like the lights are on but nobody's home." Alice gave her a sympathetic look. "I'm sure it gets lonely, but he'll be back soon, right?"

"That's right." Jenny sat up straighter. "So, the pity party's officially over. He'll be here soon."

"Good." Alice raised both eyebrows up and down. "I have some juicy gossip."

"Tell me."

Alice leaned forward. "When I was at Mama and Daddy's the other night, guess who showed up with a basket of fried chicken, fried okra, and hush puppies?"

"No," Jenny breathed. "Tell me it wasn't Ember looking for Luke."

"It was," Alice chortled. "She acted like she wasn't disappointed when she found out Luke wasn't there, but then she tried to worm her way into my parents' good graces."

"That woman is ruthless." Jenny had a sickening hunch. "Did Ember try to get Luke's contact information from your folks?"

"Yup. She was a regular Mata Hari." Alice started to giggle. "But Mama wouldn't tell her anything and got mad as a wet hen because Daddy was salivating over that fried chicken and fried everything that Ember brought. Mama's jaw got set, and she firmly packed back up all the goodies Ember was trying to unpack. You do not encroach on Mama's kitchen."

Jenny chuckled, picturing it. "Good for your mama."

"But it gets better." Alice's eyes danced with mischief. "Remember, I told you how Ember is a gold digger? She must think Luke is loaded." With studied casualness, she buffed her nails on her cotton T-shirt sleeve. "So, I mentioned Luke's unfortunate bankruptcy. Talked about how hard it was for a man like Luke to start all over from scratch, but that the paper route he'd picked up had tidied him over. Mama caught on quick and said even though Luke was poor as a church mouse, he still had his pride and that was something, wasn't it? I said it was, but Ember's face got white as flour. She practically race-walked out of their house and to her car."

Jenny burst out laughing. "Your mama's a catbird. I love it."

After they had paid the bill, they stepped outside. Alice looked at Jenny. "Even if Ember had managed to get his numbers, I think Luke would have just shaken her off. Don't you?"

Jenny thought about it and nodded slowly. "I do." Thank goodness for that.

CHAPTER 10 — SCHEMES AND DREAMS

THE NEXT DAY, JENNY WAS outside blowing leaves and pine needles off the driveway, walkways, and clearing with a backpack blower she'd borrowed from Luke. The blower was so heavy that she had to lean forward to keep from tipping backward but, man, that baby had power. A car horn honked and Jenny cut off the blower, pulled off her noise-reducing safety earmuffs, and peered down the driveway.

Charlotte was waving wildly out the window of her faded four-door sedan and pointing to the back of her car. Smiling, Jenny tried to figure out what she was pointing at. The rear of the car was almost dragging the ground and bounced up and down lazily when Charlotte hit a rut. What in the world? Pushing her sunglasses up on her head, Jenny shrugged off the blower, raised a hand, and walked over. "Hey, girl," she called.

Charlotte was too excited to bother with hello. "You will not believe the bargains I found." Jumping out of the car, she threw open the trunk, and with a Vanna White-inspired hand-movement, pointed to its contents.

Jenny gaped. The trunk was full of hand weights, jump ropes, weighted medicine balls, and padded workout bars that were piled on top of extra-thick exercise mats like the ones she remembered from her yoga dropout days. "Where did you find all this, and why did you buy it?"

"For the *Fabulous You* week, silly. And I found these at my favorite shopping establishments, the Habitat Store and the

Episcopal Women's Thrift Shop." She looked very proud of herself. "I got this whole deal for twenty-two dollars. Can you believe it?"

Jenny could. Charlotte was a professional level bargain finder. "But we don't even know if we'll have enough signed up for it to be a go."

"I already have eight women who say they're interested. Of course we'll need a credit card deposit, so we need to decide how much to charge."

"You got women signed up so quickly?" Jenny was almost afraid to believe it.

"Yup. I'm excited about it, and I think it rubbed off on the other gals." Grinning, Charlotte pointed to the back seat where even more exercise mats were rolled up or stuffed behind the seat. "The Episcopal Ladies threw those in for free because I'm a frequent customer."

Jenny grinned and pinched her lip. "So we need to find an instructor and pay her or him to come out and lead a few classes."

Charlotte held up a finger. "Or how about a do-it-yourself deal? I'll bet I could get these women to take turns leading toning and strengthening workouts. Each one could address a problem area."

"They'd be up for that?" Jenny asked doubtfully.

"I thinks so. Between all of us, we've been to a thousand exercise classes. We know all the moves. I think the point is to get away from it all and keep it low key."

Jenny saw no downside. "It's a genius idea. Let me know how I can help, but I'm turning most of the planning for this over to you. I'll pay you a good chunk of the profits for helping me."

"I don't want the money..." Charlotte started to protest.

But Jenny interrupted. "Not listening. This is the only way I'll do the event. You're excellent at this. I'm paying you for it. Deal?" She held out her hand.

Charlotte hesitated and broke into a beaming smile as she shook Jenny's hand. "Deal."

Friday morning after she'd done her chores, Jenny was keyed up. She'd caught up on housekeeping, she didn't feel like taking on a major task like raking out the potholes in the gravel driveway, and she was too fidgety to read. She knew what was wrong. Her phone conversation with Luke that morning had been more disjointed than usual. Though polite, he talked to her like she was a stranger. Then, in a final blow to her ego, he'd fallen asleep on the line. She must be enthralling, Jenny thought wryly, and then made herself stop. He was overtired, it wasn't personal, and she just needed to shift gears, or she'd really get into a funk. She needed to do something to perk herself up.

Cookies. She'd bake cookies. Comfort food. Maybe chocolate chip and oatmeal. To cheer herself up, she slipped on another vintage apron, a whimsical one featuring cats playing badminton.

Flipping through a well-worn cookbook, Jenny found the recipes she wanted. Preheating the oven, she pulled butter from the fridge and assembled ingredients on the counter. Cooking relaxed her. It wasn't only the delicious end product that she enjoyed, it was the whole process of measuring, mixing ingredients to just the right consistency, and monitoring the baking process. Soon, her kitchen would smell delicious.

As she creamed the butter and sugar together, Jenny enjoyed listening to the playlist Alice had made for her. Soulful Eiza Gilkyson sang *Coast*. Jenny loved that song. When Gregory Alan Isakov sang *Virginia May*, Jenny tried singing along to the chorus, and Dar Williams's *Fishing in the Morning* made her feel optimistic.

The phone rang just as she'd pulled the first batch of cookies from the oven. Jenny smiled when she saw the caller ID. "Hello, my favorite neighbor."

Ella Parr laughed. "High praise since you've got so few neighbors, and we're the only ones you know. Can I stop by for a few minutes? I'm bringing you a copy of my new book."

"How exciting!"

"It *is* exciting every time I get a book out into the world. Without using your cabin as a quiet she-shed in January, I would have never met my deadline," Ella reminded her.

"I was glad to have you." And that was an understatement. To have a paying guest in a slow month like January had been a big help money-wise. "Appreciate your sending me Corinne, your writing buddy. She was quiet and easygoing and said she got a ton written."

"Good," Ella said, not one for flowery talk.

"Come over. I'll trade you freshly baked cookies for more of your lake living tips."

Jenny started a pot of coffee and arranged cookies on a plate. She wasn't sure what she would have done without her neighbor. Ella was the one who had told her she needed to triple bungee her garbage cans so the raccoons didn't raid them and get the logs on the cabin treated every few years to keep them from rotting. She had given her the number for the guy who climbed her sixty-foot trees with a chain saw and limbed lower branches to keep the view to the water clear. Ella's forty years of living near a lake out in the country had made her wise in ways town people would never understand.

In five minutes, her neighbor was at the door, wearing purple sweatpants and top, a yellow down vest, and clogs. As usual, her graying blonde curls were askew and stood out at odd angles. She wore reading glasses, had an extra pair on a chain around her neck, and a spare extra one hooked in the collar of her shirt.

The two hugged briskly and settled in on the couch with mugs of coffee and a plate of warm cookies between them.

Ella pulled a book from her large purse and thrust it at Jenny. "Hot off the press. I've signed it. I told you I'd put you in the book and I did."

"This is exciting. I'm kind of famous." Jenny examined the cover. A Charlize Theron-type blonde in a red convertible was speeding down a mountain and the black car tailing her was trying to force her off the road. "What's my character like?" She hoped she was the blonde.

Ella blew on her coffee to cool it. "A harried housewife. Two kids of your own and three you inherited from your new husband."

"Am I frumpy?" Jenny frowned.

"No, you are one of those annoyingly fit mothers." She took

a large bite of cookie that sent crumbs to her lap. Bear quickly hoovered them up.

"What's my character's name?" Jenny hoped it would be a name like *Lola* or *Sugar*. So exotic.

"Anjohnette. Johnny for short. Lucky for you, I picked that name because I was going for old Southern names and considered Marvene or Lodella."

"Whew. Close call. *Johnny*," Jenny said, trying it out. "I love that name. Sporty."

"You notice unusual coming and goings in the neighborhood. Police are skeptical at first, but your clues are instrumental in solving the crime."

"Oh, *go*, me!" Jenny hugged the book to her chest. "I can't wait to read it."

Ella held up an oatmeal cookie and looked at Jenny. "These are delectable. I mean it."

"I'm going to send some home to your husband. Tell Paul again how much I appreciate his doing those renewals of vows over Valentine's Day." Since retiring from his job as an Episcopal clergyman, Paul had been at loose ends. "He seemed to enjoy doing the ceremonies."

"Are you kidding me? He loved it. Got all misty-eyed talking about it." Ella raised her glasses to her head, managed to catch her bangs in them, and her hair stood up in front.

Jenny bit her lip to keep from smiling. Ella looked like the bird she'd seen on the lake yesterday and looked up in her Audubon book. The hooded merganser was noted for its poofy hairdo.

"Time for the tips of the day, oh, wise one." Jenny grabbed her notebook and got ready to pick Ella's brain for more tips about country living. "First, do I need a chest freezer?"

Ella's eyes widened. "Well, of course you do. I'm considering getting a second one."

Jenny scribbled it down. "How about a meal-sealing doohickey?"

"Absolutely. Otherwise you're running up and down the road all the time."

She thought so. Jenny underlined *No running up and down the road*. "Any other tips?"

"Buy good cooler bags to keep in the back of your car. As the days warm up, you can run to the grocery store and do all your in-town errands without worrying your food will spoil."

Coolers and ice in back. Jenny looked at Ella expectantly. "Hit me with another."

"Get your neighbors to give you names of contractors you can trust." Ella pushed down her bangs and tried to fluff them into shape but they popped back up. "And try to schedule any work you need done around hunting season. People go MIA during those months."

Jenny scribbled notes as fast as she could. "Hit me with another," she said gamely.

"Keep fresh Benadryl in the medicine cabinet in case you, your guests, or one of the boys get snake bit. You can buy a little time on the way to the hospital."

Jenny drew in her breath sharply. Yikes. Snakes. One day soon, she'd be just as canny a country woman as Ella was. *BENADRYL!* she wrote in all caps and then cast a sideways glance at Ella. Her friend never made her feel like what she was asking was foolish. Although Jenny had never grown anything in her whole life, she wanted a garden. "I'm thinking about a vegetable garden. Organic. I want to try to put up vegetables."

"You can borrow our tiller. It's balky, but Paul can show you how to start and run it."

Jenny wrote down *Garden!* She let herself daydream about the pleasure of gathering zucchini, yellow squash, and ruby red tomatoes right from her very own plot. "Hit me."

Ella hooked a thumb toward the dock. "Your guests are going to need fishing licenses, even if they fish off the pier. You don't want anyone getting a hefty fine."

Jenny winced inwardly, thinking about her recent accidental fishing escapade. She was glad no game warden had seen her. She scrawled, *Fishing licenses.* "I can handle one more."

Ella pointed at her with a half-eaten cookie. "You might want to take a Boater Safety Course if you're going to operate a boat or Jet Ski. You can take the course online for thirty bucks."

Jenny's thoughts careened around. Yup. Even if Luke was still around, she was going to have to learn to drive boats. Nervously, Jenny scrawled *BOATING COURSE!* Popping a too-big piece of cookie in her mouth, she had to swallow hard and drink cool coffee to get it down. She gave Ella a beseeching look. "I'll get the hang of this, won't I?"

A spark of humor in her eye, Ella shrugged. "Eventually. If you don't, you can always take up crime fighting like Ahnjonnette."

"Johnny," Jenny corrected, and broke into a smile. An idea cropped up while she was finishing her fourth chocolate chip cookie and eying the oatmeal. Swallowing a bite of deliciousness, Jenny patted her mouth with a paper towel. "I have an idea to run by you."

"Shoot." Ella dunked a cookie in her coffee and chewed it. "This is sublime."

"I've got too many room vacancies in the spring and fall." She studied Ella. "Do you think you'd be up for doing a small writing retreat workshop kind of deal here? You'd charge your going rate, we'd add the cost of the cabin rentals and come up with a price."

"Hmmm." Ella looked thoughtful. Pausing her cookie munching, she rearranged some of the hair that had fallen from her hair clip, and looked surprised when she pulled a pen from her messy up-do. "I wondered where that went." She tucked the pen in her purse.

Jenny tried to hide a smile. Ella was the archetypal creative type with a bit of absentminded professor thrown in. Her husband Paul had told Jenny that every once in a while, Ella ran errands and came back into the house without turning off the car.

Ella slurped her coffee. "I've considered doing that for a few years now. I'd get a break from writing, recharge my batteries, and get to mold the minds of less experienced writers." She made an imaginary ball with her fingers and pretended to knead it energetically. "I'm up for it."

The ideas kept coming. "You said Paul was trying to figure

out how to structure his time since he retired," Jenny said diplomatically. What Ella had really said was that he was driving her mad because he kept following her around and that she was having murderous thoughts about him.

"Correct." Ella's face darkened.

Jenny was warming to her subject now. "Maybe he could do a marriage enrichment week or weekend for couples and at the end of it, do renewal of vows?"

Ella looked intrigued. "He'd be interested, and I could get that man I love out of my hair."

"I'm so glad." Jenny exhaled. Elated. She felt elated. "Talk with Paul and see if he's up for those seminars, maybe in the fall. If you can round up participants, we are on for the writers' retreat. Let me run dates by you and we'll talk about pricing. I'll help with publicity."

"This sounds grand. I'm too disorganized to pull something like this off myself." Ella pointed at her. "You, my dear, have ingenious ideas."

Jenny gave Ella a half-smile. "Being poor is the mother of invention."

The next morning was balmy and pleasant, so Jenny took her cup of coffee and sat on her front porch, her eyes resting on the lake. Mist rose from the water, every once in a while a fisherman whizzed by, and a blue heron came in for a graceful landing on her dock and stood on one leg, looking peaceful and elegant.

Jenny blew out a sigh. So much had been going on that she'd been forgetting to slow down and appreciate the wonderland that was her home. Jenny slowed her breath, rolled her shoulders to loosen them, and sank back in her rocker. A slight breeze blew up, creating rippling waves and blowing back her hair. Closing her eyes, Jenny sent up her version of a prayer.

Thank you, God, for allowing me to land in this precious spot. I am humbled to be here and grateful for Your helping me with ideas about how to keep this place afloat. I sure couldn't have come up with those plans by myself. As of now, I'm going to be more mindful about expressing gratitude to You for this life. She hesitated a moment, unsure of the etiquette. Did she just ask God to put Daddy on the line or conference him in? She decided to just jump in. Daddy, I'm thankful to you beyond measure. I love your dream for the resort, and I'm doing my best to bring it to fruition. I realize I forgot to put up that picture Luke gave me of your drawings for the resort, and I'll take care of that today. Good job on getting hold of this place. Feel free to give me advice. Hope you're doing swell up there. Oh, and Mama's coming to visit with Landis. That might be awkward for you but she's happy, and that's what we all want, right? Thanks again, Daddy. I love you. Feeling a sense of peace, Jenny slowly opened her eyes.

A male bluebird poked his head out of a nesting box, eyed her, and swooped down to sit on the branch of a pine sapling not seven feet from Jenny. With his vivid, bright blue plumage and rusty brown chest, he was a handsome guy. Jenny stopped rocking and sat as still as she could, watching him, remembering Charlotte's assertion that bluebirds bring reassurance and messages from loved ones in heaven. "Hey there, Daddy, if that's you. It's going to be another incredible day at the Lakeside Resort," she said softly. The two sat in companionable silence for a while until the bluebird flew off.

CHAPTER 11 — FABULOUS YOU

O N THE FIRST SATURDAY IN May, Jenny heard the crunch of tires and tried to be discreet as she peeked out the window as the first of the *Fabulous You* women arrived. Hoo boy. Though Charlotte had described her gym buddies as down-to-earth and not fussy, this woman looked high maintenance. It had to be Louise the lawyer, stepping out of the gleaming silver BMW convertible, wearing large movie star shades, a pencil skirt, and high-heeled boots. Pulling an enormous leather suitcase out of the trunk, she looked annoyed when the wheels didn't glide but bumped crazily across the crushed stone driveway and cedar mulched path.

Jenny met her at the door of the Dogwood. "Welcome," she said with a warm smile.

Louise raised her glasses to her head and regarded her coolly. "Hello." She waved a hand imperiously toward the driveway. "You've got gravel on that driveway."

"Yes," Jenny agreed. She'd considered paving it in gold but decided gravel was more practical.

"My car will be safe on her, right? It's brand new and I don't want it to get dinged up by flying gravel or a nicked by a passing piece of farm equipment or whatever you all use out here in the country."

Jenny hid a smile. "Your car will be safe," she assured her. She wanted to add a lie about all the bears on the grounds who liked to chew on convertible tops but decided to try to be mature. It was hard sometimes.

But Louise had her phone to her ear. "Hello?" she said in a clipped tone. "Hello?" She strode outside, searching for a signal.

Good luck finding it, Jenny thought. Feeling the blood start to pound in her ear, she took a slow deep breath and stepped back inside. This woman would be here for a week, seven whole days. What if the other women were just like her? Blowing out a sigh, she leaned her back against the door. This had been a bad idea.

Moments later, Louise rapped at the door sharply.

Jenny made herself smile as she greeted her.

"Where can I get better signal?" the woman demanded.

Jenny had made Charlotte promise to let all of her buddies know not to expect good cell service, and she'd also emphasized it in the confirmation email she'd sent to every one of the *Fabulous You* gals. She just needed to be blunt. "The cell service out here is iffy at best. If you stand on the right back corner of the dock and hold your arm up like the Statue of Liberty or go to the back left and stand still as a possum, sometimes you'll get a lucky spot for good signal," she said with authoritative nod, but then held up a finger. "If it's not overcast."

"*Still as a possum?* Tell me you are kidding." Louise went pale and was looking a little frantic. "That is unacceptable," she said brusquely.

Jenny felt a surge of temper and was trying to tone down a retort when Charlotte and a gaggle of other women showed up at the door, smiling and laughing and bumping into each other on purpose. Instead of a group of women in the late thirties to early sixties, this group looked like a bunch of fun, friendly, much younger women. Jenny breathed a sigh of relief at the pleasant, happy looks on their faces. Thank goodness.

"Hey, Jen." Charlotte gave her a quick hug. "We all caravanned out here together." She pointed to the flock of women behind her. "This is Jessie, Shannon, Dana, Melissa, Yolanda, Felicia, Rosalie, and Kelly."

Charlotte spotted Louise and enveloped her in a warm hug. "How's it going, hotshot?" she teased.

Louise's eyes were darting around almost frantically. "Things have gone haywire on a case I've been working on for eight months, and there's no good phone or internet."

Charlotte laughed gaily. "Oh, there never is." She spread out her hands, palms up. "That's the beauty of this place. You can get away from all that madness back home."

The attorney drew herself up, her mouth a thin straight line. "But this is critical business."

The redhead named Shannon patted her on the back. "We know. Aren't you the one who swore you'd start delegating more after you got that stomach ulcer?"

Nodding reluctantly, Louise was actually wringing her hands.

Yolanda chimed in. "And after all those migraines, you promised your neurologist you'd delegate more. That's what you have junior partners for, right, Louise?'

Another woman said, "She works at the same firm as Louise, so she ought to know."

Charlotte and the others bobbed their heads in agreement.

The woman she thought was Felicia craned her neck and peered over Jenny's shoulder to try to get a better look at Jenny's cabin. "Oh, wow. Is this what our cabins look like?"

"Exactly." Though a bit overwhelmed at the mass of women, Jenny waved them inside. She hoped they liked the place.

Nine women surged into her cabin like New York commuters pushing into a subway car, oohing and aahing. They petted the boys, exclaiming at the *cute* woodstove and the *darling* reclaimed barn board walls.

Though warmed by their compliments, Jenny noticed how put together the group looked. All wore subtle makeup and had manicured nails and sleek hairdos. Louise's diamond stud earrings were the size of field peas, Melissa wore an equestrian-themed silk scarf that Jenny knew had to have been expensive, and Rosalie's handsome black coat looked like cashmere. While the women chattered and looked around, she spoke quietly to Charlotte. "These women all look moneyed and polished."

"Oh, some are." Charlotte waved a hand dismissively. "My gym is in a nice part of town. But they're all good souls, even

Louise once she chills out. We'll just help them shed all that fanciness for a week. It's going to be fine."

But Jenny had her doubts. This didn't look like a crowd who did much roughing it.

Charlotte elbowed Jenny. With a face like a thundercloud, Louise was standing rigidly outside, holding her phone in the air and then pacing to another spot to hold it aloft there. Jenny wavered, considering letting Louise make the call from the hidden landline in the Dogwood but if she did, Louise would be in Jenny's cabin making calls all week. And any other women who were going through withdrawal from their devices would be forming a line to do the same. No, ma'am. She'd spelled it out clearly and repeatedly in all her correspondences that the cell service and Wi-Fi were iffy.

Jenny smiled blandly and called to Louise, "If you don't have any luck on the dock and you absolutely need cell service, the library is in town about fifteen miles away," she offered, making a vague gesture to the north.

"You can pick up signal on the right side of the parking lot at Gus's Gas-N-Git, too," Charlotte added helpfully. "That's five or six miles up the road on the right. Their pickled eggs are good, too."

Louise put a hand to her forehead and groaned. "This is not good."

Yolanda pointed to the phone clutched in Louise's hand. "Text an associate. Get them to do it."

"You need to." Shannon bobbed her head.

Louise scowled and ran a hand through her hair.

Charlotte raised a brow at Jenny and telegraphed a look that said, *Let's move on.*

Jenny gave her a quick nod. If Louise wanted to stay in her *I'm so important mode* when she had known about the iffy cell service, that was her decision. The woman could spend the week at Gus's. She was done talking about it. Jenny got busy handing out keys. "Shannon and Felicia, you two are in the Camelia. Kelly, you're in the Magnolia."

"Lucky for you girls I'm on my own." Kelly held up her key and grinned. "I'm a night owl who reads until two, and I yell at people in my sleep."

"Dana and Yolanda, y'all are in the Azalea. Melissa's in the Redbud. Jessie's in the Mimosa, Louise is in the Hydrangea, and Rosalie is in the Airstream, the Silver Belle."

"Oh, you got the coolest of all. I want a tour just as soon as I unpack," Melissa said.

"Charlotte and I will bunk here in the Dogwood. If you need anything at all, just stop by," Jenny said.

"We'll get a bonfire going in the clearing and have a little welcome to Heron Lake vino and cheese deal out there about five-thirty." Charlotte consulted a clipboard. "We agreed to do breakfast and lunch on our own, but we'll take turns hosting supper. Tonight, supper is courtesy of Dana and Yolanda."

"We did what we decided on and kept it simple and healthy," Yolanda said.

"We're having a chicken enchilada casserole with yoghurt, avocados, and jalapenos, and a big salad," the big-boned blonde named Dana announced.

There was a chorus of approval and the women murmured, *Sounds delish, Yum,* and *I'm hungry now.*

Jessie lovingly patted Buddy. "Can we borrow the dogs and Levi and give them some love?"

Jenny smiled, starting to relax. "Absolutely. Community property. Just don't feed them anything. They've perfected the *I'm starving* look but it's an act."

"I don't know about you chickies, but I'm going to get settled into that super adorbs little cabin." Dana linked arms with petite Yolanda. "Come on, roomie. Let's check it out."

The other women laughed and hurried to see their cabins.

Ten minutes later, Louise came to the door. Lips pursed, she held a bar of soap in a white washcloth.

"Hi, Louise. Everything OK?" Jenny guessed from her agitation that it wasn't.

"Is this soap organic?" Louise demanded, holding out the bar. "I am extremely allergic to non-organic soap."

"It is organic," Jenny said firmly, grateful she'd made the decision to buy only organics even if it stretched her tight budget even tighter.

The woman persisted, pointing at the washcloth. "How about the laundry products you use on your linens? If it's not organic, I wheeze, can't swallow, and my eyes close shut."

If it was that bad, shouldn't she have brought her own linens and soap? "All 100 percent organic and EWG verified."

"Good." Looking mollified, Louis turned to go but hesitated, squinting, and sniffed the soap. "There's no lavender in this, is there? My skin just breaks out in hives with lavender."

Of course it does. "It's a goats' milk soap made locally. Let me give you a fresh bar with the wrapper on so you can read the ingredients. If you can catch a signal, you could check the website, just to make sure you're comfortable with it." Jenny went to her supply drawer and handed her a bar. "If you have any more concerns, feel free to call the owner. Her name is Gemma and the number is right on the wrapper." She thought about reminding Louise again about the good signal at Gus's Gas-N-Git, but again decided to try to be a better person.

"Thanks." Louise eyed the bar suspiciously and traipsed back to her cabin.

At five-fifteen, Jenny and Charlotte set up cheese, crackers, and drinks on a table by the firepit and built a fire. Women wandered out of their cabins, exclaiming happily about their rooms, the lake, the views, and the fire.

"Happy campers," Charlotte said quietly to Jenny and called out. "Let's gather round."

Women scooted chairs closer to the fire and looked at her expectantly. In a loud, gym teacher voice, Charlotte called out, "Welcome to the First Annual *Fabulous You Fit and Healthy Week.* We are going to have a terrific time here at the Lakeside Resort." She gazed around at the others. "This week we're going to just relax and be ourselves. We're going to hike and notice nature and, best of all, enjoy fellowship with this amazing group of women." She held up a hand. "We aren't going to talk about our weight or worry about our weight. We're not going to talk about work. Try to leave all that mess at the door." She waved an arm dismissively. "We agreed that the classes we offer are not going to be high intensity boot camp classes. They might have macho names, but you know how we do it. Only exercise to your ability." She broke into a smile. "Remember, you don't need to go to one class this week. If you want to find a good spot to read and just chill, do that and don't feel the least bit guilty. That would be a week well spent."

Several women nodded their agreement.

Charlotte paused and thought for a moment. "Let's try to let go of any negative judgments we have about ourselves. We're not too old, too fat, or not fit enough." She met the eye of one camper after another. "We are perfect just the way we are. Are y'all with me?"

The women were all smiling by now and began clapping enthusiastically.

Charlotte grinned. Looking reverent, she held up an old gym teacher's whistle on a macramé lanyard that Jenny suspected was another thrift shop find. She blew it and the group went silent. "This, my friends, is entrusted to the fitness class instructor for the day, or Fitness Gal. With that role comes much power, so use it wisely."

Campers elbowed each other and smirked.

Charlotte found her clipboard. "So, fitness classes in the morning if you feel like it. We start at eight. We'll meet out here at the firepit. If it rains, we go to Plan B." She paused and gave Jenny an inquiring look. "We have no idea what plan B is, right Jenny?"

"Not a clue." Jenny gave a half smile. "Maybe y'all could read or nap."

"I love napping," Kelly pointed out, and several women agreed.

Charlotte went on. "Here's the lineup for the week. Felicia, you're leading *Perk up Your Derriere* tomorrow morning. Jessie's doing *No More Thunder Thighs*. Melissa's focused on arms in her

Ban Bat Wings class. Shannon's doing *Stretch Like Gumby.* Rosalie's doing *Cores of Quartz.* Yolanda's gig is *Killer Abs,* and Louise is doing *Squat a Lot.*"

The women groaned good-naturedly, but Jenny saw that the mood was light, and the women seemed more excited than filled with dread.

"Dana's doing *Rockin' Ropes,* a fun aerobic jump roping deal they're doing in California that's good for your legs. I'm doing a class called *Twist and Shout* that I made up myself. The class might be so-so but I've got very groovy music to go with it." Charlotte nodded proudly. "One more thing. Let's hear a few words from Jenny Beckett, the owner of the Lakeside Resort and my friend."

Not expecting that handoff, Jenny froze. But she looked at the open faces of the campers, gold-lit by the setting sun and flames from the fire. They already looked more down home than they had when they arrived. Melissa had her hair in a messy Pebble Flintstone ponytail on top of the head. The jewelry had been put away, and most women wore sweats and sneakers. They gazed at her expectantly.

Jenny swallowed hard and decided to just go with what was in her heart. "I took ownership of these cabins when I was at a low point in my life. After being dumped by a man I planned to marry, I was feeling old and not good enough. Other things went wrong. You know how that is. Trouble comes in waves." Glancing around, she saw women nodding.

"The Lakeside Resort is a haven for me. It's given me a chance to work on letting go of some of the mental chatter and concern about the judgment of others." Jenny touched her chest. "I've shored up my sense of *me.* I hope the resort works the same magic for you." She gestured to the dark lake in front of them, lit by an apricot sunset. "I hope you let yourself soak in this beauty and let yourself be still. I hope you remember the girl you were, the one who rode bikes fearlessly, got dirty, and didn't give a fig about how you looked. Have a joyful, relaxing week."

Jenny felt her face flame and put a hand to her burning cheek.

She'd meant to just say *welcome and have a good time*, but emotion had welled up in her, and the words had tumbled out.

The women were quiet for a moment, then one began to clap and then another and soon they all were clapping. Jenny looked at Charlotte for reassurance, but her friend was brushing a tear from her eye and clapping harder than everyone. Jenny sank back in her Adirondack and exhaled as she looked at the women who were smiling and sending her grateful looks.

Later, Jenny was in bed in the loft, having a shoving war with Buddy, who was trying to take over the whole queen mattress. Gaining ground, she called down to Charlotte. "Was my welcome too touchy-feely?"

"If that's you being self-critical, you said you were getting over it, so get over it." Charlotte sat cross-legged on the couch below, smearing night cream on her face. "You were perfect, sincere, and real. I think it will kick-start the week for a lot of these women. Even Louise stopped looking like she'd bitten a lemon and was following as you talked."

The next morning, after the eight o'clock workout, the air was still redolent with the smell of bacon that someone had cooked for breakfast when the campers piled into cars to follow each other over to Heron Heights Park, where hunky Ranger Emory was going to lead them on an eight-mile nature walk. Jenny stood outside and waved them off, trying to hide a smile when she saw Louise's BMW ease away, top down, with five rowdy campers crammed in, singing along loudly to the radio blaring Carrie Underwood's *Before He Cheats*. Yup, those lawyers, insurance agents, stay-at-home wives, and massage therapists were fired up about bashing a cheating guy's headlights with a baseball bat.

As the week unfolded, the women shed more of their polish. They stuck with their rotation of responsibilities for the exercise classes, too. The campers got into the groove of their routine and seemed more and more comfortable with each other. Women took long walks in pairs or threes. Melissa and Rosalie regularly took books to opposite sides of the dock and read. Jessie and Yolanda took out the kayaks even though the air was still chilly. The day it rained, the women crammed in cars that they were now referring to as girl mobiles and headed into Rutherford, a town forty miles away that had a big antiques mall. They came home with treasures and stories. Charlotte, of course, had scored the find of the day, a cornhole set in perfect condition with the Clemson Tigers' graphics on it that she'd bought for seven bucks.

After supper, campers played cornhole and did more trash talking than actually sinking any bags into the holes. For a while, several campers with strong affiliations to Carolina sports teams boycotted, claiming to be deeply offended by the Clemson Tiger, but soon they joined in and played like deadeye pros. Jenny walked by carrying a load of firewood and stopped to watch. Ms. Uptight Louise was a sharpshooting ringer even though her toss was a dainty-looking thumb and forefinger affair that looked like she was tossing seed for a bird. Jenny took some pictures and video clips that captured the fun the women were having.

Because she got so little from her telephone calls with Luke, Jenny had decided to take a new tack and send him pictures. In one shot, a group of the *Fabulous Fit* women sat by the fire roasting marshmallows as a glowing orange fireball of a sun set behind them. In another, she'd caught Buddy and Bear sitting patiently on the dock beside a ponytailed Melissa as she fished. The last shot was of Lily walking across the clearing with Levi beside her. She was chatting with the little horse, and he was gazing up at her lovingly. The last was a selfie she'd taken of her and the three boys, all nestled on the couch.

Bingo. Luke responded immediately. Jenny grinned as she read his text.

Cool pics. Are those women the Fabulous Gals? Levi's got a crush on Lily now? DON'T TELL ALICE! She'd be jealous. Wish I was in the mix with you all on the couch. Miss you.

Jenny smiled, feeling hopeful. For the first time since he'd been gone, she felt like she'd really connected with Luke. Maybe pictures of their days was a better way to communicate with him. She thought for a minute and tapped out:

Will you send me some pics of your own?

He sent back an emoji of a big blue thumbs-up.

But Jenny checked her phone repeatedly throughout the day and was freshly disappointed each time. No pictures had arrived from the land down under.

The next morning, Jenny and Charlotte walked the boys together early, and when they returned, came across Louise lounging in an Adirondack chair, engrossed in a book entitled, *Birds of the Carolinas.*

Jenny looked at Charlotte and widened her eyes. Louise did not seem like the bird-watching type.

Inside the cabin, Charlotte clasped her hands together excitedly. "I can't believe I forgot to tell you this. Guess who has a crush on hunky Ranger Emory? Louise. She asked a million questions, stuck by his side like a burr, and borrowed that bird book from him. And I think he's taken with her."

Jenny shook her head as if to clear it. "But Emory is such a laid-back nature lover. He's a granola guy and she's..."

"...a shark that needs a nice man in her life," Charlotte said with a knowing smile. "It's a perfect pairing of opposites. Wouldn't it be amazing if Louise and Emory became a real item?"

Over the week, Jenny had gotten to know Louise better and decided she was just a too tightly wound professional and not a snob. Maybe she and Emory *would* complement each other.

On Saturday, the last girl mobile drove off with campers throwing extravagant kisses and calling, *Bye little cabins! Bye Jenny! Love you, Bear, Buddy, and Levi!* The final call was, *We'll be back next year.* Jenny broke into a smile. She could have sworn that last voice was Louise's.

CHAPTER 12 —
WRITERS' RETREAT

O N THE SATURDAY MORNING THAT the writers' retreat was to start, Jenny was waiting outside when Ella tooled up in her dusty minivan.

Jenny hurried over to meet her, a squadron of butterflies revving up in her stomach. She knew nothing about writers. Were they brooding, intense, and high-strung? In the movies, they smoked cigarettes and were prone to depression. Ella seemed normal, though, if charmingly scattered. All Jenny knew was that she wanted the writers to enjoy their visit at the resort.

Ella stepped out of her car looking put together in black slacks and boots, a fuchsia V-neck silk shirt, and a wildly floral pashmina wrapped artistically around her shoulders. She hadn't worn her usual two or three pairs of reading glasses. "Good morning," she called cheerily, waving at Jenny with the leather binder she carried.

Wow. Ella looked sharp, just like the professional picture on the jacket of her book. But Jenny decided she liked her usual rumpled writer look even better. "Good morning. So glad you're here." Her mouth was dry, and her palms were sweaty. "I had a nightmare last night about your not showing up and my having to lead the workshop. I was wildly improvising, and the writers were not impressed." Jenny shuddered. "Come have a quick cup of coffee with me before the first folks arrive."

The morning was a mild and clear. The two sipped mugs of coffee on the Adirondacks and gazed out at the lake. Jenny shot

Ella a nervous look. "OK. Give me the rundown one more time on what the week will be like and what I'm responsible for."

Ella leaned back in the chair, crossed her legs, and took a sip of coffee. "OK. Here's the story. In the mornings, I give a little informal lecture and have a Q&A on a certain topic. One day it'll be creating memorable characters. The next, it might be on creating conflict. Another day, dialogue. That kind of thing." She waved a hand dismissively. "Then, we turn them loose for the whole day. They'll write and think and write some more. Each participant is responsible for writing at least four pages per day. At four, we convene, and they take turns reading what they've written and getting constructive feedback from their peers." Ella gave a wry smile. "A writer might think she's written a gem of a scene, and it might be a stinker. Heaven knows, I've written my share of them."

Jenny smiled, finding that hard to believe.

"Then you get them set up for supper," Ella reminded her.

"The caterer is coming at five-thirty and setting up outside. If it rains, she'll set up in my cabin and we improvise." Jenny fervently hoped for a dry week. "I ordered mainly chicken and fish entrees and the two vegetarian meals requested. I did what you said and got a good assortment of decadent desserts, too."

Ella gave her a thumbs up. "They'll love that. I also predict they'll drink a lot of coffee and more merlot and chardonnay than you might expect."

Jenny grinned.

A Nissan Leaf pulled in the driveway, followed closely by a Subaru. Ella gave Jenny a pirate smile and rose. "Let's get this shindig started."

At Ella's suggestion, Jenny had dragged canvas camp chairs and lawn chairs to different parts of the lakeside clearing. Early the next morning, she looked out her window and saw that five writers had already staked out their writing areas in those chairs and were writing away on their laptops. At Ella's suggestion, Jenny had run several extension cords from the cabins to the areas where they might write. Several participants had plugged in and others seemed to be using battery packs to power their laptops. A few stared out at the lake for inspiration. One woman paused her writing to jog in place and do a few frenetic pushups. All clutched coffee mugs, and one carried a big silver carafe of extra coffee lest she run low.

While the first day's reading and feedback session went on, Jenny was trying to be quiet as she loaded garbage cans into the truck to make a dump run when a woman came running from the feedback circle, her shoulders shaking in sobs and her eyes streaming tears. Though her first instinct was to go to her and try to offer comfort, Jenny hesitated, and watched as Ella strode over, and spoke kindly but firmly to the crying woman. The wind shifted and Jenny could hear parts of what Ella said: *...critical to your development as a writer...need to know how people react to your writing...good feedback is a gift to a writer.* Soon, the writer dabbed at her nose with tissues and let Ella link arms with her to lead her back to the group.

That evening, Jenny helped serve the supper that the caterers had dropped off and watched as the guests ate together. They seemed content, and it looked like they'd bonded, talking and laughing quietly as they shared stories about progress they'd made or hadn't made in their writing.

Jenny sidled up to Ella as the writer served herself a slice of pecan pie. "Everything going OK?" she asked.

"It's going swimmingly." Ella hesitated and sawed off a half of another piece to add to her first slice. "They're writing up a storm."

"I saw that woman crying earlier," Jenny said, a bit worried.

"Oh, she had trouble with the feedback the others gave about her story, but she recovered," Ella said dryly and added a large dollop of whipped cream to her pie.

"Good," Jenny sighed. "I just want everyone to have a good week." She sensed this wasn't a group that would roar with laughter, cheer at cornhole, or chat enthusiastically at the fire, so it was harder for her to read.

"They are and they will. Remember, this is a working week for them, and they're getting a lot of good writing done." Ella patted her shoulder reassuringly and walked back over to rejoin the others.

Reminded that these guests were at the resort to work, Jenny tried to stay in the background and be as unobtrusive as possible as she served them meals, changed out towels, and tidied up. She tried to keep the boys on their best behavior and initially tried to keep them in or close to her cabin, but a knock came at her door on Monday afternoon. An ethereal young blonde woman with Pre-Raphaelite curls smiled shyly at her. "May we borrow your animals? They might inspire creativity, and a few of us have pets at home that we really miss."

"Of course." Jenny opened the door wide to let Buddy, Bear, and Levi skitter outside. Honestly, no loyalty these days. But, really, she was glad the boys were getting extra attention.

Tucking a wayward curl behind her ear, the woman turned to go, looking like a Disney Princess being followed by her animal friends. She paused though and looked back at Jenny. "I can see a bluebird box from my bed. I can't tell you how pleasant it is to watch those birds flying in and out as they build their nests. I'm just sorry I'm going to miss the babies." With a finger wave, she left with her entourage.

For the rest of the week, Jenny mainly saw the boys during the day when she glimpsed them outside the window. Usually, Levi was being fawned over by the writers, while Bear and Buddy sat at their feet like Rembrandt paintings of noble dogs. Of course, the boys showed up as regularly for suppertime as factory workers punching a time clock.

That night, Jenny woke up at three, wishing she hadn't eaten those salty peanuts and drunk that whole glass of ice water before bed. When she got back from the bathroom, she saw lights and peeked out the window. Three of the cabins and the Silver Belle were lit up brightly. She smiled as she climbed back into bed. Some writers were night owls, and she felt a bond with the insomniacs.

They waved as the last writers pulled away, and Ella turned to

Jenny. "This was a productive week for these folks. They enjoyed it and I did, too. It was an invigorating break from grinding away at a book, and it reminded me of why I love writing. If you're up for another workshop in the fall or next spring, so am I."

"Count me in." Jenny kept company with Ella as she gathered up notebooks, packets of handouts, and her flipchart and headed home.

But Jenny had no time to bask in the satisfied feeling she had about the writers' group. Guests were arriving in just a few hours, including two very special guests, Mama and Landis. She couldn't wait. Before Ella was out of the driveway, Jenny was trotting to the cabins to strip beds. She had a mountain of laundry to do and wanted to get the cabins sparkly clean.

As she whirled around the Camelia with the vacuum, Jenny realized she was out of breath. Speed cleaning was good exercise, but she could see that when she started to make more money, she would need help.

As she polished mirrors and cleaned countertops, Jenny thought about her parents. Jax had had a roguish smile that was hard to resist. He'd been charming, funny, in love with life...and with Mama. Jenny had a fond memory of Jax blowing into the house after being away for weeks, finding Mama in the kitchen and sweeping her into a hug that raised her feet off the linoleum. Jenny had watched from the dining room where she'd been doing homework. Flushing, Mama had tried hard to stay mad at him for being away so long, but he'd turned up the radio and danced her around the kitchen to an Alan Jackson song. Jenny had been in her teens then and increasingly aware of the power of spark and connection. She'd gone quietly to her room, embarrassed at witnessing their chemistry.

But Mama had left Jax a few years later. Bounced checks, broken promises, wild mood swings, and no shows had finally put that marriage down. Steady, kind, considerate Landis seemed to be a much better fit for Mama, Jenny thought as she emptied trash cans. But here was a puzzle. Shady Grove was only four and a half hours from Summerville, South Carolina. Why hadn't they seen more of each other?

Jenny mulled it over as she unloaded clean dishes from the dishwasher and put them away. Mama and Landis *did* travel a lot. Five years ago, on his sixtieth birthday, the two of them had sat down and come up with their bucket lists, and then gone off on trips whenever Landis had the time. Their being busy was part of why they hadn't seen much of each other, but why hadn't Jenny made more effort to visit them?

Flushing with guilt, Jenny realized she had only made the drive to Summerville a handful of times in the twenty-some years Mama and Landis had been married. When they'd offered to come up to Shady Grove to visit her, she'd hedged, offering flimsy excuses about being too busy with work. She was a high school and middle school tutor, not the CEO of a big company. Jenny winced, remembering. Her excuses would have been transparent and hurtful.

Jenny was pulling clean, warm sheets from the dryer when it hit her. She stood stock still, realizing she'd been holding a grudge against Landis as if he had broken up Mama and Jax's marriage. Filled with remorse, she shook her head slowly. She needed to grow up. Landis was a prince of a guy who loved Mama dearly. He wasn't Daddy. That was her real beef. Even though Daddy had let her down so and been a hard match for Mama, Jenny still adored him. But now he was gone. Jenny needed to grow up and not only give Landis a chance, but make a real effort to get to know and like him. As she put fresh sheets on the beds, she vowed to do that during their visit.

She'd put Mama and Landis in the Redbud, she decided. Jenny arranged a mason jar of daffodils on their dresser and gave the cabin one more appraising look. Good. It looked good. As she checked her phone for time, she saw the date and gasped. It was May 18. She had a boat to pick up on the 24th and no idea how to hook it up, tow it, or get it in the water.

Jenny pushed both hands through her hair and held it back.

She vaguely remembered Ella mentioning public boat ramps on the lake where you put boats in the water. So, she'd have to put the boat in at one of those ramps and then drive the boat back to the resort, neither of which she had ever done in her life. Then, after safely docking the boat and putting it up on the lift at the resort — both of which seemed wildly improbable and would likely end up involving the help of a Coast Guard cutter or helicopter or whatever policing and rescuing entity they had at the lake — she'd have to figure out a way to pick up the abandoned boat and trailer at the boat ramp. Easy as pie. Cloning herself would be handy.

Jenny's scalp prickled as she felt a flash of pure fury at Luke. Where was he when she needed him? He was supposed to be here for this. He was supposed to help her. So Zander needed him. *She* needed him, and big time. Now she had to figure all this out on her own.

Knowing she was being irrational, Jenny slowed her breathing and tried the calming self-talk technique Charlotte's Serenity Coach suggested. *Calm down. You can figure this out. You can get help if you need it.* Jenny snorted at that last one. Just where was she going to get help? Charlotte knew nothing about boats. Luke's father Frank was still ill. Alice and Mike were going 100 miles per hour being pulled in multiple directions. Lifting her chin, she gave the spotless cabin a final once over and headed back home. She'd figure it out because she had to.

After a quick tidying of the Dogwood, Jenny was ready for her guests. For the first time since Valentine's Day, she had a full house without hosting a special interest group. Despite her quandary about the boat, Jenny felt exultant and hugged herself.

The blue Jeep Cherokee parked in the driveway, and Jenny could see the *Go Navy* bumper stickers on the back as she watched the middle-aged couple carry bags toward her cabin.

Jenny opened the door before they could knock and ushered in the couple. "Welcome."

The fellow gave a curt nod by way of hello. Neither the husband nor the wife introduced themselves.

"And you are the..." Jenny said expectantly.

"The Thompsons. Coy and Neecy Thompson," the fellow said gruffly as he took off his blue ball cap with *NAVY Veteran* emblazoned across it in gold lettering.

"Well, welcome to the Lakeside Resort. We're so glad to have you visit." Jenny glanced down at the reservation on her *Welcome Inn* screen, read the note she'd made and, despite their standoffishness, smiled at the couple. "Happy anniversary! Your kids gave you this month away as a present. How kind of them. How many years have you all been married?"

"Forty-five," the wife said with a wan smile as she patted gray curls.

"Almost half a century," Coy said flatly as he studied a brochure for Heron Heights Park.

"Well, that's something special," Jenny said, puzzled at their lack of enthusiasm. She'd be brighter if she was talking about a forty-fifth wedding anniversary, although, technically, she'd be almost ninety when she hit that milestone so maybe she'd just give her walker a happy shake or do a wheelie in her motorized wheelchair. Could they be tired from the drive? But glancing down, Jenny saw they were from Bonaire, which was less than two hours away. Maybe they were city folks who'd agreed to a month in the country to placate their kids. But who couldn't adore Heron Lake? Very strange. She handed them a packet of information about the area.

"This is a perfect time to be at the lake," Jenny said in her best Chamber of Commerce voice. "There's not much boat traffic yet, and the temperature is perfect. You can sleep with the windows open, and..." She trailed off. Coy was checking his watch, and Neecy was looking at her blankly.

Jenny felt a spark of indignation. Their kids had been thoughtful enough to arrange this special anniversary gift for them, and they were turning up their noses? But Luke had been coaching her on taking things less personally. Jenny would let this negativity go. Maybe Heron Lake would do its magic. She handed them the keys and pointed them toward the Mimosa. "Let me know if you need anything," she said brightly.

Coy pulled his hat back on as he hefted their bags. Jenny could see that the heavy-looking canvas tote Neecy carried brimmed with romance novels, the kind with bare-chested studly types holding ravishing young women wearing dresses with too many buttons unbuttoned. The tote was large, so it had to contain at least sixty novels. Neecy Thompson wanted to make darned sure she didn't run out of reading material here at Heron Lake. Thoughtfully, Jenny watched them walk away.

Five minutes later, Jenny was folding towels when Coy Thompson rapped sharply on her door. Bear's hackles raised and Buddy gave a low growl, but she hushed them. Swinging open the door, Jenny pinned a pleasant expression on her face. "Hey there. How may I help you?'

"There's no television in our cabins, and I can't get good Wi-Fi," Coy Thompson huffed out in the tone of a man used to giving orders. His cheeks were the colors of ripe tomatoes.

"That's right." Jenny tried to keep a benign expression on her face. Picking up a Lakeside Resort brochure, she pointed out the disclaimer she'd put in bold print in two places: **Depending on your cell service, even with the signal boosters we are using, Wi-Fi is spotty here at the Lakeside Resort. Our guests tell us that because they unplugged their devices, they talked more with one another, read, played board games, and enjoyed nature together.**

But Coy just raised his eyes to heaven. "I know for a fact that these cabins cost a pretty penny, and there's no TV and poor Wi-Fi? I've never heard of such a thing."

"It's true. We're seventy or eighty miles from civilization," Jenny said, trying to sound apologetic even though she didn't feel that way. Maybe she'd get guests checking in to take an oath on the Bible acknowledging they understood there was no TV or good Wi-Fi. Jenny handed him a flyer Alice had made entitled *Fifty Wonderful Things To Do at the Lakeside Resort,* but Coy glanced at it, scoffed, and handed it back to her.

Coy shook his head in disbelief. "No TV. In May." He tapped a finger in his palm to emphasize his point. "Today, as we speak, I'm missing the Preakness and our Navy boys playing baseball in the Patriot League Championship Series."

"Oh, dear." Jenny tried to look sympathetic.

But Coy wasn't finished. His eyes glittered with a fan's zeal as he went on. "You know what else happens in May and June? The Belmont Stakes, the Indy 500, and the U.S. Open. And as you know, Tiger's not only showing up, he's on fire."

"Goodness," Jenny said, but reminded herself she'd put the cell/TV disclaimer all over the website and the room reservation form. She used the same vague gesture she'd made when Louise demanded good cell service, only this time she pointed west. "There's a Budget Nights Motel about twenty miles up the road. I'm sure they have good cable. That may be an option."

Coy just looked disgusted and stomped off.

Good gravy. This was going to be a long month.

Before she had a chance to close her door, her phone rang. "It's a beautiful day at the Lakeside Resort," Jenny said pleasantly, trying to shake off her irritation.

"This is Neecy Thompson in the Mimosa," a woman whispered. "Do you have any cabins with two bedrooms and actual walls separating them and not this loft situation?"

"I'm sorry, but all our cabins are the same floor plan as yours." But had Jenny heard an undertone of urgency in her voice? "Is everything all right, Mrs. Thompson?"

"Oh, fine, fine," the woman said lightly. "My husband can snore like a freight train, and sometimes I find that we long-married folks can use a little...um...breathing room from each other, if you know what I mean. Oops. He's back. Bye-bye." The line went dead.

Jenny ended the call and thought about it. She knew from what she'd read about innkeeping that snoring was a big issue with a lot of couples over age fifty. Luke had told her that one of the most sought after features in the newer homes built for the Over 55 crowd was the little separate rooms off the master called snoring rooms. So maybe Coy's snoring did drive his wife to distraction, but Jenny had a hunch. Maybe the man's near panic about missing sports and his wife's request for two rooms might have less to do with their being demanding and more to do with their being unhappy in their marriage. The two could be dreading the month in such close quarters. That shone new light on the situation. The dread that she'd felt about them being guests for four whole weeks began to drain away, and she even felt a little sorry for them.

CHAPTER 13 — LONG DISTANCE LOVE

J ENNY CHECKED IN DOROTHY AND George Reed, a nice middle-aged couple from Charlotte. Next were Margie and Walter Lewis and their two pre-teen grandsons from Maryvale, Tennessee. Rounding out the crew were Kate, Lauren, and Chelsea, sisters in their thirties from Virginia. Since they lived so far away from each other, they explained, they were delighted at their reunion. The women laughed and teased each other as Jenny handed them they keys. *I was Mom's favorite. No, I was.* The three's high spirits were a refreshing changeup from the dour demeanor of the Thompsons. Fixing herself a glass of iced tea, Jenny kept peeking out the window, her stomach fluttery with excitement. Mama and Landis should be here soon.

To distract herself while she waited, Jenny got on the computer and alternated between reading an article entitled *How to Write Rockin' Press Releases* and a word document in which she tried writing an enticing blurb about the Lakeside Resort. When she came up with something appropriately *rockin'*, she'd send it to regional publications and papers for the bigger cities like Charlotte, Raleigh, and Nashville. Maybe one of them would have a slow news day in their online Lifestyle or Travel section.

The text tone sounded on her phone. Expecting it to be from Mama, she was surprised when she saw the name on the display: Lena Olson. Lena and her husband Jason hailed from Carrboro, North Carolina, and had been some of her first guests ever. The text read:

Hope you are doing well. Do you have a minute to talk?

I do! Call me, Jenny tapped out.

Jenny smiled as she thought of the smart couple who'd stayed with her over Christmas. Lena was a pleasant woman in her mid- to late thirties who'd also brought a canvas bag full of books with her to the lake, though not bodice rippers. Lena had also written a five-star review online that included a poem about *no bears, no cares, and views of water everywheres*. The whimsical poem had resulted in several bookings.

A moment later, her phone rang. "Lena, how are you?" Jenny asked warmly.

"We're both well. I hope you are." Lena hesitated. "We sent two guests to you."

"Thank you. I love referrals." Did she detect tension in Lena's voice?

"I'm not sure you're going to be so happy once I explain," Lena said, sounding apologetic.

"OK. Why?" Jenny remembered a "Problem Guests" post she'd read in the Small Hoteliers and Innkeepers Forum. Were Lena's referrals the type that skipped out on their bills or left their rooms in shambles? Tensing, she waited to hear what the woman was going to tell her.

"Today you checked in Coy and Neecy Thompson, the couple who'll be staying with you for the month." Lena's usual mellow voice cracked with tension.

From the *Ethics for Innkeepers* article she'd read online, Jenny knew she wasn't supposed to divulge any guests' names. "I really can't say, Lena. What's up?"

"Those are my parents or, as I like to call them, the fighting couple," Lena blurted and the rest of her words came out in a rush. "My brothers and sister and I were trying to come up with a present for them for their forty-fifth wedding anniversary. Jason and I had mentioned how much we enjoyed the time we had at the Lakeside Resort, and we decided to all chip in and buy them a getaway in the hopes that staying in a dreamy lake cabin would get them to fall in love again." She moaned. "What were we thinking? That was a terrible idea."

"Oh, dear." That explained a few things.

"They snipe at each other. They give each other the silent treatment. They complain about each other," Lena said wearily. "It's tough to be around."

"Why do they stay together?" Jenny couldn't help but ask.

"They're Catholic, they don't want to divide up the money, and the devil you know..." Lena trailed off. "As a rule, I do not believe in divorce, but I can't understand choosing to stay miserable. Seems to me, you either straighten yourselves out or go on down the road."

"I'm with you," Jenny said firmly.

Lena paused. "So, if they're prickly, just know it has nothing to do with you or your superb cabins. If they disturb other guests, tell them you'll kick them out. And if they decide to leave early, we'll certainly pay for the whole stay." Lena barked out a mirthless laugh. "Jason says if their arguing gets noisy, turn the garden hose on them. We just don't want their craziness to annoy other guests."

Jenny recalled several couples who'd seemed distant from each other when they'd arrived, and left holding hands and looking lovey-dovey. Bad Wi-Fi meant they had to talk, close living quarters prevented retreating from each other, and heavenly views could be a tonic. "Who knows?" Jenny asked lightly. "Maybe there's a small chance that their stay here could help."

"We are crossing all fingers and toes. But I just wanted to let you know the story."

"I appreciate it, Lena," Jenny said. "We'll hope for the best."

But when she ended the call, Jenny pinched her lip. She'd hope for the best, but she wasn't going to let any guests disturb other guests. No, ma'am. People came for a getaway, not a reality TV show where people screamed at each other.

Hearing a car approaching, Jenny jumped up, peeked outside, and saw Mama stepping out of Landis's big SUV. Flying out to the driveway, she enveloped her mother in a hug. Catching a familiar whiff of lily-of-the-valley, Mama's signature scent, Jenny kissed her cheek and held her by the shoulders to look at her. "You look amazing, Mama." And she did. Happiness became Claire. Her blonde hair was streaked with silver, and she wore it long now so it hung in a romantic braid that draped gracefully over her shoulder. Her intelligent brown eyes radiated pleasure and love.

Claire took Jenny's face in her hands. "Let me look at you, darling girl. You are just so dear and perfect. Isn't she just so dear and perfect, Landis?"

"She sure is, lamb chop." Landis grinned at Jenny. At six foot four, square-jawed Landis had a thick shock of white hair, twinkling eyes behind his glasses, and a congenial air.

Though she'd always kept him at arm's length, Jenny had always found him likeable. Landis emanated a calm and equanimity that made her believe in the possibility that everything was going to be all right.

The big man gave Jenny a hug. "Your mama's been chomping at the bit to see you. I thought she was going to slide her foot over and punch the gas once we got past Landrum."

Starting to tear up, Jenny gave Mama a second hug. "I'm just so glad you all are here and that we get a chance for a good visit."

"You may not say that after a week or two," Landis said good-humoredly as he lifted bags from the cargo area. "You know what they say. Fish and company begin to smell after three days."

"But not family," Jenny said with a smile.

Mama put her hands on her cheeks and walked slowly toward the water. "This place looks like it's from a fairy tale." Claire was quiet for a long moment. "This brilliant and beguiling lake is a miracle." She gave a swooning sigh. "In Native American cultures, lakes were viewed as life-sustaining but also holy. Lakes symbolized *the* life force, fruitfulness, and purity." Looking dreamy, she held out her arms. "I can't wait to paint this."

Jenny smiled. Mama had changed so, and in a wonderful way.

"Come on, little mama." Giving his wife an indulgent smile, Landis put a hand on the small of her back and gently herded her back toward the SUV. "Let's get our bags to the cabin and get settled in." Landis paused to take in the property and turned to

Jenny. "These cabins are handsome and set just right on a fine lot. Your daddy picked well, and it looks like you did a good job of bringing the project home."

Jenny blinked back tears, moved by Landis's acknowledgement of Daddy's vision and good choices and her own hard work. Unnerved at letting him see her vulnerable, Jenny got busy and picked up a box of food goodies from the back seat.

Looking distracted, Claire gathered her easel and a big wooden box of her paints. "I brought acrylics and watercolors, and can't wait to see the sunrises." She pointed. "I'll be right there at the water's edge or on the dock every morning."

"What happened to those lazy mornings I was supposed to get when I retired?" Landis complained good-naturedly as he picked up a large suitcase.

Arms full, Claire did a slow three-hundred-sixty-degree circle, taking in the property one more time. "The cabins and that camper are too clever and too interesting for words. Those hardwoods and pines are glorious, too, but my big challenge will be capturing the water." With a satisfied nod, she meandered toward the cabin.

"Careful darlin', or you'll walk right into the lake." Landis took his wife's shoulder and steered her toward the cabins.

Jenny liked how Landis looked at Mama like she was a treasure he'd found.

After showing the two of them the general layout of the Redbud, Landis asked questions and seemed genuinely interested in the work they'd needed to do to finish the cabins. Mama used words like *dreamy, Eden-like,* and *jewel box* before putting a finger on her chin and looking out the window again. "The muted aubergine of those dark clouds is a marvel, and the lake is having trouble deciding whether it wants to be a lapis blue or a cornflower blue."

Jenny grinned. She couldn't help her on that one. After a few more minutes of letting herself bask in Mama's praise and Landis's interest, she left them to get unpacked and, hopefully, start to feel at home.

As Jenny sautéed a chicken breast and put together a salad for supper, she peeked out the window at the clearing to see how her guests were doing.

Claire and Landis were sitting side by side in the Adirondack chairs, looking out at Heron Lake in the afterglow of the sunset, talking and holding hands. Though Mama always tried to be upbeat, Jenny remembered her as often looking like she was bracing herself for the next shoe to drop. Not now. Turning the chicken, Jenny marveled at the change in Mama. She seemed content and happy.

She thought about her mother becoming an amateur artist, and it made sense. Mama had always loved art, and some of Jenny's favorite childhood memories were of the special exhibits the two of them had attended at the Mint Museum in Charlotte. Although Mama drove them into the city with only a small amount of money in her purse and just enough gas in the tank to get home, the days were magical. Jenny recalled Mama bubbling with excitement as they stepped into the museum they referred to as the *Marvelous Mint*. They'd sighed over exhibits of artists like Mary Cassatt, Andrew Wyeth, Monet, Matisse, and John Singer Sargent. Awed, they'd stood in front of the works as Mama quietly told Jenny the history of the artist and the significance of the painting. Now, Mama was an artist who'd had successful exhibits of her own at small galleries in Summerville, Charleston, and Bluffton. Jenny scooped the chicken on her plate and dressed her salad, peeking outside again. Mama made an expressive, looping gesture toward the lake, and Landis lifted her hand to kiss it. Ahh. How sweet.

But Jenny caught a glimpse of two other new guests, the Thompsons. Coy Thompson sat on one of the rocking chairs on their cabin's small porch, whittling a piece of wood and looking like he'd rather be anywhere else but there. Neecy sat fifty feet from him on the other side of the clearing, hunched in a canvas camp chair, turning the pages of one of her steamy romances. The two were living in two separate worlds. Jenny felt a wave of compassion, but remembered how brusque Coy had been with her. Hoo boy. It was going to be a long month for those two.

Jenny sat down to her supper and realized she was fighting

the blues. Eating alone sometimes made her feel that way, so she had tried to make an effort, using cloth napkins and a real plate instead of a paper plate. Lately, she'd been trying to prepare simple home-cooked meals for supper instead of relying too heavily on frozen meals, an easy habit for a single person to fall into. Tonight, she'd even lit two candles for extra elegance, but it wasn't helping. Jenny looked at her lonely chicken breast and the empty chair across from her and took a slug of her wine. She was glad to see Mama and Landis so quietly comfortable with each other, but it had also made her more aware of her own loneliness.

Jenny made a decision. Tonight, she'd surprise Luke with a call in the early evening *his* time. She'd set the alarm. Remembering the time difference, Jenny winced. Catching him at five-thirty PM tomorrow evening meant she needed to make the call in the middle of the night her time. Jenny wasn't sure how articulate she'd be at two or three in the morning, but hopefully, Luke would appreciate her effort.

Before she dozed off, Jenny double-checked her clock to make sure she'd set the alarm properly. She had, but despite knowing this, Jenny slept fitfully and woke periodically to squint bleary-eyed at the clock. When the jangling alarm woke her at three-thirty, Jenny propped herself up in bed, slapped her cheeks softly with her hands to perk up, and called Luke.

The phone rang four times before he picked up. "Hey, you," Jenny said, her voice still raspy from sleep.

"Oh, hi there," Luke said in a polite tone he'd use when making a duty call to an elderly aunt.

In the background, Jenny heard raucous laughter, the clinking of glasses, and what sounded like loud Celtic-inspired rock. "Where are you?"

"Oh, I'm out catching a beer with Oscar, Will, and some mates from work," Luke said.

Mates? Next thing, he'd be putting shrimp on the barbie. Luke was acclimating fast. "How are you?"

"Fine," Luke shouted as the music grew louder.

"I've been thinking about you and I miss you." As soon as the words left her mouth, Jenny knew that it was the wrong thing to say and the wrong time to say it.

"I can't hear you," Luke hollered. "The call's cutting in and out."

"I miss you," Jenny called so loudly that both dogs jumped up from their spots at the foot of her bed and looked at her to see if she was OK.

Luke paused a beat before bellowing. "Me too. Look, I can't hear myself think. Let's talk tomorrow."

"OK. I'll let you go." Before she could end the call, she thought she heard a woman laughing gaily. Skittering the phone onto the bedside table, she rubbed her eyes with her fingers. Here she was trying to surprise him, imagining he was homesick and missing her. But Luke sounded like her call was an inconvenience. He was having a high old time. Shaking her head at her fatuous decision to call, Jenny switched off the lamp and snuggled back into her soft bed. But her sleep was thin, and she had crazy dreams of Luke wearing a khaki hat with one side pinned up like Steve Irwin used to wear, holding a baby kangaroo and talking about going on *a walkabout.*

The next morning, Jenny woke up tired. She was in the shower when she heard the phone. Last night's call had left her feeling stung and stupid. Rationally, Jenny knew it was just a bad time for him to talk, but it still bugged her that he was out having a rocking time with his *mates,* and she was home pining for him. Couldn't he have conveyed a little warmth? Why didn't he step away to a quieter spot and at least try to connect with her if even for a minute? The phone rang again. Instead of dashing out dripping wet to take the call, thrilled at the prospect of hearing his voice, Jenny let the phone ring.

By the time she'd toweled off and slipped on shorts and a T-shirt, Jenny had decided she was being childish and called Luke back, but his phone rang and rang. It had only been ten minutes since he'd called and it wasn't even eight-thirty his time. But Jenny saw the text from him and sagged as she read it.

Sorry we couldn't talk. Zander and leadership team want more due diligence about deal. Will be here thru July. Sorry, Jen. Miss you.

So disappointing. Jenny slumped down on the floor and Bear, Buddy, and Levi milled around her, sensing she was upset. Hugging the boys and scratching their coats with her fingernails was a comfort. Why had Luke told her news that would upset her in a text instead of waiting and telling her on the phone? She was really starting to *get* what Alice meant when she reminded her that Luke was a technical guy. He had news he wanted to convey, and he did it efficiently in a text. That item checked off his list.

Jenny shook her head, reminding herself about how steady Luke was. Though the news was disheartening, he'd call her tomorrow morning and they'd talk about it. In her heart, Jenny knew that Luke *did* love her. She could handle a few more weeks of loneliness. Jenny needed little more time at the pity party, but then she was going to try her best to brace up, get busy, and soldier on.

CHAPTER 14 —
FAITHFUL FAMILY

FOR THE NEXT TWO DAYS, Jenny kept busy and purposefully did not try to engage a lot with Mama or Landis, deciding the two needed to get their bearings and find their own routine at the Lakeside Resort. They'd be there a full two months, so unlike the weekenders who were looking for suggestions about how to pack a lot of activities, fun, or relaxation into three days, Mama and Landis were setting up a temporary home here.

Mama got right into her groove with her painting. On Sunday morning, she set up her easel and chair at a spot near the widest view of Heron Lake and asked to borrow Jenny's Audubon books so she could get the detail right on the birds she planned to include in the paintings.

Monday morning, Jenny was keyed up, very aware that she was supposed to pick up the new boat in just a few days and that she had no driver or boat tower. None of her friends or friends of friends were available to help. She looked through her Facebook friends, feeling increasingly desperate. With a *Hey, it's been a long time! Hope you're well!* as a greeting, she sent several private messages to acquaintances she'd known who might have mentioned any boating experience at all. She was scraping the bottom of the barrel. She'd give it until later tonight, but if she got no takers, she'd be forced to call Mary Parker and beg for her and her husband to help deliver the boat. That seemed pretty pathetic.

Slumping at the computer with her chin in her hand, Jenny watched, waiting for any response to her messages. Nothing. Zip.

She heard a knock at her door and smiled as she peered at the friendly, open face of Margie Lewis. "Good morning."

"Good morning," Margie waved cheerily. "We're getting out on the water. We've never kayaked before and think it would be fun. The boys are on the swim team and both Walter and I used to be lifeguards, so we're all good swimmers, but none of us have ever kayaked."

"Perfect day for it." Jenny pointed to the dock. "Let's put the boys in life preservers and get you all in vests. All the safety equipment is in the boat house. I'll walk down with you and get you situated."

Sometimes Jenny just cracked herself up when she managed to sound so boaty when most of what she knew came from obsessive watching YouTube videos on kayaking and canoeing. She and Bear had taken the kayak out a few times last week, with both of them wearing life jackets, but she was no nautical chick. She would be, though, by the end of the summer. The main thing Jenny was concerned about was safety. The kayaks she'd brought featured new technology for extra stability. Jenny hadn't skimped on the purchase of any safety equipment, from the highest-rated life jackets and vests to the two life ring throw buoys for the dock.

As they walked down to the water, Jenny offered what little advice she had. "If you stay closer to the shore, you won't get swamped by wakes from boats. There's no gradual slope to the bank. It drops off pretty quickly, so keep that in mind when you are getting launched." Margie and her husband put life preservers on their excited grandsons, donned their own life vests and floppy sun hats, waved at Jenny, and gamely paddled off.

Inside, Jenny started to sit vigil at her computer, waiting for casual acquaintances to jump at her enticing offer to help her pick up a boat. But the May morning was sunny and mild, and the day promised to be a blue sky stunner. She closed the lid of the laptop. Throwing on shorts, she corralled the boys. She'd take a brisk walk instead.

As she pressed herself against the wall to avoid being run over by the boys exiting the cabin, Jenny glanced toward the lake. Claire was getting set up on the dock for her usual alfresco painting. Wearing a purple floral kimono and a large-brimmed hat the size of a garbage can lid, she held a paintbrush and a palette and was staring at the lake, engrossed in her painting. Beside her, a companion worked on her own canvas.

Jenny squinted in the bright sunlight, trying to identify Mama's artist friend. Holy moley. Neecy Thompson had finally put down her romance novels and sat on a fold-up chair, dabbing at a canvas with her paint-filled brush. Mama and Neecy were unlikely friends, but hey, the Thompsons weren't fighting or scurrying around furtively trying to get away from each other. Coy was still whittling. Landis reclined on a lawn chair within throwing distance of the women and was reading, probably one of his espionage crime thrillers. He looked up and called out, "Ladies, do y'all need any cold water? I'm going in to get some and would be glad to bring you some."

Solicitous, gentlemanly Landis made Coy Thompson look like curmudgeonly grump. Jenny smiled to herself. Maybe a bit of Landis's chivalry and respect would rub off on the man.

When she returned from her walk, other guests were out on the water. The three sisters were in the kayaks, alternately chatting, racing each other, and using their paddles for splash fights. The Reeds were gliding along in the red canoe, Dorothy Reed pausing to trail her hand through the water. An osprey wheeled overhead, either searching for supper or headed for the nest. Jenny took it in, pleased. This was just the peaceful, convivial waterfront scene she'd hoped for when she'd imagined summer at the Lakeside Resort.

Jenny saw a note taped to her door. Curious, she opened it and saw her mother's looping scrawl.

Sweetness, Join us for supper at six-thirtyish! Landis is making his famous smoked spare ribs, and I'm whipping up gourmet, organic this and that for side dishes. Love you lots! Mama

Jenny winced inwardly. Mama used to be a fine cook, but on her fifty-fifth birthday, she announced she'd given it up, in the same determined tone people used when they declared they were giving up smoking or drinking hard liquor. She'd refocused energy on her artwork, started storing sweaters in her immaculate oven to keep the moths away, and she and Landis ordered a lot of carryout. Every once and a while Mama took a stab at cooking again but only vaguely followed a recipe and tried to remember the rest, often incorrectly. Cooking wise, that ship had sailed.

Tonight's side dishes sounded enticing, but could be gummy imitation tater tots made out of ground cauliflower or burned, seasoned sweet potato chips that drooped on your fork when you stabbed them. Though she looked forward to joining them for supper, she'd take a salad in case the *gourmet organic this and that* turned out to be inedible.

Jenny sent a quick text accepting Mama and Landis's invitation.

At six o'clock when Jenny walked over to the Redbud carrying a large green salad, Landis stood outside holding barbecue tongs as he lifted the lid of a smoking red grill with a gloved hand. The air was redolent with the spicy, tangy smell of braised meats.

"Hello, sugar," he called absently as he carefully turned over the rack of ribs and closed the grill lid with a satisfied smile. "These are going to melt in your mouth. My friend Coy from next door gave me the latest tips on ribs, and he ought to know because one of his sons participates in those Kingsford Charcoal barbecue cook-off contests." He quirked a brow. "Do you want to know the two biggest secrets of delectable ribs?"

He was so excited, she had to hear him out. "Tell me, Landis."

"Number one. Before you cook your ribs, pat them dry thoroughly with paper towels. Moisture keeps the ribs from browning. Number two." He held up two fingers for emphasis. "Press the rub into the meat to form a good crust, but you've got to let them sit like that for forty-five minutes before you cook them. That's will give you crust *and* flavor."

"Good to know." Jenny never cooked ribs, but she'd try to remember the advice. Maybe Luke loved ribs.

"Tips straight from a pit master," Landis said reverently. "That Coy's a smart guy."

Wow. Another unlikely friendship. So the Duttons had

redeeming qualities. Good. "I'll go help get supper ready." Jenny headed inside.

Mama was standing under the smoke detector, waving a dish towel at black smoke billowing from a pan. "Oh, my stars. Had a little mishap. I was making this very healthy Tuscan braised fennel and roasted butternut squash chips when I started reading an article about what influenced the greatest artists of the twentieth century. The fennel sort of melted and the squash chips ignited, but the smoke alarm did not go off." Mama looked so triumphant that Jenny guessed the smoke detector going off was a regular thing when she did cook.

Jenny opened windows and doors to helped air out the cabin while Mama used a heavy duty spatula and steel wool pads to scrape the burnt mess into the trash can.

When the air was clear and Jenny had taken out the trash to keep the cabin from smelling burnt, they both dropped onto the sofa. Claire gave her a sideways look and started to chuckle. "Glad you brought that salad."

Jenny patted her arm affectionately. "Seemed wise."

Sipping glasses of rosé, the two chatted while Landis brought the ribs in with a flourish and slid the dish onto trivets on the counter. "No touching for thirty minutes. We're letting the meat rest. I'm going to clean the grill and talk with Coy." He headed back outside.

Jenny raised a brow at her mother. "You're enjoying painting the lake."

"I'm enjoying *everything* about this place, and painting here is a treat." Her mother's eyes were sparkling. "At different times of day, the light on the water changes so. Sunrises are a miracle, and sunsets are luminous. The canoes and kayaks add vivid color. I'm just getting the hang of painting water, too. That's not as easy as it looks."

"I can imagine." Jenny liked hearing her mother's enthusiasm.

Claire pushed up her sleeves and smiled. "I never paint like this at home. I paint in that bedroom we turned into a studio, but painting outside in such a splendid setting is making my creativity and imagination flourish."

"I'm glad, Mama." She tilted her head. "I saw you painting with Neecy. What's she like?"

"Very creative. I was out there noodling one day, and she showed up with a chair and timidly asked if she could watch. I told her you can't learn to paint by watching someone else paint and got her set up with her own canvas." Claire tapped a finger on her chin. "She paints kind of energetically, almost like she's mad about something, which I would guess is the way Coy barks orders at her, but her paintings have calmed down, and I think she's really enjoying herself."

"I'm glad, Mama," Jenny said.

The spare ribs were tender and flavorful, and the meat fell off the bone, just as Landis had predicted. The three made easy conversation as they ate.

Claire patted Landis's arm. "I worried at first about neglecting this guy but he's making friends and keeping busy."

"He's been a big help to me, that's for sure." Afraid she was imposing with this next request, Jenny turned to Landis. "I've got a problem I'm hoping you can help me with. I'm picking up a used pontoon boat on Friday. It'll be the new boat for the resort."

"Good," Landis nodded approvingly.

"I don't know what I'm doing. I really don't. I'm trying to figure it out." Jenny swallowed hard, realizing she was close to tears. "Luke was going to help me but he's away."

Mama's eyes flashed, and she pressed her lips together. "Honey, we'll help you."

It was the understanding in Mama's voice that did it. Tears began to stream down Jenny's cheeks. Weeks and maybe months of holding it together and trying to press on when she did not know what she was doing all came to a head. Pressing the heels of her hands to her eyes, she made herself stop crying. In a shaky voice, she said, "We can figure it out together."

"Of course we can." Mama handed her a tissue.

"Good. So it's settled. I'll drive over with you to pick it up from the seller, we'll trailer it to the boat ramp and get it home," Landis said in a matter-of-fact tone. "Just tell me what time."

"We need to leave here by nine-thirty. Keep in mind I have never towed a boat, ever."

"We've got this," Landis said as if she'd just asked him to move a slightly heavy chair for her. He was being so kind to her when she'd had a history of being cool to downright frosty to him. Landis was a nice man. But Jenny started feeling overwhelmed again and the tears started in earnest. She blotted them with her napkin. "It's not just that. When we get the boat home, I need to learn to drive it, and I've never driven a boat. I need to be able to take guests on the boat, and take kids tubing."

"Your mama and I sailed for years, and then switched to power boats. We're happy to help. It'll be good to get out on the open water again, a stiff breeze blowing, and cruising in a well-engineered watercraft. Nothing like it." Landis rubbed his hands together. He paused, looking thoughtful. "You know, it never hurts to have another crew member on board. I'll ask our neighbor, Coy. With thirty years in the Navy, he ought to know a thing or two about boats."

Good Lord. Not that crabby man. But Jenny was too relieved and too grateful to voice any concerns about free, experienced help. "Sounds good," she said weakly.

Landis leaned back into the sofa cushions, picked up his beer, and sipped it as he looked at Jenny. "So, what do you know about boats?"

"The boat I bought is a twenty-four-foot pontoon." That was a good start, but then she ran out of gas. "The pointy end is called the bow."

Landis gave her an encouraging smile. "If you're as quick a study as your mama was, you'll be zipping around the lake in no time."

But Jenny wasn't so sure. "That gap in that dock where I'm supposed to slide the boat in looks so small. What if I crash?"

He sent Claire a twinkling look. "We crashed plenty in our days on the water, didn't we, sugar-pie?"

"Oh, my, yes. When we started with boats, we referred to our style of docking as a controlled crash." Claire chuckled at the memory. "But we got better at it."

"You'll ease into it, but even then, the trick is fenders. Lots and lots of fenders," Landis said sagely.

Jenny sent him a questioning look. "Fenders?"

"Bumpers. Lots of fat cushions around the opening and inside of the boat lift," her mother explained.

"Ah." Jenny pictured marshmallows, air bags in cars, and the Michelin Man; her shoulders dropped. "I'm taking the boating course online, and I like it. Lots of interesting videos and scenarios. But I have some questions." Knowing how little she knew, she spoke tentatively. "I don't get the rules for approaching another boat and who has the right of way, who gives way, and who stands down. That's very confusing."

"We can talk about that, but remember, don't hold your course even if it's yours to hold if the other guy forgot that lesson and isn't giving way. You need to always err on the side of caution and assume the other boater doesn't know the rules or isn't paying full attention," Landis advised with a canny nod. "So here's the rules of the road..." he began, looking animated.

Claire cleared dishes, looking pleased that her husband and daughter were talking so intently. Landis patiently and thoroughly answered all of Jenny's questions.

After they wound down, Jenny kissed them both and headed home, hugging herself with relief. Maybe she could do this. Though she'd counted on Luke to teach her the ins and outs of boating, she had solid backup from family, and that was a comforting feeling.

As she stepped into the small clearing in front of her cabin, Jenny was startled to see a red canoe she did not own leaning against the side of the Dogwood. Where had that come from?

A man's voice floated over to her. "A guy stopped by in a big black truck. Said his wife told him you were looking for a canoe, and he found one a buddy of his wanted to get rid of." An unsmiling Coy Thompson ambled over, a toothpick in his mouth.

"My friend, Mike," Jenny said softly. What a thoughtful man.

She and Charlotte had bought two gently used canoes, but they were still short a canoe, so this was a big help.

Coy tossed aside his toothpick. "I'll help you walk that down to the lake."

Shocked at his offer, Jenny worked to keep a neutral expression on her face. "I'd appreciate that."

Each hoisting an end, the two slowly walked the boat toward the dock. The canoe was heavier than Jenny had thought it would be, and she was breathing hard when they slid in into a spot beside the other crafts resting on the strip of lawn beside the water. Jenny admired her little fleet. The red, green, and yellow boats lined up on the green lawn against the blue of the lake looked like an inviting scene from the cover of a vintage LL Bean catalogue.

"Thanks, Coy." Jenny was still getting used to realizing the guest she thought was a die-hard grouch could be a pleasant guy.

He gave a curt nod. "My wife and I used to canoe." Coy rubbed the back of his head and looked rueful. "Don't know why we stopped."

"Maybe you two could take a canoe for a spin." Jenny hoped she sounded like a camp counselor, not a marriage counselor.

He squinted at Jenny. "Maybe we will. Precious little else to do around here," he muttered and tromped off.

"Have a good evening." Refusing to let her hopeful feelings be dampened by the cantankerous man, Jenny headed home.

CHAPTER 15 — DOWN FOR THE COUNT

EARLY THE NEXT MORNING, JENNY was on a ladder leaned against the boathouse, painting a section of siding that had somehow gotten overlooked by her painter, Joe, and his crew. She wasn't a fan of ladders, and her legs wobbled as she climbed it, but the painting had to be done to protect the wood. If she didn't look down and kept thinking about happier things, like Landis and Mama offering to help her, or the Jenny Colgan novel she'd started last night, or the slow but steady rise in the numbers in her business bank account, she was fine. The sun was shining, she had a good purchase, and the siding boards were soaking up the paint and looking spruce. Just three more boards to go. Jenny glanced nervously at the Redbud. If Mama saw her perched on a ladder on a dock, she'd never hear the end of it. From the corner of her eye, Jenny saw two men appear. She jumped, bobbling her small paint can, and grabbed the ladder with her other hand to keep from falling.

"Morning, ma'am," they called. Two men in a sharp-looking fishing boat with glittering paint and big engines had drifted up behind her and were fishing not four feet from her.

"Morning, men." Jenny used her arm to dab at the sweat that had instantly broken out along her hairline. Several times a week, she would see fishermen in their boats close to docks, using the whisper-quiet trolling motor to fish. She'd only been spooked because she'd turned around and they were there.

Resuming her even paint strokes, Jenny had a thought. "Men,

if I have folks fishing off the pier, what should they use for bait or lures and what are they fishing for?"

The man with the amber wraparound sunglasses and the long-billed fishing cap called out, "Largemouth, striper, crappie, and catfish. Best lures are spinnerbaits, crankbaits, buzzbaits, and poppers. For live bait, greasy chunks of hot dog."

"Thanks." Jenny tried remembering the lure names but could only recall greasy hot dogs and decided that would be the official bait of the Lakeside Resort.

Later in the morning, Jenny sized up the area she'd decided might be good for her garden, a large rectangular spot of ground with good sun. Standing with her hands on her hips, she glanced at the sky, trying to figure out where the sun rose and set.

Landis ambled over, wearing baggy khaki shorts, a golf shirt, and a rumpled bucket hat. "Good morning. What are you up to?"

"Good morning." Jenny smiled. "I'm putting in a garden and want to pick the best spot."

Landis rubbed his chin and looked around, his head tilting as he noted the arc of the sun. "Looks like a fine spot you've chosen."

She gave him a crooked smile. Landis had such a reassuring way about him. Why had she wasted so much time keeping him at a distance? Pulling wooden stakes and a ball of twine from a canvas bag, Jenny handed him a hammer, and the two went to work making an outline of her garden.

"Jenny, have a look at the landing, and try to do it discretely," Landis said softly, pretending to adjust the angle of the stake.

Looking out from the sides of her sunglasses, Jenny glimpsed a sight she'd never imagined she'd see. Coy and Neecy Thompson were paddling the red canoe out in the lake by the dock. The picture would have been romantic, except Coy was raising his voice at Neecy. Because the two weren't paddling in sync, instead of gliding along through the water in a straight line, the canoe kept circling. They were going nowhere fast.

"Oh, dear." Jenny's idea of a romantic canoe ride bringing the couple back together went up in smoke.

"Arguing couples in boats. That rarely ends well." Landis shook his head ruefully.

The voices from the canoe grew louder. Coy's voice was authoritative, and Neecy's responses were angry. Her stomach tensing just hearing the conflict, Jenny tried to tune it out and asked Landis for his opinion about the best placement for different vegetables. A moment later, they heard a splash. Jenny looked up in alarm. Neecy Thompson apparently had had her fill of her husband's Captain Bligh behavior and jumped over the side. Jenny's eyes darted wildly to Landis's. "Do we need to go help them?"

He pretended to adjust his sunglasses as he sized up the scene. "She's a strong swimmer. First-class breast stroke. He's paddling behind her, apologizing and asking her to get back in the canoe. Life vest is holding up well." He shrugged. "Water temp is in the seventies. Let's let them keep their pride." He squatted and repositioned the stake to tighten the twine. "We never saw that little incident."

Jenny leaned down to help him and cracked a smile. "What incident?"

"Good girl." Landis swatted away a fly and retied the stringer. "We saw this more often than you'd think when we sailed. Man overboard, or woman usually. A fellow would shout out one too many orders, and over the wife would go."

"Coy needs to pay attention to how nicely you talk to Mama. Maybe it would rub off on him."

"He has a few rough edges," Landis said mildly. "Sometimes it's hard for these guys that got to high ranks in the military to forget they're not captains or admirals at home."

"Good point." Jenny hadn't thought of it that way.

It was Wednesday morning and as soon as she woke, Jenny threw on shorts and a T-shirt, excited at the prospect of going to the Parrs' house to pick up the tiller they'd offered to lend her. She couldn't wait to get started on the garden.

The morning was gray and drizzly, maybe a good day to take a first run at tilling up the soil for her garden, especially since the past two weeks of solid sunshine had left the ground hard. Sipping her coffee as she looked out the window, Jenny pictured her thriving garden. She'd been reading up on successful vegetable gardening without using pesticides or harmful fertilizers. Part of her plan was to follow Mr. Levi around with a bucket and start a pile of his...organic fertilizer. She knew she needed to let it season so as not to burn her plants, and she needed to put the pile away from the cabins so there'd be no unpleasant odors. If she added coffee grounds, banana peels, eggshells, and gently tossed in a family of worms, soon she'd have a grand pile of goodness to nourish her vegetables. She'd seen organic vegetable spikes in catalogs, too. Those would be fun to try.

Since it was still cool in the mornings, she'd plant lettuce, cabbage, and spinach, then put in warmer weather plants like okra, red bell peppers, yellow and green squash, and carrots. She wanted to experiment with brussels sprouts, Swiss chard, beets, and kohlrabi. Jenny also wanted to try a few plants just for fun or because they were pretty, maybe a few rows of Silver Queen corn, sunflowers, and purple lavender.

As the boys came back in from what had to be a muddy romp, Jenny tried to towel off their feet as they came in the door, but they were slippery characters. The floor was full of muddy paw and hoof prints. Jenny mopped the kitchen floor, wondering if she could teach all her animals to wipe their feet. The bucket of soapy water soon turned brown, and Jenny dumped the filthy contents outside and refilled it. She'd just taken the first mop stroke with fresh water when she felt a jab of sharp pain in her lower back. Jenny went rigid, whimpering. If she moved a centimeter, the pain shot through her like a dagger. Slowly and painfully, she edged over to the sofa and managed to reach for her phone. "Mama," she whispered. "Can you come over here? I need you."

An hour later, Jenny was lying on the couch with a heating pad under her back. If she leaned a bit on her left side, the pain was an eight instead of a ten. Mama had given her two anti-inflammatories and half of a muscle relaxant that the doctor had given her last time this had happened. Jenny breathed a raggedy sigh and thought it might be possible that she would walk again.

Claire had been bustling round the cabin, getting Jenny comfortable and putting up the mop and bucket. Finished, she dried her hands and sent Jenny a worried look. "Sweetheart, do you think you need to see a doctor?"

"No. It's easing up a bit," Jenny said quietly. "I've had this before, and it usually lets go after about a day." She tried to shift positions and cried out. She *had* to start doing her stretching exercises again.

Looking worried, Claire put a glass of ice water on the table beside her. "You need rest, sugar. Let us help. I'm going to ask Landis to forward your phone to ours. We can take any calls that come in. We'll take care of the animals, too," she said firmly. "You've been working way too hard. That can't help your back."

Jenny thought about wearing that backpack blower, lifting bags of mulch, carrying the ladder to the pier, and hefting bags of dog food from her trunk. No wonder her back had called a time out. She knew Mama was right, but had a niggling concern. "I need to get that tiller from the Parrs' house. Ella and Paul are headed out of town. I don't want to wait until they come back to get it. Some of the vegetables need to be planted now, the broccoli, beets, collards, and..." A jolt of pain shot through her, leaving her breathless.

Claire winced in sympathy and gently smoothed Jenny's hair back from her forehead. "I'll ask Landis to go get it."

Cautiously raising one finger, Jenny pointed at the counter to a bowl of keys. "Have him take Luke's truck. It's got a hitch, and he can haul the tiller in the utility trailer."

"Got it." Claire said. "Just rest now. We'll take care of everything."

Jenny felt the heat soothing her screaming muscles and closed her eyes. She'd try to sleep, and hope the worst of it was over when she woke.

When Jenny finally did wake, she did an experimental wiggle

of her back and hips. Sore, but not a fraction of what it had been, and none of that shooting, searing pain. Thank heavens. Carefully, she raised her arms above her head and did one little stretch and then another.

The house was too quiet without the dogs and Levi. With one steadying hand on the counter, Jenny slowly walked to the sink and greedily drank a tall glass of water. Blinking, she looked at the clock on the stove. One o'clock, the next day. Good grief. She'd slept or dozed twenty-four hours. That meant Luke had called and reached Mama or Landis. Good, she thought meanly.

She heard an engine backfire, catch, and rumble throatily. Still walking as slow as a sloth, Jenny pulled back the curtains and peered outside. Eyes wide, she studied the scene.

A grinning Landis was being dragged around the garden by a large rear-tine tiller that was effortlessly churning up large areas of dirt. Wearing noise-protecting earmuffs over his ball cap, he looked like he was having the time of his life. Coy Thompson, his fellow farmer, wore a wide-brimmed hat and earmuffs and was actually smiling as he raked churned-up dirt and formed raised rows for planting. When he smiled, Coy was actually good-looking in a craggy, Jeff Bridges kind of way. Landis cut off the tiller, and the two men cackled about something, looking as carefree and happy-go-lucky as college boys.

Claire smiled at Jenny as she walked past the front picture window holding a tray and rapped gently at the door. Walking haltingly, Jenny opened it. "Hey, Mama."

"Hey there, sugar pie," Claire said as the dogs and Levi swarmed inside. Bear and Buddy were so glad to see her that their whole bodies wagged and they were smiling doggy smiles. Levi did the prancing step and head tossing that he did when he was excited.

Jenny patted, rubbed, and reassured the boys, then sent Claire a grateful look. "I was glad you were here yesterday. Thank you."

"I was happy to help. You feeling some better?" Claire's concern shone from her eyes.

"I am." She took the tray her mother offered. Mama had

prepared a meal she couldn't ruin, a green salad with a boiled egg and sliced chicken.

"You need someone to take care of you when you're sick," Claire said, a note of reproach in her voice.

"Most of the time, I do a pretty good job of taking care of myself." Jenny just didn't have the energy to get into that discussion again about how she needed a husband. She put the tray on the kitchen counter and tilted her head toward the window. "Landis and Coy look happy as puppies. I've never seen Coy look like he's enjoying himself before, and he's kind of cute."

Claire smiled. "Those two boys have hit it off."

Jenny remembered she'd lost a day. "Did Luke call?"

"Oh, yes. We had a nice little chat," her mother said nonchalantly, her face the picture of innocence as she fluffed couch pillows.

"What did you talk to him about?" Jenny hoped Mama hadn't made it sound like she was at death's door. He had enough to worry about.

"I told him you'd hurt your back but were on the mend. After that, we just talked about day-to-day things." Claire picked up a dish towel and began drying glasses in the dish rack that Jenny knew were already dry.

Jenny sensed there was more to it than that, but Mama wasn't talking. She'd ask Luke about it when they talked tomorrow. "Come for a drink tomorrow evening, Mama," she said impulsively. "We've been so busy that I haven't really had a chance to talk with you."

"I'd love to," Mama said briskly. "Now, unless you need me, I'm going to head back to the cabin. I'm meeting Neecy to paint at two o'clock, and Dorothy Reed and Margie Lewis are joining us."

"You've got a real painting class going," Jenny said. "That's impressive."

Claire looked pleased at the compliment. "I'm hardly qualified as a teacher, but we enjoy ourselves."

After she left, Jenny eased herself to the floor and did some more light stretching. She lay on the floor with her rear end against the wall and propped her feet up. The tight muscles in her back loosened. Aaah. Jenny vowed to take better care of herself, and she'd start today.

The next morning, Luke called her just after six AM. "How are you, Jenny? I heard you were down for the count." He sounded worried.

"I'm better," she said, giving her back an experimental stretch.

"Your mama told me all that you've had going on with worries about money and getting the cabins booked. She said you'd been learning to tow the boat and drive it. I'm proud of you, Jen."

Though warmed by his compliment, she felt a wave of exasperation. "But I told you about all that. Every little bit of that. Don't you remember?"

Luke hesitated. "I heard it but didn't really get it. I've been going so fast that I don't think I've been listening very well to you," he admitted.

Jenny quickly weighed letting him off the hook, but she felt a steely determination to stand her ground. "You're not listening well to me, Luke. I think you get about a quarter of what I tell you."

"I'm sorry," he said, sounding genuinely pained.

"It makes me feel like I'm alone, and I don't like it." Jenny felt a lump in her throat, realizing she was close to tears. She'd been holding in these feelings for weeks now. "Luke, I need you to tune into me. I'm scared you're slipping back into your old workaholic ways. You're the most important person in my life, and I need to feel connected to you, even if you're 10,000 miles away."

He groaned. "You're right, and I'm so sorry."

Jenny felt herself soften. "I forgive you, but let me in your life. Come into mine and show more interest. I need you."

"I need you," he said fervently. "You are my whole world, Jenny."

Smiling hard, Jenny blinked back tears. "And you're mine. I can't wait for you to get home and for us to start our lives together."

"Soon, Jen. Soon." Luke sounded resolute.

"Good." She hoped with all her heart that he would do better, but she'd be watching him.

As she ended the call, Jenny put a hand to her mouth, remembering what he'd said to her at the restaurant before he left. *No woman will ever come between us.*

But what about his work coming between them?

CHAPTER 16 — JENNY
AT THE HELM

O N FRIDAY MORNING, JENNY PULLED slowly into the driveway, making a wide arcing turn to avoid clipping trees, guests' cars or the edges of the cabins with the empty boat trailer she was towing. When she put Luke's truck in park, she shook out her hands. They were cramped from driving white-knuckled for forty-six miles to the Parkers', to the boat ramp, and then back to the Lakeside Resort. So relieved to be back home in one piece, Jenny felt like kissing the ground.

Hopping down from the high seat, she hurried over to the clearing and put a hand over her forehead to block the sun as she peered out at the water. Jenny's heart ticked up a beat as she saw her gorgeous boat come into view, cutting gracefully through the water, leaving wide arcs of frothy white wake behind it. Landis was at the helm, and Coy sat beside him in the first mate's seat.

Claire, Neecy, Margie, and Dorothy were all painting in the clearing but stopped to admire the approaching vessel. Mama called, "That's about the prettiest boat I've ever seen," and the other women chorused their agreement.

"Thanks. I think so, too." Jenny broke into a smile as she headed down to the dock, feeling a heady mix of pride and excitement as she watched the fast boat approach. Her boat was a beauty. Slowing, Landis lined up the bow with the boat slip and floated into it, slick and easy. Jenny sighed appreciatively, knowing he was making it look easy to put an eight-and-a-half-foot wide boat into a ten-foot slip. Maybe she could learn to dock a boat like that before she started drawing Social Security.

Landis smiled broadly at her and Coy gave her a thumbs-up. "Rides like a dream," Landis called as he tossed her a line. "Lake water levels are high today. Just to be on the safe side, always tie us off once we get raised up." Coy turned the lever to the lift and the boat rose slowly out of the water.

Jenny tied the line around the piling the best she could, not sure that a modified bow was a good knot. The three walked up to the cabins. Tilting her head, she looked at the two men. "Did Luke and I do a good job picking this boat?"

"You certainly did," Landis said firmly, and Coy jerked his head in a nod of agreement.

"So tomorrow is my first lesson, right? Are you men still on for that?" she asked.

Landis tapped the watch on his wrist. "See you on the dock at nine o'clock sharp."

"Zero nine hundred hours," Coy clipped out, but a smile played at the corners of his mouth.

That evening, Jenny laid kindling and wood in the small firepit Luke had had a stone man build as part of her Christmas present. Though the main firepit in front of the cabins had proven to be a big draw for guests so far, she liked having the privacy of an owner's firepit between her cabin and the Silver Belle. Lighting a match, she enjoyed watching the flames catch and grow.

Claire walked over to the Dogwood wearing a flowing floral cotton dress and sandals. Her cheeks were a tawny gold from the sun, and her hair was clipped loosely to the top of her head with a tortoiseshell barrette. She looked relaxed, pretty, and a good twenty years younger than her age. Waving at Jenny, she smiled dreamily and paused to take in the lake. "That yellow ochre sun, those waves sparkling like diamond on gentian blue water...This place is enchanting."

Though she was getting used to her mother's waxing poetically, Jenny still felt as proud as if someone had complimented her on the brilliance or handsomeness of Bear, Buddy, or Levi. "I love it here, Mama." She gestured to a chair. "Come sit. Let's have that glass of wine." Stepping inside, she brought out two stemless glasses and an open bottle of a sauvignon blanc she'd splurged on in the over-ten-dollar section of the grocery store and was saving for special occasions.

The two women sat companionably, enjoying their first sips of the clean, crisp wine. Claire turned and studied the Silver Belle. "The sunlight just sparkles and dances on that shiny metal. I must paint that, too."

Jenny sighed happily. "I love everything about the Belle, but I haven't even taken her on one real camping trip. One of these days, I'm going to take her out on the open road."

"You should. She's too pretty to stay at home." Claire tilted her head to the side. "Why haven't you done that yet?"

Jenny shrugged. "I've been too busy getting this place going, and I don't have anyone to take care of the resort while I'm gone."

"Ah. Well, you'll get that worked out," Claire reassured her.

In the clearing, Landis and George Reed were battling it out with Coy and Walter in a cornhole tournament. Neecy sat reading her novel, but she'd moved her chair twenty feet closer to the clearing and seemed to be surreptitiously watching the competition. When Coy hooted at a wisecrack George made, Neecy looked up, smiled briefly, and returned to her book.

Jenny watched with interest. "How's Neecy doing, Mama? I know she's enjoying the painting, but are she and Coy getting along any better?"

Claire wore a half-smile on her face as she watched the men play. "They're both happier because they're out of their rut. Coy is a teddy bear somewhere under that gruff exterior, but he barks at Neecy. She pays him back by withdrawing into her romance novels. But something about this place is changing things up. He's being more polite and respectful. Her jumping out of the canoe because she couldn't stand him anymore seemed to get his attention."

Jenny grinned, remembering. "How about you? I know you

and Landis usually do a lot together, but you both seem to be doing more on your own. Is that OK?"

"Surprisingly, yes. I adore painting here, and I've met all these nice women. Landis is having a ball and making new friends." Claire tapped a finger to her lip. "I think I like it. We can both do our own things, meet for supper, and have new things to talk about."

"I'm developing a little bit of a dad crush on Landis. He's so easygoing and upbeat," Jenny admitted, trying to pinpoint what made him so endearing. "He's been right there when I've needed advice or help, and doesn't make me feel stupid for needing it."

Claire gave her a knowing look. "I'm so glad you've given him a chance. He's the kindest man, and he's so good for me."

"He lets you be yourself and loves you to pieces."

"Exactly." Claire nodded slowly. Twirling her wine glass in her palm, she looked reflective. "He's not your daddy, and I know you struggled with that."

"I did for a long time," Jenny admitted. "I've let go of that, though."

"Good. The past is the past," Claire said firmly. Pushing back strands of hair that the wind had teased from her hair clip, she cast a sideways glance at Jenny. "I grieved your daddy's passing more than I thought I would. How I loved that man." Taking a sip of wine, her eyes sparkled in amusement. "Jax could charm the birds out of the trees. I don't know how many deals he made by amplifying his Southern accent and doing that *Aw shucks, I'm just a country boy* routine he used." Frowning, Claire rubbed her eyes with her fingers. "I wish I'd known enough to recognize his illness." Mama gave a wan smile. "With Landis, we take care of each other. I've learned more about who I am, and he thinks that's just fine and dandy." She put a hand over her heart. "I swear, the good Lord sent me that man special delivery, and I'm so grateful he did."

"I am, too," Jenny said quietly.

"You sound serious about Luke. Tell me more about him."

Mama shifted in her chair so she could look more squarely at Jenny.

"Oh, he's wonderful. He's smart, and kind and good to me." Jenny knew she was gushing but couldn't help it. "He's a steady guy, just like Landis."

"Steady is good," Mama said. "So he's in Australia now."

"Yes, he's been there for a few weeks now. It's a temporary project, though, and he'll come home before long." Then the penny dropped. Luke had been so attentive during this morning's phone call, as if he'd had some sort of epiphany. Jenny had a sneaking suspicion his epiphany might be related to his conversation with Claire. "Mama, what *exactly* did you say to Luke the other morning?"

"I just gave him a little update." Claire waved her hand like it was no big deal. "I filled him in on your back. I told him how it had happened, and that it was no surprise given how hard you'd been working all on your own." Mama suddenly seemed intent on studying the lake instead of meeting Jenny's eyes.

"Did you say anything else, Mama?"

Claire examined her nails. "I may have mentioned that I was disappointed that he couldn't be here to help you."

"You said you were *disappointed*?" Mama had pulled out the big guns. "That word strikes fear in the hearts of Southern men, and you know it."

Claire dimpled prettily. "So much more effective than telling a man you're upset with him."

Jen covered her eyes with her hands, feeling the heat of embarrassment. No wonder Luke was falling all over himself to apologize. "I wish you hadn't done that."

Claire lifted her chin, looking defiant. "I'm glad I did. You know our family history. Men seem to think working like the devil is an excuse for not being there for their loved ones, and it's not. Women who make the mistake of being too understanding can let their men to veer off course and possibly wreck a relationship and a family." She held up a hand. "I know I shouldn't have interfered, but I just had to."

Jenny nodded, realizing *she* needed to speak to Luke as directly as Mama had.

"I'm sorry for interfering," Mama said.

Jenny heard the tremor in her voice, and felt a stab of compassion. Taking her mother's hand, she squeezed it. "It's OK, Mama. Everything's OK."

The next morning, Jenny was wide awake before sunrise, revved up and feeling equal parts eager and anxious about today's boating lesson. She was also exhilarated at the prospect of talking with the new and improved version of Luke. After Mama being *disappointed* in him, yesterday's conversation had been so wonderful

After a quick shower, Jenny sat on the porch in her bathrobe enjoying her coffee as she peered at the bird box closest to her cabin. Yesterday, she'd cleaned debris from the nesting box after the last couple hatched their babies, raised them, and moved out. She'd felt a wistful pang, realizing the male bluebird who'd sat on the branch of the pine sapling and kept her company for a little while probably had moved on. But as she sipped her coffee, she went stone still as she watched a new bluebird pair fly around, light on the box and peer inside. Gosh, the bluebird real estate market was hot.

Glancing out at the lake, she saw a boat gently drifting along. At first, she thought the owners were just driving slowly, but she looked again. No one was at the helm. Peering more closely, her heart began a staccato beat. That was *her* boat meandering down the lake. Jenny threw on clothes and raced to the dock, shocked at how high the water was. The lake had risen almost two feet since yesterday.

Shimmying into a life vest, she grabbed a boat hook and a paddle, launched the kayak, and began paddling furiously toward the boat. Thinking about the knot she'd used to tie the line to the piling, Jenny felt burning shame. The girly bow she'd tied hadn't held. She should have asked the men to help her tie a sturdier knot but hadn't. Never again, she vowed, as she caught up with the boat. After several unsuccessful tries, she managed to hook the trailing line with her boat hook and pulled her kayak toward the boat. Quickly scanning the exterior, Jenny blew out a sigh of relief. The boat looked like it had weathered its free-roaming. No scratches, dents, or any signs of damage. Thank goodness. Jenny slowly towed the boat back toward the dock and managed to slip it back onto the boat cradle. This time, she tied it off with a triple-tied bow. Then, trying to remember that week at Girl Scout camp thirty-two years ago, Jenny added what she thought might be a square knot.

Glancing around the cabins, she saw no lights. Grateful that she hadn't been seen wrangling her own boat, Jenny slipped into the Dogwood. At the computer, she pulled up books on tying nautical knots and ordered several, including one called *The Knotty Boater*. As a bonus, the book came with a practice board complete with cleats, eye bolts, and two lengths of a rope attached. She could hang it on the wall beside her desk, and when she needed a break, practice tying nautical knots. The author claimed the Bowline, the Clove Hitch, the Cleat Hitch, and the Square Knot were the basic *must know* knots for the boating life, but the Double Half-Hitch, Sheep Bend, Anchor Bend, and Trucker's Hitch could get a boater out of tricky situations. Jenny liked all the names, but shivered a little when she imagined what tricky situations the author was alluding to. One thing she knew, she wasn't going to risk not knowing how to tie a decent knot. That rookie mistake would never happen again.

At a few minutes before *oh nine hundred*, Jenny waited nervously on the dock. After she'd ordered the knot book, she'd done more reading about the nuts and bolts of operating a pontoon boat. Seemed like an awful lot to remember. Her palms were clammy and her stomach in a Bowline or a Half Hitch or some sort of sturdy knot as she watched Landis and Coy stroll down to the dock, each holding a cup of coffee.

"Morning," Jenny shoved her hands in her pockets to keep from wringing them.

Landis smiled. "Good morning."

Coy gave a squint which could have been his version of good morning, and glanced around. "Lake's up."

"Sure enough. We should have raised the boat higher in the lift last night but we got lucky." Landis sipped his coffee. "All that rain last week just flows right to the lake from creeks and lakes upstream."

Jenny decided she'd keep this morning's kayak adventure to herself.

"You need to learn the boat and the engine," Coy said out of the corner of his mouth as they stepped onto the boat. At the helm, Jenny swiveled her head and took in the length of the boat before her and the length of the boat behind her and breathed out a shuddering sigh. Holy Mother. What had she gotten herself into?

"Now, just ease it into reverse." Landis smiled pleasantly, looking as relaxed as if he were sitting down to Sunday supper.

Her mouth dry as corn starch, Jenny tried to just ease it into reverse, but they roared out of the boat house backward. Quickly, she shoved the throttle back into neutral. Both men's heads slung forward and back, but they managed to keep those preternaturally calm expressions on their faces.

"Maybe just a touch easier," Landis suggested, dabbing at the coffee that had sloshed all over the front of his shirt and shorts.

Coy's clothes had coffee stains, to, but his face was implacable as he looked serenely out at the horizon.

"Let's try it again," Landis suggested.

Her heart skittering, Jenny glanced behind her and inched the boat into reverse, this time managing to just sling the men's heads some, but not as bad as before.

Coy raised a brow at Landis. "She's getting the hang of it."

The rest of the lesson went well, although her putting the boat in forward involved some head slinging in the other direction. Maybe that would be good from a chiropractic standpoint, she thought crazily. Jenny kept wiping her sweating palms on her shorts, because they seemed to be part of the reason she was rocketing them around.

To be on the safe side, Jenny inched the boat along the lake.

At one point, two speedy kayakers overtook them, but she didn't care. "Doing good, girl," Coy called out from time to time.

After a while, Jenny was comfortable enough at the helm that she could almost breathe normally. Landis asked for her phone and took a picture of her at the wheel. "You can send that to your mama or put it on your website," he said with a proud smile.

Though her mouth was probably twisted in a rictus smile, Jenny would send that picture to Luke, too, so he could see her in the gorgeous boat and hopefully remember what he was missing.

Though both men claimed her first time piloting the boat had been a success and that she showed real potential as a captain, Jenny's legs still shook as she walked up the dock with them. "I don't know what I would have done without you all." She pointed at the blotches of coffee stains on their clothes. "If you get those to me, I'll run them through the wash with a stain remover, and they'll be good as new."

At least she was good at laundry.

Back home, Jenny wished she could tell Luke all about her lesson. This morning's kayak rescue of the drifting boat meant that she'd not been home for his call. Replaying in her mind how warm he'd sounded when they'd talked last, Jenny decided she'd make another middle of the night call her time and surprise Luke right after work.

Jenny carefully set the alarm and was jangled when it woke her at three-fifteen AM. "Hey. Luke."

"Hey, Jenny." Luke sounded rushed and a bit out of breath.

"Do you have a few minutes to talk?" She hated how tentative she sounded.

"Sure I do. I couldn't talk with you this morning. How was your day?"

Jenny started with the highlights of the boat drifting off and the slow speed chase in the kayak.

Though he said, *Really* and *Good* at all the right times, Luke sounded distracted.

"I had my first boating lesson today, too," Jenny said in a peppy and upbeat voice, determined to make her life sound so interesting that he'd put down whatever he was doing and actually pay attention to her for a few moments. "It was very exciting."

"Neat. How'd you do?" Luke asked warmly.

There it was. That engaged, caring tone that she loved. "I'm a little erratic now. I rammed into the dock and almost dumped Landis into the lake. I need to work on easing the boat into gear." She flushed with embarrassment just thinking about it.

Luke chuckled. "It's hard at first, but it gets easier with practice."

"What's been going on with you?" Jenny asked.

"I met with the engineers in Research and Development and visited the call center."

"To see if you all would be a good match?" Jenny hoped she had it right.

"Right," Luke said. "So, their technology is compatible with ours and..." He stopped talking. A phone rang, and then went quiet. Luke must have taken the other call, because in a somewhat distant voice, Jenny heard him say, "Hey, Zander. Yes. Yes. Can you hold on one second?"

He was talking on his cell and the landline? Jenny couldn't believe it.

Luke came back on the line. "Jen, hang on. This will only take a minute."

"OK." Jenny rubbed the sleep from her eyes. But the time dragged on. Glancing at the phone, she saw she'd been hanging on for almost seven minutes. Luke had either gotten caught up in a longer conversation than he'd anticipated, or he'd forgotten she was holding. At the nine minute mark, Jenny stabbed a finger at the phone and ended the call. She pressed her fingers to her temple as her blood started a slow boil. She tossed the phone onto the bedside table with a clatter. Ten minutes later when the phone rang, Jenny turned it off, rolled over, and tried to go back to sleep.

CHAPTER 17 — GALS ON THE OPEN ROAD

THE NEXT MORNING, INSTEAD OF popping out of bed to greet the morning, Jenny was groggy and grumpy. She hadn't been able to go back to sleep after that call with Luke. It was way past the boys' usual breakfast time, so Buddy and Bear took matters into their own paws, climbed up to loft, loomed over her like two big turkey vultures, and just stared at her. Jenny groaned and tried to ignore them, but between the dog breath and Bear planting a paw on her shoulder and leaning in to check her vitals, there was not a chance. Reluctantly, Jenny rolled out of bed. Opening the blinds, she turned on the phone and saw two voicemails from Luke. She just didn't want to hear any more excuses or apologies. Jenny hit delete.

After airing and feeding the boys, the coffee finally brewed, and Jenny raised the mug to her lips for that life-affirming first sip when the phone jangled shrilly. Startled, Jenny spilled hot coffee on her fingers and dabbed it with a paper towel. She looked at the caller I.D. Charlotte. "Hello?" Jenny croaked cautiously, sounding like a pack-a-day smoker.

"Good morning! How are you on this fine day?" Charlotte burbled.

Jenny groaned. "Can you dial back the cheerfulness? I didn't sleep well."

"Sure. Better?" She now sounded like a merry librarian.

"Better." Jenny finally got a good long swallow of smoky coffee. She might live. "What's up?'

"All sorts of things. I've been kissing babies and eating rubber chicken on the campaign trail. And, oh, oh, oh! I got my first paying client. So exciting!" Charlotte chirped. "Can I come see you tonight? I can stay in the Belle, and we can catch up."

"Sure." Charlotte would distract her from her man troubles.

"Ta-ta for now. I'll be there by five o'clock, and I'm bringing wine and pizza."

"Good." Jenny hung up and stretched.

Settling into her favorite spot on the couch, she raised the mug to her lips again for that so important second sip when a text tone dinged loudly. Again with the dribbling. Jenny steadied herself and got another good swallow down before she checked the text.

The text was from Alice and read:

Baby is coming along. All good here. Hope the same for you. How is my brother behaving?

Jenny leaned her head back and closed her eyes. She just did not want to get into that topic this morning. She tapped out, *Busy!* and added emojis of dogs' footprints, a duck, a bluebird, and a powerboat whizzing along the water. Maybe Alice would be distracted by the emojis and not catch the subtext. She hit send.

After a quick shower, Jenny checked emails and social media. A few more people had made reservations, filling the last remaining open spots in the summer. Halleluiah! Today was Saturday, so The Reeds, The Lewises, and the sisters from Virginia would all be checking out. After they checked out, Jenny had a mountain of laundry and four cabins to clean before the next full house of renters arrived.

Jenny idly glanced out the window and gaped. She had staff, and she didn't even know it. Landis slapped Walter Lewis on the back and turned to exchange contact info on his phone with the Reeds. Coy looked positively jaunty as he helped load the Lewises' grandsons' duffels into the car and put the Virginia girls' luggage in their car. Claire and Neecy were heading towards Jenny's cabin, chatting and chuckling as they walked with guests who were packing up. Pausing, Claire embraced Margie and Dorothy and Neecy followed suit. The house party was over for the time being, but based on the friendliness of the goodbyes, Jenny guessed some of her guests had become fast friends over the week.

A knock sounded and Jenny swung open the door to see Claire and Neecy carrying buckets, mops, and cleaning products they must have gotten from the shed. "Cleaning crew reporting for duty," Claire said. She and Neecy saluted and then broke into giggles.

After telling them that she couldn't possibly impose on them to help, and them telling her equally stubbornly that they were indeed going to help clean, Jenny assigned the two of them two cabins. By the time she'd finished tidying the Hydrangea, Neecy was adding a final polish to the Magnolia and Mama had peeled off yellow rubber gloves and closed the door of the Camelia. They all pitched in and cleaned the Azalea in record time.

While the three were at the laundry shed putting away vacuums and cleaning supplies, Jenny turned to Mama and Neecy. "I can't thank you two enough. Neecy, I don't know how you got roped into this, but I appreciate it."

Neecy shrugged good-naturedly. "I like staying busy and your mama said your back went out on you this week." She put both hands at the base of her back. "That happens to me every so often, and it makes me just want to curl up in a ball and make the world go away."

"Exactly." Compound that with overtiredness and being disappointed by a man she thought she could count on but couldn't, making the world go away sounded appealing. But Jenny had work to do, checking in arriving guests, responding to inquiries, writing a breezy, upbeat summer newsletter, and taking the boat to the marina to get gas. Thankfully, Landis and Coy were riding shotgun.

Jenny was growing more confident with the boat, but was grateful the two men insisted on riding along when she took it out. Though the two tried to act casually and talked about how they *couldn't turn down an opportunity to get out on the water*, Jenny knew they were doing it to help her grow more confident as a boater. This past week, she'd taken guests out for two lake cruises and taken the Lewis boys tubing and had done pretty well. Knowing Landis and Coy were right there to help was so reassuring. Since Jenny had come to really care about Landis and grumpy Coy was morphing into helpful Coy, she never wanted them to leave.

Midmorning, Jenny finished the newsletter and tried to decide which photos to include in it. The most appealing shots were of the sunset cruises in the boat, mist around the cabins in the golden light of dawn, and the blue heron standing peacefully on the dock. Every time she had thoughts of Luke, she shooed them away and tried to concentrate harder on work. Mama appeared at the front window, smiled tentatively, and tapped on the glass with a fingernail. Jenny beckoned her in.

Mama slumped on the sofa, and pressed her fingers to her temples. "I've gotten some bad news..." she began.

Jenny tensed. What kind of bad news? Cancer? Early Alzheimer's? They'd lost all their money on bad investments? "Tell me, Mama."

Claire threw her hands up. "Landis just got a call from the builder at the Over 55 community where we're moving. It's been pouring in Asheville for weeks, and they are way behind schedule. We thought we'd be moved and out of your hair here by August 5 at the latest, but now it looks like it's going to be September 1 before they finish our house." In a quavering voice, she added, "If the rains continue, the completion date gets pushed out even further. It may be the end of September before we can move." Claire's face was red and it looked like she was fighting tears.

Jenny blew out the breath she'd been holding. "Good Lord, Mama. I thought you had tragic news. This is nothing." Jenny slid closer beside her on the sofa and put an arm around her shoulders. "I'm glad to have you stay longer."

Mama looked like she wanted to believe her but frowned. "You have reservations for August and September. We can't interfere with your business," she said. "Two months was overstaying our welcome, and now we're talking about month three."

Jenny thought quickly. "I'll offer the Silver Belle to guests who have booked your cabin, or the boys and I will move into the Belle and we'll rent them the Dogwood."

Claire looked doubtful and shook her head no. "We just can't continue to impose. We'll move into one of those executive stay places. There's one right off I-40 near Asheville that looks very nice."

"Stop, Mama. I've loved having you and Landis around, especially with Luke away. You've been good company and so helpful with everything. You need to stay."

Her mother opened her mouth to protest again when she paused, her eyes widening. "Didn't you and Charlotte have to cancel your camping trip because you had no backup?" Beaming, she pointed at herself. "Guess what? You've got backup."

"I couldn't ask you two to babysit the Resort," Jenny said.

"Why not? How long has it been since you had any time off?" Mama gave her a stern look. "You're overtired. You've been going nonstop since fall of last year. Your immune system is probably precarious and Dr. Oz says the immune system is the bedrock of your health." Claire nodded as if that was that.

Jenny started to argue with her and then stopped. Why? Why was she not accepting help that she needed and that was willingly given? Claire and Landis knew the ropes and would enjoy being backup innkeepers. Mama had a knack for engaging guests with her art and encouraging them to notice the beauty of Heron Lake. Landis was the friendly, avuncular senior statesman whose calm demeanor helped guests relax. The resort would be in the best hands. Mama was right. Jenny felt a spark of excitement. She needed to go on that trip.

"I'm going to take you up on your offer." Jenny opened her arms and hugged her mother.

Claire looked delighted. "Thank goodness. For once, I can help take care of you."

Jenny blinked looked at her. "What do you mean, Mama? You always took care of me."

Claire put her hands to her cheeks. "My biggest regret in life is not leaving Jax sooner, for your sake. I'm afraid I exposed you to…uncertainty and chaos."

Jenny could see the pain in her eyes. "Mama, you did the very best you could. Daddy did the best he could. You kept me safe in so many ways and were always there for me."

Claire drew a shuddering breath and gave a wan smile.

"I have so much love in my life; love from you and Landis, from Luke, and from my wonderful friends." Jenny circled a finger around the interior of the Dogwood. "Look at all the goodness and security I have in my life because of Daddy. I've landed on my feet and so have you." Smiling, she pointed out the front window at Landis who was on the dock helping a young father teach his son to cast a fishing rod. "So, can we stop with the regrets?"

Claire nodded slowly and broke into a relieved smile. "We can sure try."

Late that afternoon, Charlotte arrived in a flurry of horn toots, *yoo-hoos*, and high-pitched sugar talk for the boys. "Bear, you are a precious boy. Mr. Buddy, I could just sop you up with a biscuit. Hello, Levi my love, my sugar booger. Your Auntie Charlotte's finally here."

Smiling, Jenny helped her friend carry her floral duffel to the Belle, and the two settled in lakeside with a delicious thick crust pizza with tomato, spinach, artichoke, fresh basil, and extra cheese. Jenny watched as her new guests emerged from their cabins and began to get to know the property. The Olsons, a couple who looked to be in their early seventies, held hands as they walked to the dock. Two gangly teens checked out the cornhole board, and June Rogers, a newly divorced woman from Charlotte, examined the kayaks. Jenny had learned that guests typically did this exploring on their first day here. Everyone was doing fine.

After a quick catch up, Jenny gave Charlotte an inquisitive look. "So, missy, tell me about your new paying client. How did that all happen and what's the job going to be like?"

Eyes shining with excitement, Charlotte held up a finger as

she finished chewing her bite of pizza. "So, last time I was here, I was driving back to Celeste and I stopped at Gus's Gas-N-Git for a little something to eat. They make the best chili dogs." Charlotte took a sip of wine. "A woman was having trouble getting the gas cap off on her SUV, so I helped her. She saw the bolts of fabric in my back seat and asked me if I was an interior designer. I said yes, indeedy, I was. I saw her Heron Lake bumper sticker and casually mentioned that I'd done some work at the Lakeside Resort and she got all excited because she'd read the yuppie and the skunk story in the *Heron Lake Herald* and adored the pictures of the Silver Belle." Charlotte shook her head in at the coincidence. "She and her husband are both bankers from Charlotte. They just bought a house at the lake and are getting ready to retire here full time. So, I gave her my card, and the rest is history." She threw up her hands. "So, I'm going to start working on their house next month. I told her I'd give her alternatives to the strictly nautical designs that people fall back on at waterfront homes."

"I'm proud of you," Jenny said. "You'll do a fantastic job, and their friends and neighbors will ask for your contact info. You'll be in demand fast."

"I hope so." Charlotte held up crossed fingers and reached for another piece of pizza. "Give me your news. Everything going well here? Your mama and stepdaddy good? How's Luke?"

Jenny gave her the update, glossing over her frustration with Luke, but Charlotte's eyes narrowed.

"He's not acting right," she said darkly. "Maybe Ashe or Landis needs to have a little man-to-man talk with him."

Jenny snagged a third piece of crusty deliciousness. "Nah. Let's let him be. I don't want to force him to show up. Either he will or he won't."

Charlotte looked impressed, but slightly suspicious. "You're being so mature. I'd want to scream at him or buy a ticket to Melbourne so I could yell at him in person."

"I'm tired of thinking about it." And she was. Worries about Luke had taken up way too much thought space lately. Jenny turned to Charlotte. "Are you up for some fun?"

"Always." Charlotte rubbed her hands together. "So are we talking lunch out, supper out? A movie?"

"Better," Jenny promised. "Mama and Landis's construction got delayed, and they're insisting that I take time off and they babysit the resort. If you can come, we're leaving on Thursday for a ten-day all-girl adventure and shakedown camping trip in the magnificent, newly refurbished Silver Belle."

Charlotte whooped. "I am so in. So, where are we headed? We talked about seeing the lighthouses down on the coast or going to the mountains and visiting waterfalls. I'm up for either."

"Let's think." Jenny rested her feet on Levi, who conveniently happened to be napping in a location where she would have put a footstool had she had one. She scratched his back with her toes and thought about logistics and practicalities. "Let's do the waterfalls. It's our first trip hauling the Belle, and I'm guessing it would be a long trip across the state and all the way to the Outer Banks."

Charlotte whipped out her phone and fiddled with it. "My mapping program says seven-and-a-half hours by car, so we'd be looking at eight to nine hours towing the camper." She blew out a sigh. "This whole towing a trailer business makes me nervous. Maybe we should just creep down the highway like one of those Student Drivers." Charlotte giggled nervously.

"We'll keep the blinkers going the whole time," Jenny teased, but she was nervous about it, too. "It's going to take some getting used to, but we can do it." She tried to remember what she'd learned during her only experience towing the Silver Belle from Shady Grove to Heron Lake. "The mountains are going to be a challenge. We'll need to know how to tow up hills and down. What if the campsite's on a hill? We need to not roll away while we sleep."

Charlotte agreed. "Can you generally plan the itinerary and then hand it off to me to nail down the details? I'll find us out-of-this-world vistas, waterfalls, and campsites, and make reservations. We can both work on a list of food and supplies to take and research instructions for towing and camping with

Airstreams. We'll watch a lot of YouTube and take notes between now and then. We'll get the hang of it."

"We will." Jenny was starting to feel a buzz of anticipation at the prospect of ten days on the road with no responsibilities.

"Good," Charlotte was quiet for a moment and then broke into a peal of happy laughter. "We are going on a grand adventure. I'm so excited!"

Two days later, Jenny and Charlotte secured the Airstream to the ball hitch on the truck. The woman in the tutorial they'd watched got her rig hitched in five minutes, but it took them a half-hour to be confident they'd gotten it right.

"All chains secured. Signals working." Jenny eyed the backside of the trailer, reminding herself to take the wheel chocks with them to prevent rolling.

"Check the right blinker one more time," Charlotte hollered from the open window of the driver's seat.

Jenny made sure her friend could see her in the side mirror and gave a big thumbs-up.

The two packed their provisions in the camper, double checking for essentials like sunscreen, wine, bug spray, summer sausage, and lots of bacon in case they decided to go low-carb, chips and Cheetos in case they didn't, dental floss, their own pillows, drinking water, a bundle of seasoned oak, and five fake logs to encourage the fire on rainy days.

"Remember, the fellow in the Good Sam video said to put 10 to 20 percent of the weight in the front of the Belle and evenly distribute the rest so the tongue didn't have too much or too little weight. Are we doing that?" Charlotte asked.

"I think so." Jenny pinched her lip and glanced around. "Hopefully, the Belle won't fly off the hitch or go scraping down the interstate, throwing sparks."

Charlotte gave an exaggerated shudder. "Let's hope not."

Jenny loaded the last of the groceries into the tiny refrigerator. Luke had put in as big a fridge as he could, given the size of the tiny kitchen, but it was still small. They'd need to stop to restock groceries along the way.

Mama and Landis poked their heads in the open door. "You two doing OK? Need any help?" Landis asked.

"I think we're good." Jenny looked at them, remembering two things she'd forgotten to tell them. "On the Fourth of July, remember to keep the boys inside with the white noise machine running and the TV on loud so they don't get spooked by the fireworks." She gazed at Landis. "Ella and Paul say the lake gets really busy on holiday weekends, so maybe you can do the boat rides and tubing earlier in the day."

He nodded. "Got it, boss."

What if they needed help fast? "If we break down or have problems with accidentally rolling away or have problems with..." Jenny hesitated, having temporarily run out of possible disasters.

"...with wolves," Charlotte added helpfully.

Jenny just looked at her and then back and Mama and Landis. "Will you come get us?"

"Immediately." Mama had a flinty look in her eyes.

"You have all the AAA Carolinas and Good Sam info and numbers?" Landis asked.

"We do." Jenny reached over to the seat to tap a packet of information and emergency numbers that Landis had put together for them. Add that to the file folder of info Ashe had researched for them, and they had their bases covered.

Mama's eyes filled with tears, and she brushed them away with her fingertips as she stepped into the Belle to envelop them both in hugs. "We love you both and hope you have the trip of a lifetime." Landis joined her inside and put an arm around all of them. The four of them stood bunched up like that for a long moment, feeling the love.

CHAPTER 18 — EVERY PICTURE TELLS A STORY

A T FIVE-THIRTY THE NEXT MORNING, Jenny slipped on the clothes she'd laid out the night before, grabbed a cup of coffee, and looked around for a moment, silently saying goodbye to her beloved cabin. Though beyond excited about the trip, Jenny would miss everything in her little world: the boys, the cabin, the lake, and Mama and Landis. But still, her step was light as she walked next door to the Belle. She and Charlotte were off on a grand adventure.

In the truck, Jenny suddenly felt nervous about driving and about the whole trip. Wiping her clammy hands on her shorts, she pulled on the seatbelt.

Charlotte cocked her head. "You sure you don't want me to start off behind the wheel?"

"I'm good," Jenny lied. She wanted to get underway before her bravery wore off. Starting the engine, she again felt intimidated as she looked at the dazzling array of gauges and instruments on the dashboard of Luke's truck. She and Charlotte had taken the truck for several spins with and without the Belle, and she was fairly comfortable driving it, but they were on their way to the steep grades and curvy bends of mountain roads.

Jenny reminded herself of how much they'd practiced. She and Charlotte had found a large empty parking lot at a trucking company and driven around, getting the feel of the rig. They'd accelerated, done gradual breaking, turned, backed, and parked.

They kept reminding each other to use their cameras and mirrors, something the friendly instructional fellow had really emphasized.

"You can do this, girl." Her friend sent her an encouraging look.

"I can." Jenny gave a wan smile as she shifted into drive. "You double-checked our reservations, right?"

"I did," Charlotte assured her. "We're staying at highly-rated campgrounds with super views. I ran them by all the new friends I've made on the RV forums, and they said you'd picked well. You are looking at a proud member of both the *Carolina Campers* and the *Cardinal Campers*." She held up her phone, smiling proudly. "If we have any problems with the Belle, all I have to do is give them a ring. What nice folks," she said, shaking her head at her good fortune. "We have friends everywhere. We got invited to a potluck supper, a craft show, a prayer group, and a salsa dancing class. They even have AA meetings," Charlotte said happily.

Jenny nodded, only slightly reassured about their new friends. She pictured jackknifing, careening off a steep mountain road, getting stuck up to the axles in mud, and unknowingly dragging a gas station overhang behind them down the interstate. She felt herself start to perspire and sent a quick prayer up to God or Jax or whoever was available, asking for help in her not wrecking them once they got underway.

As she carefully stepped on the gas, the engine in the big truck responded immediately. Jenny tried telling herself that this was no different than driving her SUV. But her car was the size of a pinto bean compared to Luke's truck, and her car didn't have a twenty-foot, thirty-seven-hundred-pound hitchhiker tagging on the back of it. Wide turns to avoid clipping stop signs, lampposts, and other cars, she reminded herself. Brake early and gently. Rapid fire, she did a mental rerun of all the instructional videos she'd watched on how to pull the travel trailer.

Charlotte stretched languorously and slipped on sunglasses. "Ah, the highway calls and the journey begins," she trilled.

Technically, they were still only a mile and a half from Heron Lake, and if Jenny kept driving this slowly, they'd reach the first waterfall by autumn. Tentatively, she pressed more firmly on the gas pedal. Responsive, the truck now whooshed along the road out of town. Jenny was getting used to the feel of towing, but her anxiety amped up again as they merged onto I-40, which was already busy with truck traffic, RVs, and SUVs with roof cargo bags on top. She gripped the steering wheel tightly and obsessively peered at the mirrors and cameras to make sure she hadn't accidentally flung off the Belle at curves in the road. Twenty minutes later, Jenny's breathing slowed, and she started to relax. "This isn't so hard," she said, but kept her eyes drilled on the road in front of her.

"You're driving well." Charlotte sipped coffee from her steel cup.

"Thanks," Jenny said, concentrating. A minivan that was tailgating them passed them with a roar. She shot a glare at the speedy driver who passed them, but it was a little white-haired lady with a *Born to Quilt!* bumper sticker on her car. Jenny glanced at her speedometer. Sheesh. She was going fifty in a seventy-mile zone. Sheepishly, she hit the gas. But she was getting the hang of it. Jenny started to breathe more normally. "Let's take some not too strenuous hikes, pack lunches and picnic by the waterfalls. I planned free time, too, and if we ever want to chuck the schedule and just go with the flow, I say yes."

"I do, too." Charlotte tapped her itinerary with a finger. "OK, so here's our plan. Our first waterfall is Carolina Glade, which has got 4.8 stars from visitors. On to the town of Crest Mountain, which has cool art galleries and crafts stores. We hit Swannanoa Valley Museum & History Center, which Mama said was so interesting. We mosey south to Panther Falls near Lake Lure. We slide south to Grayson, which is supposed to be charming and has restaurants the foodies love."

"Let's eat wonderful food this trip. We don't have many restaurants near the lake, and I miss good food." Jenny said wistfully.

"I agree." Charlotte traced her finger on the map. "At Flat Rock, we visit the Carl Sandburg house, pat his precious goats, and attend a play at the Flat Rock Playhouse. Oh, they're doing

South Pacific, which is so romantic." She sighed. "We hit Sunray Falls, which is supposed to be fab and just a short distance from the road. That's a plus because of my delicate ankles."

Jenny had never heard a word about Charlotte's ankles being delicate, but she just nodded gravely and adjusted the sun visor.

"We head west toward Dupont State Forest, stopping on the way to see Rushing Water Falls. Then we visit Honeymoon Falls. I just love that name. After that, Summers Day Falls, which is supposed to be extra beauteous and has a plunge pool. That will involve a bathing suit, which I have mixed feelings about," Charlotte said primly. "But I may change my mind when we get there. Then, Sliding Rock Falls, where you can slide, I presume." She looked over at Jenny and smiled. "I like the names of these other waterfalls, too. Laughing Falls, Yellowstone Falls, and Skinny Dip Falls. That last one will never happen, by the way."

Jenny smiled. "Gotcha."

"We start easing north again, weaving our way toward Asheville, and stop there for the day. I love that town. So scenic, with a stellar music and arts scene, plus fab food galore. We need to swing by the River Arts District, where you can tour galleries and studios of all sorts of artists — glassblowers, painters, potters, and the whole enchilada. There are oodles of wineries and breweries we may want to stop and visit along the way. If we have time and aren't waterfalled out, we head up to Pisgah National Forest and visit some of those falls. And then we head back to Heron Lake." She patted Jenny's knee. "You did an excellent job planning this."

"Thanks. I tried to..." But she was interrupted by the trill of her phone. She quickly glanced at the clock. Six-thirty. It had to be Luke. She'd dodged his calls for the last two days. Jenny looked at Charlotte. "That's Luke. Can you get it?"

Charlotte pursed her lips. "I'd be happy to." She picked up and said crisply, "Good morning. This is Jenny's assistant, Charlotte."

Jenny could hear Luke's baritone through the line and grinned, glad he'd be puzzled by reaching Charlotte and not her.

"Oh, I'm so sorry. She's driving and couldn't possibly speak with you now."

Jenny cracked a smile. Charlotte had suddenly developed a British accent.

"Yes, we are in your truck, towing the Belle, and we're off on a grand getaway. We'll have free time, not a care in the world, and we'll meet lots of super people." Charlotte gave her an exaggerated wink.

Yup. She sounded like Claire Foy in *The Crown*. Jenny smirked and shook her head.

"Surely, I'll tell her you called. Yes, I'll can certainly ask her to call, but no promises. We'll be very, very, very busy," Charlotte sounded regretful, but as she ended the call, her eyes glittered and she did a fist bump. "Yes. We'll take your *busy* and raise it to *very, very, very* busy. Hah!"

Before their last call when Luke left her hanging on the line, Jenny would have been bothered by what Charlotte said to him, but now she just didn't care. He deserved a dose of his own medicine. She gave her friend an approving nod. "Sounding very posh this morning, girl."

Charlotte shrugged modestly. "I try."

Their first waterfall was *a mega-hit*, according to Charlotte. Crest Mountain was charming, and they navigated through the small town without any problems. On a few turns, Charlotte hung almost halfway out of the window to double-check the passage of the Belle, but still, they'd deemed that side-trip a success. Charlotte found a few unusual pieces of blue and green pottery and purchased them even though they weren't on the discount table, and Jenny bought a pretty-sounding wind chime that was made of old silver spoons, forks, and knives.

They found their campground for the next two nights, a small family-owned place with big sky views. Jenny pulled into their campsite without taking out any neighbors' RVs or lampposts. After a hair-raising hard list to the left that had them skittering and grasping at the countertop, they'd figured out how to level the travel trailer. They'd hooked up the power with Charlotte reading aloud the instructions from her phone, but they'd been successful.

For supper, they cooked turkey burgers over an open fire and roasted s'mores afterward. Charlotte cooked a few extra, declaring they *paired divinely* with wine, and insisted they take their drinks and sticky snacks to a nearby bluff with a clear view of miles and miles of mountains.

Jenny finished her s'more and tried in vain to get the sticky marshmallow off her fingers. with a paper towel. "How are things with Ashe? How's the campaign?"

"It's going well." Charlotte sighed happily. "This whole business of getting nominated by peers, people who know him and respect him, has done a lot for his self-confidence."

"Falling in love with you has done a lot for his self-confidence," Jenny pointed out.

Charlotte smiled. "When men know that they've got a woman who loves them, it perks them up. Ashe is funnier, sillier, and more assertive than when I first met him," she mused and then yawned. "Remind me again why you're mad at Luke. I know he's been too caught up in work and has not been attentive."

"He has a long history of being a workaholic. He said he let it ruin his first marriage and vowed he'd never act that way again, but I think he's slipping back into it." Jenny tilted her head back and studied an extra bright star, wondering idly if it was the North Star.

"He's not been very aware about how scary and hard it's been for you to get the resort up and running," Charlotte observed, and tried dunking her s'more in her wine. It must have been tasty because she took a bite and did it again.

"That is so true," Jenny said, surprised at her own vehemence. "All this business stuff is old news for him, but it's been very scary for me. I don't like not knowing what I'm doing."

Charlotte leaned back on an elbow. "You know, the problem with you is that you never look like you're struggling. You have this calm demeanor, and if someone asks you how you are, you always say *fine*, even if your hair is on fire."

Jenny gave a rueful laugh. "Lots of practice with that. Our house was chaotic growing up, so I got good at looking calm."

Charlotte nodded. "You used to fool me from time to time, but you know how savvy I am." She tapped her forefinger to the side of her nose.

Jenny just smiled.

But Charlotte looked reflective. "Think about it, though. Luke gets dropped in a foreign country with a huge and complicated task. He's worried about the success of the company and all its employees. He's lonesome, and he's working like a son of a gun. It sounds like he's trying his hardest to get home to you."

Jenny mulled it over and nodded miserably. "All true."

"And Luke is a decent, kind man who seems to love you. You don't want to throw that away, do you?" Charlotte's voice was kind.

Jenny thought about it. Jax had taught her to expect men to let her down, but Luke wasn't like that. He was making mistakes, but she couldn't push him away because he wasn't perfect. Jenny was far from perfect. Luke's being distracted and inattentive made her feel unloved, though, and that would have to be fixed. "I don't want to give up on him."

Charlotte leaned all the way back in the grass and put both hands behind her head. "Then, fix it, girl. You may need to wrestle with him on the work issue, but you can help him with that."

"Hmmm." Jenny thought about Mama's advice about not allowing men get away with letting work take priority over love. She turned to Charlotte. "I'll fix it, but I don't want to make it too easy on Luke, or he'll never take me seriously. I'll do it my own way and in my own time."

"Works for me," Charlotte said, sounding drowsy.

The sky was black velvet with the pinpricks of yellow stars. The quarter moon hung low in the sky, and the only sound she could hear was the rustling of the breeze and the high-pitched sound of tree crickets. It was a quietly glorious night, and Jenny was relieved about her decision.

They both kept yawning, and headed back inside.

As she sat on her couch slash bed, Jenny was toeing off her sneakers when she heard a muffled voice calling, "Hello? Hello-oh?" Snatching the phone from her back pocket, she stared at it, dismayed when she saw the caller ID. She'd accidentally dialed Luke with her rear end.

Charlotte walked by slathering cold cream on her face and humming.

Jenny held the phone to her chest and hissed, "I called Luke by mistake!"

Charlotte just rolled her eyes. "Well, talk to him, silly."

"Uh, hey, Luke," she said gracelessly.

"Everything OK?" he said tersely.

"Oh, it's fine. I accidentally dialed you with my rear end."

He chuckled. "Well, it's still good to hear your voice. I'm headed into a meeting that I'm leading. Can I call you back later?"

"Last time we talked, you left me on the line for ten minutes," Jenny said evenly, trying to tamp down the irritation that she felt just thinking about that.

"I'm so sorry. Please forgive me. The negotiations are heating up, so I'm working late and not sleeping much. Zander wants to be involved in every little detail even though he delegated this to me, and he's 10,000 miles away." He blew out a sigh of frustration. "I've got to go, but can we please talk again soon? Maybe in the morning your time?"

"I don't want to talk to you just yet," she said stubbornly.

"How about we try sending pictures again? I liked that," Luke said with quiet intensity.

"You never sent me any pictures, though. I sent pictures but you didn't bother to reciprocate," she reminded him.

"Please. I'll send some tonight, and I'll hold up my end of the deal this time," he said imploringly.

"We'll see. Good night," Jenny murmured and ended the call. Throwing herself on the bed dramatically, she scrubbed her face with her hands, but she was smiling.

A foaming toothbrush in her mouth, Charlotte put a hand on her hip and looked at her. "Yes?"

"I wasn't ready to talk yet. We're sending each other pictures instead."

"Odd, but nice. I like it," Charlotte mumbled. She swished out her toothpaste and dried her mouth with a towel. "And good for you for making the overture, even if it was an accidental butt call."

When she was lying in bed waiting for sleep to come, Jenny felt lighter than she had in days. If Luke held up his end of the deal and sent her pictures, her mind whirled with what pictures she wanted to take and send him. Surely shots of the waterfalls, her and Charlotte sitting around the campfire, the Silver Belle looking spruce in its slot in the campground. For the first time since Luke had left, communicating with him might even be fun.

The next morning, Jenny felt a fluttery excitement as she checked her texts. Luke had sent her pictures of the Spartan hotel room where he'd been staying for the duration of the trip. His room looked bland and far from homey. The building that headquartered the company he was working with was a typical chrome and glass skyscraper in the business district. Neither suited warm, real, country, quirky Luke. Charlotte was right. He was far from his element and had to be yearning for home. Jenny started to feel guilty and made herself stop. She even waited a day before she sent him photos. Let Luke see what is was like to twist in the wind for a while.

Jenny and Charlotte enjoyed learning the history of the valley at the Swannanoa Museum, located in a 1921 firehouse designed by the lead architect of the Biltmore House. Panther Falls were high and dramatic. Jenny took a few selfies of her and Charlotte with their feet in the water. They explored picturesque Lake Lure, known for its role in the movie *Dirty Dancing*. Outside Baby's Bungalow, one of the *Dirty Dancing*-themed cabins, Charlotte took a picture of Jenny striking a hip slung, arms-wide version of what she guessed might be a dramatic dancing pose. Cheesy but funny, Jenny decided. Luke would like it.

Every night before bed, Jenny picked three of the photos that best characterized the day and sent them to Luke. Jenny sent a picture Charlotte had taken of her sitting at the campfire and added a little heart emoji.

Jenny and Charlotte got into a comfortable traveling routine. They stopped when they wanted to, took detours if an attraction caught their eye, and played hooky some days, just going on a spontaneous hike or lounging outside in lawn chairs under the striped awning of the Belle, drinking coffee and reading, ignoring their plans for the day.

Mama sent texts with pictures: Landis and Coy waving as they drove by in the boat towing girls on a knee board, Landis looking proud as he held a white platter of brilliant red tomatoes from the garden, Mama sitting at the easel with Bear, Buddy, and Levi sitting around her like art groupies. After showing them to Charlotte, she sent them on to Luke. He could use a dose of home.

One evening, the two of them sat on a bench overlooking the valley, watching the glittering stars come out. "Looks like you could just reach up and touch them," Charlotte said dreamily, and took a sip from her paper cup of pinot grigio.

Jenny just nodded, almost hypnotized by the moonlight. She swirled her own wine around. She was as relaxed as she'd been in a long time, but had a niggling worry. Jenny turned to Charlotte. "In this morning's pictures from Luke were a few shots of him and some of his teammates from work. He'd mentioned Will a few times, who is the chief liaison from the other company. I'd pictured Will as a big hipster-looking engineer with a bushy beard." Jenny scowled. "Will is a short for Wilhelmina, and she's a knockout. What is it with these women with men's names?" she grumped, thinking about her old fiancé Douglas's new wife, Aiden.

"OK." Charlotte shrugged. "So he has a pretty co-worker."

But Jenny remembered Ember's practically throwing herself at him and his delayed response. She took a healthy swallow of wine. "Luke worries me. He can be so naïve about women."

Charlotte cocked her head. "He strikes me as a faithful as a good dog."

"I know. I need to work on trusting him." But Jenny pictured Will claiming she had car trouble and needing a ride home, or stopping by his hotel room with work that *had* to be hand delivered or…Her stomach got so balled up she could hardly breathe. Jenny touched her thumb to her forefinger. "I need to let it go. Zen living, here I come."

"That's the spirit." Charlotte refilled Jenny's wine cup with a bottle she'd stuffed in her oversized purse.

"Can you tell me which of those meditation apps you've been using? Maybe I'll give one of them a whirl." Jenny was doubtful, though.

"Sure. They calm me down," Charlotte said.

"I don't want to get too calm, though," Jenny said wryly. "Being revved up is part of my charm."

"So true." Charlotte gave her a reassuring pat on the back, and the two went back to their stargazing.

Later, the lights were out and Jenny was drowsing, almost asleep.

Charlotte's voice floated over to her from the bed on the other side of the trailer. "I was thinking about falls at Summers Day and Sliding Rock. We should do it."

"OK," Jenny said sleepily but woke up enough to be confused. "Do what?"

"Swim. Get our swimsuits on and do the plunge pool and the rock sliding board and loll around in the water."

Jenny groaned. "My legs and arms are white as rice, and I still have my winter weight." Her thighs reminded her of rice pudding.

Charlotte snorted. "I keep my winter weight. Remember our Fabulous You mantra. 'We are lovely just the way we are. We are not in our twenties and we shouldn't expect ourselves to look like out twenty-year-old selves, especially in bathing suits.'"

"True." Jenny plumped her pillow and laid her head back down. "And no one will know us."

"Not a soul," Charlotte agreed.

"You know, I don't want to be one of those women who doesn't want to swim because she doesn't think she looks good enough in a suit or is worried about getting her hair wet. This whole trip is supposed to be a just *say yes* kind of deal, right?" Jenny mused aloud.

"Yes, ma'am."

"OK. We swim tomorrow at the plunge pool, and we'll slide at that rock."

"Goody," Charlotte said and soon began a gentle, ladylike snore.

CHAPTER 19 — HOME AT LAST

T HE NEXT MORNING, JENNY WOKE at five and spent a half-hour breathing rhythmically, listening to her dreamy-voiced meditation gal and allowing her thoughts to *drift in and drift out.*

Afterward, Jenny quietly pulled on her sneakers and tiptoed past Charlotte, who snored like a quietly purring cat. Locking the door behind her, Jenny made her way to the walking path around the campground that ran along the ridge and offered views of blue peaks and verdant green valleys. Walking briskly, Jenny drew in deep breaths of the good, clean air. She was going to let go of all this worry about Luke. She rubbed her forehead. So much room for misinterpretation when you couldn't talk with someone in person. Long-distance relationships were for the birds.

When she got back to their campsite, Charlotte was outside frying bacon on an electric skillet. Jenny sniffed. "Someone should make a perfume that smells like that."

"Men and dogs would just follow you around," Charlotte said. "There's fresh coffee brewing inside."

While she poured a mug, Jenny's text tone sounded. Glancing at it, she smiled. Alice. Her friend wrote:

How is the all-gal adventure travel trip going? We miss you. Tell me y'all's ETA for coming home. Bringing a belated housewarming surprise gift, a must-have for the resort. Sending buckets of love.

Knowing Alice, the gift could range from the practical to the crazy. Jenny grinned and let herself imagine what a *must-have* would be in her friend's mind. Maybe a Little Free Library inside an old British phone booth? Possibly an extravagant tree house or an over-water zip line? Jenny shuddered inwardly, recalling an offhand comment Alice had made about it being easy to set up an axe-throwing target. Maybe that was her housewarming gift. Who knew with Alice?

Grinning, Jenny tapped out a response:

Having fab time. Home one or two on Saturday. Hugs to you, your hubby, and the little bean. XOXO

At Summers Day Falls, the two carefully picked their way down the rock-strewn path, grateful for the support of their sports sandals. They wore bathing suits under their shorts and tees. Jenny carried a small tote containing towels, sunscreen, hats, and cold drinks. The backpack cooler slung over Charlotte's shoulders contained delicious-looking boxed lunches they'd picked up that morning at a bakery called Baby Cakes.

Jenny smiled as she heard the rushing water and smelled the fresh, clean scent of water and ozone. When they came into the clearing at the plunge pool, she sighed at the now-familiar sight of rainbow prisms of light around the rushing falls. Several families were already swimming. Three women sat on a large, partially submerged rock and chatted happily.

Charlotte gave her a mischievous grin and said quietly, "No one here looks like they hit the gym four times a week."

Jenny broke into a smile. "They look like normal everyday people, just like us."

The day was clear and sunny and the sky a crystal-clear blue. The two shrugged out of their clothes and gasped and laughed as they eased in the cold pool of water. After paddling around for a while, they propped up on the side of a rock ledge and let the waterfall rush over their heads and shoulders. Sunning themselves on a boulder, they dangled their feet in the water. When they got hungry, they found a picnic table that was positioned so close to the waterfall that cool mist drifted over them. The two munched on rare roast beef sandwiches on freshly made sourdough bread, pecan pound cake, and chunks of fresh, sweet cantaloupe. "I'm going to start swimming more when I get home," Jenny announced.

"Absolutely." Charlotte popped a chuck of juicy melon in her mouth. "I see more picnics in our future, too."

Their next home-away-from-home was outside of Asheville in a large but highly-rated campground. They parked and hopped out to register at the office, which was in a general store. Golf carts whizzed by. A sleek motor home pulled out as another rolled in. A family rode by on bicycles. A young couple with a baby were erecting a pop-up camper. Several men practiced their short games on a putting green.

After finishing their paperwork, the two of them poured themselves cups of complimentary coffee and poked around. Jenny thought about how quickly their vacation was passing. She turned to Charlotte. "Let's grab more gusto on the rest of this trip. Let's rent bikes, swim at the pool, and laze in the sun. Let's rent a golf cart so we can tool around and check out the campground."

Charlotte's face lit up. "Let's do."

After they got the Silver Belle situated, they rented a snappy red golf cart with LED lights woven into the top *for night driving and bling,* the manager told them with a smile. They glided around the grounds, circling a pond and cruising on a mountain-view path. They got friendly waves and smiles from other campers, passed couples walking their dogs, and admired other RVs. Jenny elbowed Charlotte, pointing at golf carts with custom bodies made to look like a Bentley, a Batmobile, and a vintage turquoise Bel Air with fins.

They stopped back by the office for a pit stop and when Jenny came of the ladies room, Charlotte was standing in front of a calendar of events posted on the wall and talking with a white-haired man about the best sights to see in the area. Jenny sidled up beside her and studied the jam-packed calendar. Next weekend was for bluegrass fans, the following for shag dancers, and next month featured a gospel-singing weekend.

Charlotte peered over at her. "You can't be bored here, can you?"

The fellow chimed in. "Y'all should have seen the Fourth of July extravaganza. Everybody dressed up and decorated their rigs, and we had a patriotic parade with the golf carts. The fireworks were top-notch."

Jenny nodded. "That sounds like fun."

"It was." The fellow gestured toward the calendar. "Did y'all see we're having a square dance tonight? Some of our campers are big dancers. They've got the music and can call, too. You should come." He bobbed his head enthusiastically.

"I'm afraid we can't..." Jenny began, edging away. She didn't know these people. She was a dangerous dancer who had once fallen doing a line dance to *Achy Breaky Heart* and created a domino effect of downed dancers.

Charlotte jumped in, blasting the fellow with her smile. "Of course, we'll be there."

As they glided back to the campsite with Charlotte at the wheel, Jenny glared at her. "Why did you say we'd do that? Remember that little...kerfuffle last time I danced? There could be a warrant out for my arrest." She pulled out her trump card. "Plus, we don't have anything to wear."

"I thought we were staying open to new experiences on this trip." Charlotte gave her a beseeching look. "Come on, Jenny. Let's go. If we hate it, we'll leave, but we need to stay at least an hour." Casually, she added, "Plus, I read about the square dance ahead of time and brought real authentic dresses for us online, the ones with poofy skirts."

Jenny sighed, knowing how futile it was resist Charlotte when she got an idea in her head. But she thought about it. She was the one who'd been talking about grabbing gusto just two hours ago. Grudgingly, Jenny started to smile. "OK, but I'm doing this just because I want to see what we look like in those outfits."

That evening, Jenny glanced in the dresser mirror, disbelieving. She looked like a real-life square dancer. Her coral red skirt had scalloped ruffling and was supported by layers of crinoline that belled out gracefully and made a swishing sound when she moved. Her red-and-white calico blouse had a V-neck, more ruffles, and peasant sleeves. She glanced over at Charlotte, who looked just as authentic in her square dancing dress, a print with bright lemons floating on blue-and-white stripes. "You outdid yourself. These outfits are very cool."

"Thanks." Charlotte gave her skirt an experimental flirty flip back and forth.

Jenny frowned. "Problem is, now we look like we know what we're doing on the dance floor. I'm not sure watching those YouTube videos is going to help us when the music starts."

"Come on. We'll wing it, and we'll have a ball." She handed Jenny her phone. "Will you take a picture of me so I can send it to Ashe and show him what he's missing?"

Jenny obliged. After Charlotte took one of her, they were off to the dance, rustling as they walked to the golf cart.

Forty-five minutes later, the five-piece band was playing crowd favorites like *Cotton-Eyed Joe* and the fellow in the Stetson hat was calling out prompts. Jenny was laughing at her missteps while being swung round and round by a grinning, sure-footed man with a white beard and a big belly. "You're getting it, girl," he said encouragingly and delivered her to her next partner.

Through the *Orange Blossom Special*, *Pistol Packin' Mama*, and *Red River Valley*, the other dancers were friendly and forgiving. Jenny stopped worrying about being a clumsy rookie. Her dancing improved when she stopped watching her feet and trying to count the beats. Starting to get the hang of the allemande left and right and facing the sides, Jenny found she was out of breath, grinning, and having a blast. She spied Charlotte in another square, and she seemed to be enjoying herself, too, laughing as she moved her skirt with her hands from side to side during a do-si-do.

Back home, Jenny yawned as she hung up her dancing clothes. "So fun," she said, pausing to chug a bottle of cold water. "I don't know how I let you talk me into that, but it was so much fun."

"I told you so." Charlotte pulled on pajamas. Pausing to tap out a text on her phone, she crawled into her bed and called out sleepily, "Good night, Jen."

Jenny's text tone dinged, and she reached for the phone, her heart beating faster. Text messages at night might mean terrible news. But when she saw the message was from Luke, her heart beat staccato. They hadn't been writing each other or even captioning the pictures they exchanged. This was different. She sat up straight and read it.

Good night, twirling girl. From pics and video clips, looks like you had a ball. Tell that tall, good-lookin' rancher dude that you're spoken for. I miss you. Luke

She hadn't sent Luke any pictures yet but recalled Charlotte taking a few shots of her at the dance. Jenny peered over at her friend, who was burrowed down in her blankets, just a tip of black curl on her pillow. "Charlotte, did you send Luke anything?"

"I may have," she said in a muffled tone.

"Clips of me dancing with a good-looking man?" Jenny hardly remembered the guy because she'd been concentrating on doing the next dance move right. Plus, she'd just tripped the thin man in overalls, but he'd bounced right back up and resumed his Allemande Left.

"Possibly."

Jenny sank onto her bed. "You're friends with Luke? You text and email him?"

"Of course, silly." Charlotte popped her head up, a pretty, tousled-haired prairie dog trying hard to look innocent. "Any friend of yours is a friend of mine."

"Mother of pearl." Jenny rubbed her forehead.

Charlotte gave an open-mouthed yawn, complete with an exaggerated two hands above the head stretch. She turned over and closed her eyes. "Good night, flower. Sleep tight."

"Night." Turning off the light, Jenny lay with her eyes wide open. Grabbing her phone, Jenny reread each word of Luke's text and couldn't help but smile. He was a little jealous and she was *spoken for*. How lovely.

As she cracked eggs in a bowl the next morning, Jenny found herself humming what she thought might be *King of the Road*, one of the songs from last night that had really gotten the crowd going. Charlotte was singing in the shower as Jenny went outside, put turkey sausage on the griddle ,and just stood there for a moment, admiring the softly lit morning.

Camping made her feel like a lighter, younger, more carefree version of herself. Back inside, she inhaled deliciousness and peeked in the oven to check on the nicely browning blackberry muffins she'd whipped up, and looked over the scrambled eggs in the pan.

Her thoughts turned to Luke and his nice but somewhat cryptic note. She wanted to call and ask him twenty questions about work, Will, and was he still in love with her, was she really spoken for, and what exactly did that mean. Instead, she picked up her phone, found the shot she'd taken yesterday morning of her and Charlotte wearing rumpled shirts, their hair in messy ponytails, looking cheerful and relaxed as they sat beside the campfire and discussed the plans for the day.

In the frame, she'd managed to catch a part of the gleaming travel trailer behind them with its red-and-white striped awning fluttering in the breeze and a backdrop of the mountains. As she sent it, she felt a rush of satisfaction. With no note, the photo could be just a casual trip pic, a reminder of what he was missing, or even an *I miss you, too.* She'd let Luke decide.

The drive home to Heron Lake was a much more relaxed affair than their white-knuckled departure. Instead of grasping the wheel with a death grip and keeping her eyes riveted on the road ahead, Jenny had an elbow on the open window and enjoyed the warm breeze as she drove with easy confidence. Excited about almost being back home, Charlotte called Ashe several times. She had a slew of nicknames for him, too, including *honeybun, babycakes, sweet pea, boo,* and *punkin.* Jenny smiled wryly and turned up the radio to tune out the mushy talk. *You are too adorable. No, I missed you more.*

When Jenny pulled the truck into the driveway of the resort, Mama ran from the Redbud and embraced them both. Mama looked pink-cheeked, rested, and happy as she fussed over them.

"Oh, we were so lonesome without you, but knew you were having a ball. Come on in. Let me get you some iced tea. Is it too early for a glass of wine? I can't wait to hear all about it."

Just then, a golf ball soared through the air and landed neatly at Jenny's feet. She gave her mother a quizzical look as Landis, Coy, and an older fellow in madras plaid shorts strode into the clearing, pulling rickety-looking golf carts loaded with clubs in bags that looked like they might date from the Eisenhower administration. "Fore," Landis called too late and beamed as he trotted over to greet the girls. He warmly hugged both her and Charlotte, and Coy gave them each a strong handshake. The fellow who made up their threesome hung back and held up a hand in a wave.

Landis pointed at him with his head. "That's Chester. He and his wife are guests in the Hydrangea. He's currently number one on the leaderboard because of a lucky ricochet off a pine tree that landed him on the green and he birdied. But we've got three holes to go, and we're closing in on him fast."

The three men cackled. Landis gave them a two-fingered salute. "We'll let you all catch up and see you at supper."

Neecy smiled and waved at them from the chair in her usual reading spot and, to Jenny's amazement, Coy walked over to her and dropped a kiss on her head. Neecy twinkled up at him and went back to her novel. Coy found a ball that they hadn't seen and hacked up a sandstorm as he got it from the makeshift sand trap. The three golfers strode off.

Jenny and Charlotte looked at each other and started to giggle.

Claire put her hand to her mouth and burst out laughing. "Those boys went to the Fire Department rummage sale yesterday and each bought sets of old golf clubs. I think they paid ten dollars for the three sets of clubs and the carts." Her eyes sparkled with amusement. "They've been playing in the field behind the cabins and apparently this clearing is the third hole."

Charlotte whipped out her phone and tried to make a call, her brow furrowed. "I'm going down to the dock to see if I can get a signal. I need to call Ashe." She trotted off.

"I need to see my men." Jenny called for Buddy, Bear, and

Levi, and as the three spotted Jenny, they approached at a gallop. The dogs swarmed around her while Charlotte took a one-on-one moment with Levi to sincerely apologize for abandoning him.

"How did they behave?" Jenny asked.

"Oh, they were perfect gentlemen. Such good manners."

Jenny crouched and gave them all good rubs and sugar talk while they kissed her, leaned against her, and gave her soulful looks. "I missed you so," she murmured, feeling a wave of pure love as she gently stroked Levi's muzzle.

They were interrupted by the rumbling growl of a large motor and the blare of a horn. Both of them looked up and saw the big black truck with extra brawny tires ease down the driveway.

Jenny waved and explained to Claire, "That's Luke's sister, Alice, and maybe her husband, Mike. She said they'd be stopping by with a belated housewarming present."

Linking arms with her mother, Jenny grinned and walked over to greet them. The windows had a light tint to them, so she wasn't sure who was driving, but Mike stepped down from the truck and shut the door. With his broad smile, all-American good looks, and wraparound sunglasses, he looked as sharp as one of the NASCAR drivers. "Welcome home," he said, suddenly looking shy.

Jenny gave him a hug and just as she introduced Claire, the other truck door opened and Luke stepped out. Jenny's breath stopped as his eyes locked on hers.

Scarcely believing her eyes, her heart slammed against her ribs, and she found it hard to breathe. Jenny raced around the truck and flew into his arms. "Luke," she cried.

"Hey, baby girl," Luke murmured. He hugged her tightly, lifting her off the ground, and gave her a kiss that left her breathless. When he let her go, she pulled him close for one more euphoric kiss.

Alice stepped out of the truck, gave a whoop, raised her arms, and did a hopping victory dance. Happy tears streamed down her face. Encircling Luke and Jenny in a quick hug, she walked over to Claire, introduced herself and Mike, and the three walked off to give Luke and Jenny some privacy.

"What are you doing here?" Jenny finally managed to ask. "I thought you'd still be gone."

Luke gave a slow smile. "I'm home for good."

Jenny shook her head as if to clear it. "But what about Zander and the project?"

Luke rubbed his chin with his hand. "They're almost at the finish line. Zander's been chomping at the bit to get to Melbourne and iron out all the details, and the doctors just cleared him to fly as long as he brings a caregiver." He smirked. "His full-time helper is a few years older than he is and holds his feet to the fire when he does something knuckleheaded. I think Zander's smitten."

Jenny smiled. "So, no more flaky models and actresses." But she was having trouble taking it all in. "So, you just decided it was time to come back?"

Luke looked chagrinned. "Alice called me and reminded me of the mistakes I'd made in my past. She told me straight out that I was being a fool for risking things with you. I was coming to that conclusion on my own, but she just gave me a shove in the right direction."

"I'm so glad," Jenny said in a voice that trembled with emotion. "So you just told Zander you needed to go?"

"I did," Luke's said, his voice flinty. "I told him I wasn't going to risk ruining love."

Jenny tilted her head. "And Zander said OK?"

"I didn't really ask him. I told him. He trusts me and relies on me, but he has other staff members that can help button up this deal." Luke looked chagrinned. "I realized that maybe I liked being the guy who could save the day, but Zander has other talented, devoted folks that could have saved the day, too."

"I'm so proud of you." Jenny touched the side of his face and gazed into his denim-blue eyes. "I've missed you more than I can tell you."

"I missed you, and I won't let this happen again, Jenny. No more getting caught up in work," he promised.

"I promise I'll hold you to that," Jenny said sternly but broke into a foolish smile. "And you don't ever have to go back to Melbourne again?"

"I'm home for good." Luke reached into his shirt pocket, pulled out a black velvet box, and held it in the palm of his hand. "I brought you something," he said, his eyes fixed on hers.

Jenny's eyes widened.

Putting an arm around her shoulder, he steered her toward the others. "Now, let me go meet your Mama. I need to get down on one knee and make it all official. Then, we've got a wedding to plan."

A Special Invitation

Dear Reader,

Thank you so much for reading *Summer at the Lakeside Resort* and spending time with me at Heron Lake. Hope you loved this book.

I'd like to ask for your help. Reader reviews are the most powerful tool for making my book successful. While the story is fresh on your mind, would you please go to your favorite online retailer and write a review?

As always, I am so grateful for your support.

Susan Schild

A NOTE TO MY READERS

I am so grateful to you all for your appreciative comments and reviews. So many of you have said how much you love Heron Lake and the Lakeside Resort story. Some tell me you wish you could book a cabin and come stay for a while! Here's what I think my readers have in common:

1. You enjoy reading about heroines your own age having adventures, falling in love and building a happy life. We women over forty are pretty interesting!

2. You also liked the fact that Jenny and Luke, their friends and family care about other people and try to do the right thing. Many of you do, too, although the news from the world could make you think you in are in the minority. So, keep the faith and know that there are a lot of other kind, caring, good people out there just like you.

Come visit me again at the Lakeside Resort in May of 2020.

LOOK FOR MY NEXT BOOK

Reader friends, mark your calendars! The next book in the Lakeside Resort series, *A Wedding at the Lakeside Resort*, will be released in May of 2020. Look for more friendship, fun, inn-keeping mishaps and a dreamy wedding!

Levi, Bear, and Buddy send their love. They'll be waiting for you.

ABOUT THE AUTHOR

Susan Schild writes heartwarming and wholesome novels of love and family featuring women over forty bouncing back from trouble, having adventures, and finding their happily ever afters.

A wife and stepmother, Susan enjoys reading and taking walks with her Labrador retriever mixes, Tucker and Gracie. She and her family live in North Carolina.

Susan has used her professional background as a psycho-therapist and management consultant to add authenticity to her characters.

Please follow Susan on:

BookBub: https://bit.ly/2tHuDzu

Facebook: https://www.facebook.com/authorsusanschild/

CPSIA information can be obtained
at www.ICGtesting.com
Printed in the USA
LVHW050718081019
633524LV00011B/888/P